A

TOO SOON DEAD

ALSO BY MICHAEL KURLAND

THE ALEXANDER BRASS MYSTERIES

The Girls in the High-Heeled Shoes (February 2016)

THE PROFESSOR MORIARTY NOVELS

The Infernal Device

Death By Gaslight

The Great Game

The Empress of India

Who Thinks Evil

TOO SOON DEAD

AN ALEXANDER BRASS MYSTERY

MICHAEL KURLAND

TITAN BOOKS

Too Soon Dead
Print edition ISBN: 9781783295364
E-book edition ISBN: 9781783295371

Published by Titan Books
A division of Titan Publishing Group Ltd
144 Southwark Street, London SE1 0UP

First Titan edition: November 2015
1 2 3 4 5 6 7 8 9 10

A CIP catalogue record for this title is available from the British Library.

Printed and bound in in the United States.

To Jack and Stephanie and Edith and Max and Mary
and Madeleine and Morgan and Rusty and Sybil
and all who love them

INTRODUCTION

My father was a reader. He read everything from historical novels to detective stories to encyclopedias, even a few science fiction novels and an occasional racing form. And I grew up reading through his library, *The Diary of Samuel Pepys*, *The Saint Meets the Tiger*, *Adventures in Time and Space* (the Healy & McComas anthology that turned me on to science fiction—still a great book), *The Three Musketeers*, and whole shelves of wonderful fiction and essays from the 1930s. When I decided that I wanted to become a writer, at the age of 10, the people I wanted to emulate were Cole Porter, Samuel Hoffenstein ("the Poet Laureate of Brooklyn"), Noel Coward, Dorothy Sayers, Rex Stout, Dashiell Hammett, and especially Robert Benchley and Dorothy Parker. (And, I must admit, Mark Twain and Gilbert and Sullivan, but I digress.)

In my imaginings I would have an apartment on Central Park South, right across the way from George, or possibly Ira Gershwin, and spend the days in happy banter with Benchley, Thurber, Parker, and the staff of *The New Yorker*. In the evenings, if I wasn't attending the opening of a new Sam and Bella Spewack play, I would sit down at my Underwood Standard and type out deathless prose. If only I had a time machine. And, of course, modern antibiotics.

The Alexander Brass novels are the offspring of my love affair with the 1930s. I have him as a columnist for the *New York World*, a fine newspaper which, in real life, died in 1931 over an inheritance dispute, and which had a sign over the city editor's desk: "Never write down to your readers—anybody stupider than you can't read."

The title of the second book, *The Girls in the High-Heeled Shoes*, comes from a 1930s era toast my mother taught me:

Here's to the girls in the high-heeled shoes
That eat our dinners and drink our booze
And hug and kiss us until we smother
And then go home to sleep with mother!

Perhaps a bit non PC for today, but certainly heartfelt.

In the tales of Alexander Brass I have tried to recreate the feel, the atmosphere, of what it was like to be alive in the 1930s, to be part of a generation that was forced to grow up fast in the middle of a great depression, and who developed that rarest of talents, the ability to laugh at themselves.

MICHAEL KURLAND
12 February 2015

1

It was about eleven in the morning when I arrived at the *New York World* building. Mel the elevator boy worked at telling me a complicated joke as he took me up to the sixteenth floor. Something about Mussolini and the Ethiopians. If there was a punch line, he lost it without noticing somewhere between the eleventh and twelfth floors. I chuckled appreciatively as he stopped and pulled the elevator door open. It was the least I could do.

I brushed the last touch of March snow off my gray tweed topcoat and kicked the last trace of March slush off my black wing-tips before I pushed open the door to Brass's outer office. A fat man I'd never seen before stood in front of the reception desk, shaking his chubby forefinger at Gloria. "Oh, no," he said in a surprisingly high voice, "I can't talk to you." He raised a pair of fleshy pink hands in shock at the suggestion. "Either I get to see Mr. Brass himself or I go peddle my papers somewhere else, little lady. I don't talk to anyone but Mr. Brass. Personal."

The fat man could see, but he could not observe. Anyone who would call Gloria Adams "little lady" would call Jack Dempsey "buddy." The description was technically accurate: Gloria stood about five-two in her stockings, and she was certainly a lady; but the connotative content of the phrase was all wrong. Strangers meeting Gloria for the first time became tongue-tied searching for the proper salutation. "Madam" sprang to mind, and was immediately rejected. "Your Royal Highness" was formal enough, but wide of the mark. Most people, speechless, would merely bow or curtsey, although a few especially perceptive foreigners had been known to kow-tow. Foreigners have a sense of the fitness of these things that we Americans lack.

Gloria was in her late twenties, and cold and blond and beautiful. Looking at Gloria, one knew instinctively that she was possessed of knowledge that the rest of us could merely guess at, and that this knowledge ennobled her and made her immune to human emotion. I thought of her as the Ice Princess, and sometimes dreamed—*ah*! the things I dreamed. After reading either too much or too little of the works of Dr. Freud, I had decided that the reason I found her so attractive was probably the result of something that happened in my childhood that I didn't want to know about. But I digress.

I crossed the room and tossed my pearl-gray fedora onto the peg reserved for it, and turned to Gloria, who was smiling a welcoming smile sweetly up at me. The smile that said this is *your* job. And welcome to it. Then she turned off the smile. "This is Mr. DeWitt," she told the fat man, indicating me with a slight nod of her head. "Perhaps you could explain it to him. He is Mr. Brass's personal assistant." Which was not exactly accurate, but was close enough for New York jazz.

I took my topcoat off and hung it with due care under the hat, while looking our guest over thoughtfully. He used the same time to look me over, and I could only hope that he was getting more enjoyment out of his view than I was out of mine. I saw a man who looked to be around forty, of medium height, overweight in all directions, with a pasty-faced complexion that suggested that sunlight was not his favorite form of illumination. He was not drastically obese, but his fat was the loose sort that looks like it has been laid on with a trowel.

The buttons on his soiled white shirt were pulling away from the buttonholes, and the shirttail had come out around the sides. His belly pushed out the fabric so that it hung over the top of his pants, obscuring the belt. The jacket of his double-breasted blue serge suit may have been his size at one time, perhaps ten years ago when lapels that wide were still in style, but today it would resist strongly being buttoned across his wide front. His hair was long on the right side, and the strands were combed over the balding top in a vain effort at concealment. All in all he was not the sort of man a well-brought-up young girl would bring home to Mother.

"What's this all about?" I asked, doing my best to sound stern and friendly at the same time, since I wasn't sure in which direction I would have to lean.

"He wants to see Mr. Brass," Gloria said.

"I want to see Alexander Brass," the plump person said half a beat behind her. "I don't want to see no one else. I don't want to talk to no one else. And Mr. Brass will want to see me, I bet."

"If you want to see Mr. Brass," I told him, "you're going to have to talk to me. That's the way it is. Nobody sees Mr. Brass unless they talk to me first. Especially if the nobody is somebody that Mr. Brass doesn't know. My name is Morgan DeWitt. What's yours?"

The fat man cocked his right forefinger and pointed it at my nose. "Listen, you," he said. "No names. I didn't ask you to throw your moniker at me, did I? I came all the way to see Alexander Brass, 'cause I got something for him. But it's personal, see. But he wants what I got, you can bet on it. And if he don't, there are other newsies in town."

I noticed a fleeting smile pass Gloria's lips. She was probably thinking how Brass would react to being called a "newsy."

In any other office, in any other business, the man would have been out on his ear by now. But Alexander Brass had a syndicated column to write every day. "Brass Tacks" paid the salaries of Gloria Adams, his researcher, fact-checker, and general know-it-all; and myself, his right-hand man, general gopher, and do-it-all; as well as that, of Theodore Garrett, Brass's personal cook, handyman, and bouncer, and assorted other assistants, researchers, interviewers, informants, and supplicants as the need arose. It was the reason the *New York World* supplied Brass with this fancy suite of offices on the sixteenth floor. It paid the rent on the twelve-room penthouse apartment at 33 Central Park South that Brass called home, and allowed Brass to indulge his taste for old books, expensive booze, and toys of all sorts. The latest being the Packard sedan that I had just picked up at the showroom. Other parts of the world might be depressed, but the offices of Alexander Brass in the

New York World building on Tenth Avenue and Fifty-ninth Street, Manhattan, were doing fine. And "Brass Tacks" was the reason why. Oh, there were a few other things, like "After Dark," the weekly column appearing in forty-six cities other than New York that fulfilled its readers' worst fears—or best fantasies—of what life in Gomorrah was really like; like "Alexander Brass Speaking," the half-hour radio show that went out on transcription to—at last count—137 stations around the country; like his fees for speaking engagements, which were exorbitant.

But "Brass Tacks" was the heart of it all. Nine hundred and fourteen newspapers in the United States and Canada expected "Brass Tacks" to titillate their readers over breakfast every day but Saturday with cleverly phrased gobbets of fascinating facts concerning the great, the rich, or the merely notorious. And to explain to them in a simple and fascinating way the issues of the day, and tell them what to think about this and that. And fascinating facts of the sort that make news are seldom volunteered by those whom they concern. Instead they come from some of the most unlikely people. Our motto was "You never can tell." Which was why the desk in the lobby had instructions to let anyone up who looked even reasonably kempt, provided only that they were not foaming at the mouth or waving a sharp-edged object about. Usually they talked to Gloria. She was a good listener. Men had been known to confess to major crimes just to see if they could get her to look impressed. So far no one had, to the best of my knowledge. And I kept track.

On the other hand, there were a lot of nuts in the world, and Brass had his share of enemies. The fat man looked like an unlikely candidate for homicidal maniac of the year, but, like I said, you never can tell.

"Give me a hint," I told the fat man. "Something I can take inside to tell Mr. Brass. If you've got something good, you don't want to take it anywhere else. Mr. Brass is the best newsy in town."

The fat man thought it over. "You got an envelope?" he asked.

Gloria opened a drawer in the desk and pulled out a business envelope.

"Nah," the fat man said. "Bigger." He made an indefinite-sized box with his hands.

Gloria produced an eight-by-ten manila envelope, one of the kind where the flap ties closed with a string. The fat man took it and turned his back on us for thirty seconds. Then he used the stapler on the desk to staple the flap shut and held the envelope out to me. "Give this to Mr. Brass," he said. "Tell him to open it private-like. Then he'll see me. And don't you open it!"

I examined the envelope. "Well, it's too skinny to be a bomb," I said. "And it doesn't wiggle around, so it's not a poisonous viper."

"What are you talking about?" the fat man demanded.

"You'd be surprised. We had a bomb once. I'm still waiting for the poisonous viper."

I took the envelope in to Brass, who was sitting in his office with his feet up on his giant desk, staring out his window at the Hudson River, which flowed beneath his feet, give or take a few blocks, filling much of the available view. "Good morning, Morgan," he said without looking around. "It's a gray day. Did you get the automobile?"

"I did, Mr. Brass," I told him. "It's in the garage on Ninth Avenue. You'll have to arrange with the garage manager to get a permanent parking space."

"I thought I had two," he said.

"Yes, sir," I said. "The Cord and the Lagonda are in them."

"Ah!" Brass said. He swung his feet down off the desk and swiveled around to face me. He was shorter than I by a couple of inches—I'm about five-ten; lighter than I by a few pounds—quite a few, actually; I'm about one-sixty, and built solid without too much extra flesh on me, but Brass has one of those slender bodies that look like they were made to wear tuxedos. He had sported a brush mustache for fifteen years, until the day, two years ago, that Adolf Hitler had been appointed chancellor of Germany; now he was clean-shaven. I had told him that I couldn't see the resemblance, but he shaved anyway.

"I have been staring at this sheet of paper for the past hour, and I am not inspired," he said, indicating the Underwood typewriter on his desk, with its sheet of white paper still pristine around the roller.

"You were staring out the window when I came in," I said. "Inspiration doesn't write your columns, perspiration does."

He glared at me, but since I was quoting him—something he had said recently in an interview to a writer's magazine—he didn't reply.

"I have something for you," I told him, extending the large manila envelope toward him. "Wait until I leave the room to open it."

He eyed the envelope suspiciously. "Why?" he asked.

"I'm not supposed to know what's in it," I told him.

Brass shook his head. "That's ridiculous," he said. "I have no secrets from you. At least, none that could be contained in this."

"I agree," I said. "But the gentleman who handed it to me to give to you insists that you open it in private. Incidently, he won't give his name."

"What does he look like?" Brass asked.

I described him while Brass stared thoughtfully at the little ivory Chinese god on one corner of his desk and weighed the envelope in his hands.

"It doesn't sound promising," Brass said when I was done. "I would prefer that he were well tailored and well spoken; then he might have something I'd want to see."

"You want a diplomat bringing state secrets," I said.

"Of course," Brass agreed. "Don't you?"

"I don't know. A nice, juicy murder might be fun."

"Not for the victim."

"There is that," I agreed.

"Well," Brass said, "I might as well open this. Stand across the room; that should satisfy the requirements."

"I'll even turn my back," I said. "Let it never be suggested that we journalists are not honorable."

"Heaven forfend!" Brass agreed, slitting open the envelope as I turned and walked over to face the Pearson landscape on the far wall. I was particularly fond of the castle in the right-hand corner of the picture. I had always wanted to be somewhere where I could look at a real castle.

There was something more than a moment of silence.

"Son of a bitch!" Brass said, sounding at least surprised, and possibly awed.

I turned around. Brass almost never cursed, so whatever was in the envelope was probably worth a view. He had put whatever-it-was on top of the desk and was staring down at it. "Let me guess," I said. "It's a nude picture of Marie of Rumania."

"I'm not sure who the woman is," Brass said.

"What?"

"Come look at this."

I crossed around to his side of the desk and looked down. There was a photograph of a man and a woman lying on what appeared to be a large, fluffy rug. To be more precise, the man was on the rug, face up, and the woman was straddling the man. There was no clothing in sight. They both seemed to be enjoying themselves. Perhaps they were playing Find the Pony. The camera had been above them and to one side, so that the man's face—among other things—was clearly in view. The woman was almost as clearly visible, except that her face was in shadow.

The picture looked pretty much like what it was—a pornographic photograph—and nothing exceptional along that line. The girl was attractive as far as I could tell—and I could tell pretty far—but the man was, if anything, a bit chubby and a bit old for that sort of thing. I couldn't understand what had provoked Brass's reaction. I peered closely at the photograph.

I whistled thoughtfully between my teeth as I realized what Brass had noticed. "Son of a bitch!" I said.

2

"Go retrieve the fat gentleman and bring him in here," Brass ordered. "And stay in here with him when you return—I don't think a private conversation would be useful."

"Gotcha, boss," I said.

"And don't call me 'boss,'" he told my back just as I reached the door. "And for that matter, you would do well to expunge 'gotcha.' The next great American novelist will probably not be a vulgarian."

He was hitting me where it hurt, but I didn't wince visibly as I closed the door. When, fresh out of Western Reserve College and even fresher in New York, I had applied for the job with Brass, I had told him that my ambition was to be the next great American novelist. The next day, when he called me back, he had simultaneously offered me the job and strongly advised me not to take it. "It can't do you any good as a writer," he had said, "and it may destroy your talent and ambition."

"Jobs are not that easy to come by at the moment, Mr. Brass," I had told him. "And I've never had any strong desire to become a lumberjack, or a coal miner, or a missionary, or any of those other jobs that writers are supposed to get so they can put it on the back of their book jackets. I've always thought that to learn writing one should be around writers."

"This isn't writing that goes on here," he had told me, "this is plumbing and mortising with words. This is a literary yard-goods store, not a fashion house."

"On the contrary, sir," I had told him. "You have a terse, cleaft style that I've always admired."

"Style!" He had shaken his head. "You start on Monday."

And so I had. That was in September 1931, about three and a half years ago. I'm still at it. And I still admire Brass's style. And I still haven't written the Great American Novel. Oh, I've started it a few dozen times. As a matter of fact, I just started it all over again last week. I had about six pages done now.

They call me Percival. I was born in a monastery in Brooklyn Heights. My mother, in an ecstasy of misplaced zeal, had joined the Order of Supplicants of St. Sebastian while she was carrying me, lying about her sex and possibly a few other things. The monks, being an introspective and essentially incurious crew, effected not to notice. Those few who did notice kept silent for reasons of their own.

That's how this version begins. I can't decide whether to call it *The Supplicant* or *The Uncivil War* or *Money Well Spent*. Perhaps, as I understand they do with babies in primitive societies, I should refrain from naming it until I'm sure it's going to live. Maybe I should give it another fifty pages or so.

The fat gentleman was sitting in one of the four cane-bottom chairs in the reception room, shifting his weight impatiently from side to side. The chairs are French, done in the style of Louis XIV, or XV, or whichever Louis was into furniture. They're copies, but they were copied so long ago that they're antiques in their own right by now. They were given to Brass by a mobster named Francis "the Chin" Capitello in return for a favor Brass had done the mobster involving Capitello's daughter Isabella and a trombone player named Sid. Brass had not considered what he did a favor for Capitello, but for the daughter, and he hadn't wanted a reward, and he didn't like the chairs much anyway, but there you have it. And if the fat man broke the chair he was sitting on, Francis "the Chin" would never understand it.

"Mr. Brass would like to see you," I told him.

"I thought maybe he would," the fat man said, pushing himself to his feet. The chair creaked, but it held. He marched into Brass's office with all the grace of an indignant goose, and stopped in front of the big desk. He glanced down at the envelope, which was neatly centered on Brass's desk blotter. "I thought you'd see me," he said. "Send your errand boy out of here so's we can talk."

Brass leaned even farther back in his swivel chair and examined the fat man, who stolidly met his gaze.

"Mr. DeWitt stays," Brass said. "If you want to talk to me, talk. If not, get out."

The fat man took a half-step backward and raised his hands in a mock gesture of warding off physical attack. "Sure, sure," he said. "If you trust him in this kind of business..." He looked around him. "Got a chair?" he asked.

I pushed a solid wooden chair over to the desk, and he plumped himself into it. Pulling a reasonably clean white handkerchief from his breast pocket, he mopped his face. "Let's get down to business," he said.

"Start with your name," Brass told him. "I always like to know to whom I am speaking."

"Not part of the deal," the fat man said. "You don't have to know my moniker for us to conduct business."

"Just what kind of business is this?" Brass asked. "Why did you give me that picture, and what do you expect me to do about it?"

"That's the question, isn't it?" the fat man replied. "You did recognize the john, of course."

Brass repositioned the envelope slightly with two fingers. "The man in the photograph has a superficial resemblance to Senator Childers," he said. "But I don't know how that resemblance was achieved."

"Superficial, hell," the fat man said, sounding annoyed. "It's him. You know it's him."

"That's just what I don't know, sir," Brass said. "I don't know the provenance of that photograph. Perhaps it's a clever composite. Perhaps it's merely a chance resemblance. Perhaps it's an actor made up to look like the senator. I don't know. Do you?"

"It's no composite," the fat man said. "I got the negative—I could tell. A chance resemblance? Hell, it would have to be his twin brother. An actor? What would be the point?"

"What *is* the point?" Brass asked.

The fat man sat upright in his chair. "I don't know," he said, "but I bet I'm going to find out. I have some ideas." He reached into his jacket pocket and pulled out a rubber-band-wrapped packet of photographs, which he tossed on the desk. There were, perhaps, thirty of them. "Take a look at these," he said.

Brass took them up and shuffled slowly through them, examining each one closely. Three of them he peered at for a long time before going on. "Very, ah, imaginative," he said finally, looking back up at the fat man. "Why are you showing me these? I won't pay you anything for them. If you try selling them to anyone else, you might get some money, but you might be buying a lot of trouble."

The fat man grinned. "I'm not selling you anything," he said. "I'm making your life more interesting." He leaned forward and pushed several of the photographs toward Brass with a pudgy forefinger. "A United States senator, a big-shot lawyer, and a judge. All playing bury-the-pickle with girls who are certainly not their wives, whatever else they may be."

"And the others?" Brass asked. "There are photographs of seven or eight different men here."

"I haven't found out yet," the fat man said. "Judging by the company which they are in, I figure they are important persons. I figure you can look them up for me. I figure you won't be able to resist doing just that."

"Is that what you want from me?"

The fat man shook his head. "I want you to hold these pictures for me until I come back for them. Then we can exchange information. You can tell me who these other gents are, and I can tell you where these photos came from. Or then again, I might not. You might say I'm buying insurance."

Brass leaned back and put his hands together in front of him, fingertip to fingertip. "I see," he said.

"I thought you would," the fat man said, "you being such a wise guy." He leaned forward. "I don't know enough about those pictures yet, but I intend to find out. I'm leaving them with you as a sort of insurance policy. You can't use them unless I tell you more about them. Like you said—they might be faked. Although we both know they're not. So I'll come back and tell you more about them. Or I won't. Depending."

Brass stared into space somewhere over the fat man's left shoulder. "I don't like being used," he said. "It goes against my policy. If I let one punk use me once, there'll be a line of them outside the door tomorrow."

The fat man waved his hands in front of him like a first-base umpire trying to decide whether the runner was safe or out. "You offend me," he said. "I see this as a sporting proposition. In return for temporarily sticking some pictures in your desk drawer for a while, an act which costs you no sweat, and maybe taking a glom through your photo morgue, you get a shot at a story that could be right up there with Fatty Arbuckle."

"I don't know what kind of insurance you think I'm giving you. These pictures," Brass said, poking at the nearest one with his finger, "pictures like these—they can't be used for anything even if they are real. At least not by me. You do realize that?"

"Of course," the fat man said. "You being an honorable guy. But you don't get it yet." He leaned forward, putting his chubby palms on the desk. "The tale I'm offering you is not these old guys humping the broads, no matter who they are. It's where they came from. It's who took the pictures—and why."

"Who did?" Brass asked. "Didn't you?"

"Gracious sakes, no," the fat man said. Honest, that's what he said. I didn't expect it either. "Gracious sakes, no." Perhaps he had been an altar boy.

"Gracious sakes, no. But I think I know who did. At least, I know who knows who did. And that tale may well be worth telling."

"How did you get the pictures?"

"That would be telling." He stood up. "I must go now. You will be hearing from me shortly." He gestured toward the pile of photographs on the desk. "Keep those," he said. "Don't show them around. Don't tell the cops. And don't try to find out who I am. That could be trouble for both of us, if you go nosing around. Even me nosing around is liable to create some waves, and I got a sensitive nose. Give me time to get some more info. Maybe a couple of days—maybe a couple of weeks. I'll be in touch." The fat man headed for the door.

Brass pushed himself up from his chair. "I make no promises," he said.

"I'll be in touch," the fat man repeated over his shoulder.

Brass watched the door close behind the fat man and then picked up the in-house phone and jiggled for the operator. "Give me the city desk, will you?" he asked.

"Ben? This is Brass. Any legmen loose at the moment?" He stared thoughtfully into space. "Billy Fox? Good. Can I have him for a couple of hours? No—no trouble, just a tailing job. It may be a story, I can't promise. Thanks. Stick him on the phone." Brass drummed his fingers on the table. "William? This is Alexander Brass. I want you to tail someone for me. Find out who he is and where he goes. But don't let him know. Lose him if you have to. Right. Bring whatever you find out up here to me. I can't promise a story, but I'll give you a buck-an-hour bonus and I'll stand you to dinner. Right. He's headed down in the elevator right now. Fat man in a blue double-breasted. Not very neat. You can't miss him. Just run down three flights and pick him up in the lobby. Okay. Good luck."

While Brass was talking I went over to the table and took a look at the pictures, leafing through them one at a time. There was little to attract the connoisseur of smut to them. Were it not for the prominence of some of the practitioners, they were trivial and repetitious examples of the art. The only conclusion I reached was that stout elderly men should not allow themselves to be photographed in compromising positions; they looked ridiculous. One of them was actually young and handsome, and fairly athletic-looking. He seemed to be enjoying himself. Three of the oldsters also looked like they were having fun; the remaining few looked grim, as though it was a difficult job, but somebody had to do it. The girls—and each fellow seemed to be with a different girl—were uniformly young, well built, and happy-looking.

I tossed the pictures back on the desk as Brass got off the phone. "If this is the latest thing in calisthenics," I said, "it ought to sweep the country."

"What do you think of our friend?" Brass asked.

I shook my head. "He's using you for something."

"So he intimated. But what are his goals, his motivations? What, if anything, does he see in these pictures besides couples coupling? Is he a simple blackmailer? But then, why give me the pictures?"

"I give up," I said.

Brass handed me the photographs. “Go down to the morgue and see if you can identify these men. I’m pretty sure about two of them, but I’d like it verified.” He tapped the picture of the handsome young man. “In this case,” he said, “I think the identity of the lady is what will interest us.”

“Oh,” I said. “I didn’t think of that.”

“I thought it was obvious,” Brass said.

I grunted and headed for the door.

3

The research department of the *New York World*, which we experienced newsies called “the morgue,” a huge room punctuated by two rows of pseudo-Greek columns, took up much of the sixth floor. It was the domain of Michael Fredric Schiff, a skinny old man with large ears, a thin, pointed nose and chin, oversized, arthritic knuckle joints, and an encyclopedic knowledge of everything that had happened in the world for the past half century. Schiff guarded his rows of file drawers full of clippings and photographs with the zeal of a mama bear guarding her cubs, and he always seemed to be able to go right to any required bit of information. After thirty years in this country he still spoke with a vaguely middle-European accent. The rumor was that he had been a college professor in his native land, but had been forced to flee when he was caught in the bed of the daughter—or, some said, the wife—of an anti-Semitic government official.

Schiff kept the room cold, probably to discourage loitering, and wore a dark brown wool sweater with a row of tiny buttons, keeping all but the top one buttoned so that just the knot of his tie peeked out. He sat behind his battered oak desk and peered at me as I posed the problem to him.

“Let me see the pictures,” he said, pulling over a swinging-arm desk lamp and snapping it on. “I might be able to save you some time.”

“I’m not sure if I should show them to you,” I said.

"You might as well," he said. "They're going to end up in here sooner or later anyway."

"I doubt that," I said. "These are—different."

"Oh," he said. "Like that. We've got those in here too, my boy. Listen, you see that cabinet?" He pointed to a dark corner of the room.

"Which one?"

"Never mind which one. It is sufficient for you to know that it exists: a cabinet full of pictures that would shock a Swiss pimp."

"Are they particularly unshockable?" I asked him.

"So it is believed where I come from," he told me. "But if you don't want me to see your photographs—"

"Here," I said, passing them over to him.

He examined each one carefully, dragging a magnifying glass out of the top drawer to take a closer look at a couple of them. He said, "Hah!" He said, "Humm." His expression gave no indication that he thought anything in the pictures the slightest bit unusual. He went over to the bank of filing cabinets near the hall door and began pulling drawers out and leafing through the files, pausing to pull up an occasional picture and compare it with one of those in his hand.

After a couple of minutes Schiff returned to his desk and, taking a thick, stubby fountain pen from his shirt pocket, printed a list of names on a sheet of yellow paper. "I have numbered the pictures in pencil," he told me, "very small, on the back. Here are the names to go with the pictures; all but two. That is, I have identified all but two of the people, who are, let us call them, the primary subjects of interest in these pictures." He held up one from the back. "I assume that in this one, while you might like the name of the young man with the large member, what you are primarily interested in is the woman's name."

"Mr. Brass assumes the same thing," I told him.

"Good. It's on the list. Leave these two pictures with me, and I'll see what I can do about putting names to them." He capped the fountain pen. "A notable assemblage. I assume that these photographs were taken for purposes of blackmail. Is that so?"

"I don't know," I told him.

Schiff folded the yellow sheet neatly in half and handed it and the pack of photographs to me. He shook his head. "Imagine that it was ingestion instead of fornication that was taboo," he said. "Then people would have illicit trysts with ham sandwiches, and elderly men would be held up to ridicule for lusting after young, shapely Bartlett pears."

I put the photographs in my pocket. "And sharply dressed men would accost you on street corners," I suggested, "offering hamburgers."

"Just so," he agreed. "With not *too* French, french fries."

I pulled the morgue file on each name on his list and took the assortment back upstairs to Brass. He was swiveled around in his chair facing the typewriter and staring with murderous intensity at the blank page. It would not be a good time to interrupt him. I left the files and the photos neatly on a corner of his desk and retreated to my own office to ponder the possibilities. There were six names on the list:

Bertram Childers
Gerald Garbin
Ephraim L. Wackersan II
Pass Helbine
Suzie Frienard
Stepney Partcher

It was quite an exclusive group of photographer's models. Bertram Childers, senior senator from New Jersey, was regarded as a long-shot Republican contender for president in the next election. He couldn't beat Roosevelt—hell, nobody could beat Roosevelt—but if FDR happened to have a heart attack, or was caught in bed with a teenager of either sex, or was proven to have Jewish blood or be a secret agent of the pope—a couple of dozen letters a week came into the paper accusing him of one or both of these high crimes—then Childers had a good shot against anyone else the Democrats could run.

Gerald Garbin, naked playmate number two, was a judge of the New York State Superior Court, and had a reputation for strictness and severity. Felons sentenced by Judge Garbin could expect to spend an extended time away from home.

Ephraim L. Wackersan, Junior, president and son of the founder of Wackersan's Department Store, our number three, was a stickler for cleanliness and uniformity. His employees were checked every morning for personal hygiene and grooming. Hair on men had to be kept short, and on women, long. No facial hair was permitted.

Number four, Pass Helbine, millionaire philanthropist, was working on his third marriage, but aside from this exercise in sequential polygamy—a minor character flaw in this day and age, when, as Cole Porter puts it, "Anything Goes"—his life was the stuff of which hagiographies are written. The six Helbine Houses, where a down-and-out citizen can get a good meal, a shower, and a place to sleep for a dime, and if he doesn't have a dime he can wash dishes, are models of philanthropic endeavor.

The woman, Suzie Frienard, was an attractive blonde who had not yet seen her fortieth summer and looked even younger. Were it not for the extreme youth and vitality of her partner, one might have thought she was just one of the girls. From the view of her charms in the photographs, I certainly wouldn't kick her out of bed. Her husband, Dominic Frienard, was a major contractor in the New York City area. It would be hard to walk more than ten blocks in any direction without walking over or past Frienard-poured concrete.

The last person on the list, Stepney Partcher, was the senior partner of Partcher, Meedle and Coster, a very political law firm. The file had little about him, since the firm employed a public relations expert to keep all of their names out of the papers. What these six people had in common, besides wealth and a presumably inadvertent appearance in smutty photographs, was not revealed in their files.

The staccato sound of Brass pounding the keys of his Underwood wafted its way through the door of my little office. Can sound waft? Well, I guess it can now. We novelists bring life and vigor into language. Can I call myself a novelist when I haven't been published? Can I call myself a novelist when I haven't yet finished a novel?

Brass spent a long time every day staring at a blank sheet of paper, but when he actually started typing it usually went pretty fast. When he was done he'd let it sit for an hour or two, and go over it with a blue pencil, and give it to Gloria to make sure it didn't contradict any obvious facts or natural laws, or anything he'd written previously. Gloria has an eidetic memory, which means that she never forgets anything she sees or hears, as though her other attributes weren't frightening enough. Then she passes it to me to type a final draft to send down to editorial.

Brass claimed not to be a perfectionist, and he affected a low regard for his own prose, but he regularly achieved the sort of subtle turn of phrase that would sneak up on the reader and whack him on the back of the head when he wasn't looking. Brass's description of Senator Burnside as having "delusions of adequacy" got Brass denounced on the Senate floor. I particularly admired his recent description of singer Bessie Elliot as wearing a red silk dress that was "just too tight enough."

While Brass typed I concentrated on sorting through the mail. The letters fell into about six standard categories as well as "too nutty to deal with" and "the boss better see this one." It all got answered except a portion of "too nutty to deal with," which was too nutty to answer. The six standard categories would receive versions of six standard but personalized form letters.

My favorites were the letters from convicted criminals explaining, usually voluminously and in pencil, why they were innocent. Brass was one of the six members of the Second Chance Club, a group that worked to free people wrongly convicted of major crimes. The only problem was that everyone whose freedom had been curtailed by the court thought himself innocent, and wrote to Brass to prove it.

Gloria and I shared the pleasure of typing the replies to the rest of the mail. When the backlog got too big, Brass would get one of the city-desk reporters who needed some extra money—and they all always needed extra money—to help us cut it down. Billy Fox, the reporter who was out following our fat friend, was one of the regulars at the old L.C. Smith typer in the hall.

One time I pointed out to Brass that H.L. Mencken, a fellow newsy who worked for the *Baltimore Sun* before going off to found his own magazine, was reputed to have an all-purpose reply that he used for his mail: a postcard with a rubber-stamped message that read, "Sir or Madam, you may be right."

"Mencken does not suffer fools gladly," Brass had replied. "A habit that makes introspection difficult."

I'm still not sure how that applies, but now I answer Brass's fan mail with no further complaints. Which, I suppose, was what he had in mind.

I waited a full five minutes after the typewriter had stopped clacking before I returned to Brass's office. His column, triple spaced on yellow copy paper, just like he was a real working reporter, was in the wire basket. Brass was staring out the window at one of the day boats making its way up the river toward Albany.

"What's the column on today?" I asked.

"Nightclubs," he told me, still staring down at the Hudson River traffic. "The solid citizens of the Midwest never tire of hearing about nightclubs. Set the most innocuous story in a nightclub and it acquires sinful innuendo by proximity."

For Brass, as for most New Yorkers, the Midwest was an area full of corn and cattle, with an occasional buffalo, where nothing of note ever happened, which began on the other side of the Hudson and continued to the Pacific Ocean. I did not suffer from this character flaw, having parents and a sister in Ohio.

Brass turned to face me. "Fox isn't back and he hasn't phoned in," he said. "It's almost four o'clock."

"Perhaps he followed the subject to somewhere in the Midwest," I suggested, "and the last stagecoach has already left." Brass stared at me with the expression of someone who has just discovered a new but not very interesting insect in his soup. "Perhaps," he said.

"So," I said, hastening to change the subject, "what do you think of our list of distinguished perverts?"

"Perverts?" Brass raised an eyebrow. "They've been caught in the act of performing perfectly normal sex acts with reasonably attractive partners of the opposite sex. If there is any perversion involved, it would be with the photographer. Although I suspect he had a commercial motive. The fact that publication of these pictures would cause each of the subjects insupportable embarrassment is a comment on our vestigial Victorian social mores, not on the activities portrayed."

There was nothing to say to that, so I did so. Brass handed me the pictures. "Wrap these in something and put them in the safe," he said.

"Schiff still has a few of them," I said, going over to open the safe. "There are two subjects he couldn't identify. What about the files?"

"I want to look them over. Tomorrow morning you can return them and see if Mr. Schiff has satisfied our curiosity."

4

I live on West Seventy-fourth Street between Amsterdam and Columbus avenues. The neighborhood used to be, so I understand, mostly Italian with a smattering of Irish. Now added to the mix are a heavy sprinkling of out-of-work actors and dancers with a soupçon of starving writers, composers, and poets. Of course, "out-of-work" is an unnecessary modifier in this year-of-the-breadline 1935. Actors and dancers have one advantage over the rest of the population: They're used to being out of work, it's their usual condition. They call it "between engagements," but that doesn't make it any easier to pay the rent.

My room is on the third floor front of a five-story brownstone rooming house which was a private residence once, several ages ago. Faded signs of its former glory can be discerned in the scrollwork on the baseboards and the walls; in the ornateness of the long disconnected gas fixtures still in some of the rooms; and in the interior doors, meant to separate dining room from drawing room from library in the long ago, but which now have multiple layers of paint welding them shut. My room is large enough for my belongings and my needs. The furniture: bed, night table, dresser, stuffed chair, wooden chair, table, and a sort of abbreviated wardrobe in the corner big enough for two suits and a bathrobe, all came with the room. I have added my clothing, a couple of framed photographs, and a 1911 Underwood typewriter that I got at an auction for three bucks. I could afford a new one, what with my steady employment with Alexander Brass, but that wouldn't make me a better typist or a better writer. The typewriter, which works fine, sits on the table, which sits by the window so I can look out while I try to write.

I got up the next morning at six-thirty, as usual, so I could spend two undisturbed hours at the typewriter before I had to leave for work. One of the advantages of working for Brass was that he never got to the office before eleven, and all that he asked of his employees was that they were there when he arrived. I always tried for ten, so I would be sure to be there by ten-thirty. I showered in the communal bathroom and by seven was sitting at my ancient machine.

The love that I felt for Melinda transcended passion, and took me to another level of reality. Colors were shifted in their spectra, sounds were selectively magnified, and the Earth was tilted to the right. Everyday events were embodied with mystic significance. A trip to the grocery store became an odyssey through alien streets to an incomprehensible land. I could read portents of our relationship in the empty candy wrappers and crumpled cigarette packs that littered the sidewalk in front of her door. From behind drape-covered windows people peered out and whispered, "Melinda and Percival were meant for each other." Pigeons strutted about the street muttering, "Melinda and Percival, could there be a doubt?" I was sure there were no heights to which our love could not ascend, if only I could somehow manage to make Melinda aware of my existence.

I stared at the passage I had just written and realized that the words I had given to my fictional hero Percival exemplified two facets of my own life. First, that I knew absolutely nothing about sex, aside from the mechanical details, and even less about women; and second, that I was perhaps vaguely bitter about this fact. I wasn't interested in sex as sex, I told myself, but in the act of love—the coupling of two minds to create a finer, greater whole. (And what would Dr. Freud say about that particular construction?)

It wasn't that I hadn't done my share of adolescent fooling around in the rumble seat of an old flivver or the last row of the

Valley Grande movie house with a girl who was as curious about these powerful emotions and desires as I was. But Mary Beth had, to my eternal regret, been able to curb both her desires and my own. And my romantic experiences since this lovely but strong-willed young lady had been nil.

Not that I didn't know love. I was constantly falling in love. I didn't exactly fall out of love again, but merely allowed the newer love to supplant the older. Sometimes the loves lasted as long as a week or two, sometimes no more than a couple of hours. Usually—hell, invariably—the object of my affection was innocent of any knowledge of my feelings and thus of the need to reciprocate. It was my firm belief that the entire rest of the human race, both sexes, was secure, self-assured, and confident, and that I was the world's only schlemiel—a word that I picked up from my next-door neighbor, Pinky, a retired circus clown of the Jewish persuasion. Pinky pointed out that if there was a word for it, there were probably other people doing it, but this failed to cheer me up.

This makes me sound like the Innocent of the World, in the running for the Candide prize when next it should be awarded. But it wasn't lack of knowledge that hampered me; three years working for Alexander Brass and listening to the stories that he printed—and the ones he couldn't print—has given me insight into the "tangled web we weave when e're we practice to conceive," as a noted English actress put it. Anatole France said that a critic is like a eunuch in a harem: He sees the trick done nightly, and he hates himself for not being able to perform. Well, I sometimes sympathize with that eunuch.

While I was staring at the page of ardent text in my typewriter and wondering whether to place it on the pile of manuscript pages that was slowly growing on a corner of my desk, or in the wastebasket, my telephone rang. I was the somewhat harassed possessor of the only private phone in the building. There was a pay phone in the second-floor corridor that even Mrs. Bianchi, the landlady, used. But when Brass wanted me outside of office hours, the need was often urgent, and he wanted to be able to get me. The boys and girls in the building kept the hall phone tied up for hours arranging their professional and personal lives. So Brass paid for the phone in my room and I had a constant fight to keep my neighbors from using it without seeming actively hostile.

I picked up the phone. "Hello?"

"Brass," Brass said. "Be downstairs in five minutes. I'm picking you up in a cab." He hung up.

I pulled out my hunter pocket watch—the legacy of a deceased uncle—and snapped it open. It was five minutes to eight. This was definitely an unBrasslike hour to be up, much less to be picking me up in a cab. I pulled the blinds from the window and looked outside to reassure myself that the world hadn't ended during the night, or that Fascist goon squads were not setting up machine-gun posts on the corners. All seemed tranquil.

I put my tie and vest on and shrugged into my jacket. A Checker Cab was pulling up as I stepped out the door four minutes later. Brass pushed open the back door and I climbed in. Brass, as always, was immaculately groomed—dark red bow tie perfectly butterflied below his chin, every hair in place. This was particularly impressive considering that it was two hours before he usually got up. Brass was out until at least two every night, associating with the sort of people who make New York the City That Never Sleeps, and supply such good copy for his column. Then he goes home to make notes for his column. Sometimes he even writes it before he goes to bed. In bed by four, up by eleven makes a man wealthy and wise if he writes about the playgrounds and playmates of Gotham. Healthy, we don't worry about here. Some day we'll move to the country to get healthy.

"Who are we rescuing this morning?" I asked as the cab pulled away. Brass's hasty excursions were usually to rescue some Gothamite who had gotten himself into a scrape with the law, or with one of the outlaws with which the city abounds.

"Too late," Brass said. "He's beyond rescuing."

I looked at him, awaiting an explanation, but Brass just stared out the window.

We went through the park at Eighty-sixth Street and turned right on First Avenue. On Eighty-second Street we turned down toward York Avenue and I saw a cluster of police cars, both marked and unmarked, in the street ahead of us. We stopped in the middle of the block, just before the police cars, and Brass told me to pay the driver. By the time I had handed the cabby a couple of quarters and told him to keep the change, Brass was out of the car and headed toward the trio of uniformed cops standing in front of one of the tenements. I had to scurry to catch up.

The officers recognized Brass. Very few cops on the island of Manhattan wouldn't recognize my boss. He liked to write up the heroic exploits of the uniformed force, even as he castigated the arrogance and graft of their bosses. And he was always good for a ten-spot if one of the uniforms brought him something interesting in the way of information.

"Mr. Brass," a thin cop with prominent ears said, nodding to us as we approached.

"Henderson, isn't it?" Brass asked.

"That's right, sir. Go on up. The inspector's expecting you."

As we started up the steps a black station wagon pulled up to the curb. The writing on the door panel said, office of THE CHIEF MEDICAL EXAMINER: CITY OF NEW YORK. I Suddenly had a strong feeling that I knew what we were going to find upstairs.

The tenants of the building were in the corridors, clustered about the staircase. They were in various stages of grooming and dress, having put aside whatever they were doing to share in the vicarious excitement of the police investigation. On the landing two flights up we found Inspector Raab.

Inspector Willem Raab was a large, florid man with a round face and a body that was getting rounder with every passing day. But under the excess poundage was a solid, muscular frame that had served him well during his thirty years on the force. Originally Dutch or Flemish, or one of those European seafaring peoples, he had jumped ship in New York when he was seventeen and promptly been arrested for beating the crap out of someone who had tried to pull the Murphy game on him. When he got out of jail a week later the officer who arrested him asked him if he wanted to join the force. "They needed men with a lot of muscle, a sense of moral righteousness, and not too many brains," he was fond of explaining. If so, he had cheated them. As chief of the homicide squad for the past seven years, he had shown a high degree of intelligence as well as the tenacity of a bulldog.

"Brass," the inspector said, making it sound like an expletive.

"Inspector Raab. Where is he?"

The inspector stepped aside. "Through there. Don't touch anything."

There were eight or ten doors along the corridor, stretching on both sides of the landing. The first door to the right of the landing was open, and we went in. It was the front room of a three-room flat, kitchen ahead and to the right, and bedroom to the left. Two men from the fingerprint squad were inside the apartment dusting various surfaces.

There were few pieces of furniture in the room. A desk with an old battered typewriter against one wall, and an ancient mimeograph machine a couple of feet from the other wall, gave one the feeling that the apartment was not used as a domicile. There was a sort of couch between the two doors across the room. Hanging from a nail over the couch was a badly lithographed calendar with an illustration of a portly German in leather pants saluting the World with a large stein of beer. Underneath the picture was a motto: "We Are Too Soon Old and Too Late Smart." Below that hung the month of March, with about half the days x-ed off.

Lying partly on but mostly off the couch was Billy Fox, who would no longer get any older. The last we'd heard of him, he was going off to follow our fat purveyor of pornography. Was this where the fat man had led him? I looked up at the calendar. Too soon dead, I thought. I didn't want to look down again, but I couldn't help myself.

His head and one arm were on the couch. His throat had been cut. And the blood had drained out of the wound onto the couch, and thence to the floor below, where it formed a clotted black puddle about two feet across.

He was wearing a brown suit and neatly shined brown shoes. From the way his right leg had twisted I could see that there was a hole the size of a nickel in the sole of his right shoe. I wondered about the other shoe. I wondered about the piles of paper with mimeograph printing on them that I saw scattered about the room. I went over and knelt down to get a look at one without touching it. For a second I couldn't figure out why I couldn't read it, and then I realized that it was in German. That was understandable. This was on the edge of Yorkville, a major German area in Manhattan.

I wondered how many Germans lived in Yorkville. I wondered what the papers said, and who had used the room as a printing office.

I stared at the bloody dead thing on the couch that had yesterday been a friend, an occasional drinking companion, and a professional comrade, and wondered what had happened to him. And why. And where I could go to quietly throw up without annoying the men working in the room.

5

Brass stared silently at Fox's body for a minute, and then walked around the room carefully, peering through doorways, poking into corners, and looking over the shoulders of the technicians dusting the room for fingerprints. After roaming about what the police like to call the crime scene for far longer than I thought necessary, he returned to the corridor and I gratefully followed.

"Okay," Raab said. "Give." The skinny detective standing next to him, whose name was Greene, pulled his notebook out of the pocket of an overcoat that looked about two sizes too large for him.

"His name is—was—William Fox," Brass said. "He worked as a reporter for the *World*. Legman on the city desk."

Inspector Raab looked as though he'd just tasted something sour. "I knew that when I called you," he said. "Tell me something I don't know."

"I thought perhaps you wanted proper identification," Brass said.

"We'll let his mother do that," Raab told him. "What was he doing here?"

"I have no idea," Brass said.

"Ben Ogden, your city editor, tells me otherwise."

"He's not my city editor," Brass said sharply. "I have a syndicated column; I am not employed by the *World*."

Inspector Raab smiled an unsympathetic smile. "Aren't we testy this morning," he said.

Brass sighed and nodded. "Yes," he said. "I am annoyed—principally at myself. I sent Fox out, perhaps to his death, on what was essentially a whim."

Greene made his first note. Inspector Raab pulled a pack of Old Gold cigarettes from his jacket pocket and stuck one in his mouth. "Let's hear it," he said, patting his pockets in an unsuccessful hunt for a match. Greene pulled a Zippo lighter out of his pocket and lit his superior's cigarette before the quest could degenerate into a comedy routine.

"A gentleman came to see us yesterday," Brass said. "He wouldn't give his name. He offered to sell me some pictures. He was not specific as to what they showed, but assured me that I would find them interesting. I refused to deal without seeing the merchandise first. He refused to show the pictures until I had paid for them, which put us at an impasse. He left in a huff. I called the city room and arranged for Fox to follow the huff, so I could discover who the gentleman was and where he came from. I did not hear from Fox again."

Brass paused while Greene struggled to get the words down in his notebook. I stared at Brass with silent admiration. Among the attributes of his that I admired, I would now have to add that he could lie like a trouper. But why would he bother?

"Do you want me to repeat any of that?" Brass asked Greene.

"No, I'll get it, just give me a moment to catch up," Greene said, flipping over the notebook page and continuing to write.

"You really should have your men take courses in shorthand," Brass told Raab.

"Sure thing," Raab said, tapping his cigarette ash onto the linoleum floor. "You never saw the man before?"

"Never."

"He didn't tell you what the pictures showed?"

"Not a hint, except that I would consider them worth the money."

"How much did he want for them?"

"Two thousand dollars."

"That's not much for the *World* to pay, if they were any good," Raab commented.

"I keep telling you, I am not the *World*. The money would have come from my pocket."

Raab nodded. "Just what I was thinking," he said. "If the pictures were newsworthy, why didn't he take them to the city desk? Why you? And why wouldn't he show them to you? If they had any value, looking at them wouldn't eliminate it, it would merely verify it."

Brass shrugged. "Some people have very strange ideas," he said, "of which they refuse to be disabused. Elderly gentlemen approach me regularly with plans for perpetual motion machines. One otherwise unexceptional banker is convinced that small people from under the Earth are going to invade upper Broadway through the subway system. He believes this because he has noticed a scarcity of nickels, which he reasons are being hoarded by the underworld creatures for use in the subway turnstiles."

Raab stared unblinkingly at Brass for a minute and then shifted his gaze to me. "Did you see this shy visitor?" he asked.

"Yes, sir," I told him.

"What did he look like?"

I tried to look at Brass without seeming to, to see if I could get any clue as to how he wanted this question answered. Brass was looking impassively at Inspector Raab. Having an indistinctive dislike of lying to the police, I took a deep breath and described the fat man to the best of my recollection.

Raab turned to Brass. "Do you agree?" he asked.

"Quite an adequate and accurate description," Brass said. "Young Morgan would seem to have an eye for detail."

"Have you anything to add?"

Brass considered. "The man's shirt collar was soiled, and there were stains on his hands," he said. "Principally on his right hand."

Raab took a last drag on his cigarette, dropped it on the linoleum floor, and twisted it out with the sole of his shoe. "One of the great unwashed, eh? What sort of stains?"

Brass shrugged. "Ink stains, dye stains—I didn't get that close."

Raab stared morosely at the shredded cigarette on the floor. "I've got to stop smoking," he said. "You think this fat man did this—killed Fox?"

"If you just want an opinion, then no, I don't think so. He didn't seem like the sort of man who would solve problems in such a violent and foolish manner, although of course I can't be sure. But if you are asking whether I think Fox's death is related to my sending him to tail the fat man, how can I think otherwise? I am culpable, I admit it."

"Don't get overly dramatic," Raab said. "You didn't slit his throat. And whoever did, we'll get."

Alan Shine, a small, balding man who was the *World's* ace crime reporter, stuck his prominent nose around the corner of the stairs and followed it onto the landing. "Inspector Raab," he greeted. "Brass. DeWitt. A hell of a thing to wake up to. Is it really Billy Fox?"

"Yeah," Raab said, gesturing with his hand. "In there. Don't touch anything."

Shine went to the door of the apartment and looked in. A *World* photographer we called The Peanut because he stood something under five feet tall appeared on the staircase and lugged his Speed Graphic over to the doorway. After giving one long, expressive whistle he screwed a flashbulb into its holder and went into the room. Flashes of light brightened the doorway as he captured the death of a *New York World* reporter on film.

For a long moment Shine just stood by the door, watching The Peanut at work, and then he took his hat off and turned away. "Shit!" he said. "He owed me twenty bucks. I guess I'll have to write it off."

"That reminds me," Brass said. "Was Fox married?"

"Yes," Shine said. "Cathy. A little blonde. She worked as a hatcheck girl at the Hotsy Totsy Club before Legs Diamond was knocked off and the place closed. As a matter of fact, you once did a piece on her. You called her 'the moxie girl.'"

"Oh, yes," Brass said. "A cute kid. Wanted to be a singer. I wondered what happened to her."

"She gave it a try. Singing, I mean. She's been working at night spots around town. Right now she's working at some club way downtown in the Village. Shit. Someone will have to tell her."

"Cathy Wild," Brass said. "I've heard her sing. A little joint in the Village. The Blue Lamp. About a year ago. I was there with Winchell. He was furious when the owner—Fat Bess, her friends called her—wouldn't pick up the tab, and he stormed out. I stayed and paid. It was worth it; she has a good voice, really sells a song. I never realized she was the same girl." He shook his head. "I'll take care of telling her about, ah, this," he said, turning to Raab. "Thank you for calling me. I wish I could tell you more."

"Yeah, well," Raab said. "Maybe the tail job he was doing for you had nothing to with it. Maybe someone else he owed twenty bucks to caught up with him."

"Say, Inspector—" Shine said, stepping forward.

"Yeah, yeah, I know," Raab said, holding his hand palm-up like a stop sign. "Just a little humor."

"Well, you ain't funny," Shine said.

He stood there for a minute twisting his hat in his hands as though he expected to wring truth from the felt. "Listen, Inspector, if you need any help on this—you know..."

"Yeah," Raab said. "I know."

Brass turned and trotted down the stairs, and I followed after muttering good-bye to those on the landing. When we reached the street Brass turned west and walked quickly down the sidewalk, his hands shoved deeply into his overcoat pockets. By the end of the first block he had entered what I thought of as his walking fit. Walking served as a release for Brass, and a way of focusing his thoughts, and he did a lot of it. But sometimes when he walked he shut everything else out and just walked and thought, or brooded, or whatever you would call what was going on inside his head. At these times his pace was rapid and he was just aware enough of his surroundings to avoid running into any moving objects. When a walking fit was on Brass it was hard for me to keep up with him.

I had some questions I wanted to ask him, but they would have to wait until he slowed down, a sign that his concentration was broken and he would again be aware of the world. He turned left on Madison Avenue and headed downtown and I followed. I wished I could tell how long the fit would last. I would just as soon take a cab to wherever he was going to end up and meet him there. Maybe I could have some breakfast or at least a cup of coffee while I was waiting for him.

On Fourteenth Street and Fifth Avenue he stopped. I was about half a block behind by this time, and it took me half a minute to catch up with him. He, I noted, was breathing normally. Aside from a pronounced flush on his face, that pallid visage upon which the sun seldom shines, there was no sign that he'd just walked three and a half miles at a speed usually reserved for soldiers on a field exercise. I, on the other hand, was breathing heavily, and I could feel my heart beating under my white broadcloth shirt.

"Did you eat breakfast?" he asked.

"Not today," I told him.

"Come on," he said. "We'll go to Kohl's. My treat."

Five minutes later, and not a moment too soon, we were seated at a back booth in Kohl's Delicatessen on Sixth Avenue. Maxine, our aging, plump waitress, who was possessed of the broadest smile I've ever seen on a human being, and who used it indiscriminately on all her customers, was filling our coffee cups and taking our orders. Below her blue waitress uniform she wore bedroom slippers that flopped when she walked. She never wrote out a check; she didn't need one.

"I have a question," I told Brass as Maxine flopped off to the kitchen to yell our orders to the chef.

"I'm sure you do," Brass said. "I have an answer. Let's see if they match."

"Why did you lie to Inspector Raab about the fat man? I've known you to refuse to tell the police something you wanted to withhold, but never before to just lie about it."

Brass leaned back into the corner of the booth and surveyed his surroundings. "What would you have had me tell him?" he asked.

"Well, for one thing, we have this bunch of photographs in the office safe that just might have had something to do with Billy's murder, in some indirect fashion," I said.

"Sarcasm becomes you," Brass said. "You wear it like a shield before the armor of your righteousness." He took a deep breath and stared at me intently for a minute. Then he said, "Consider the consequences of what you propose. The photographs might well have something to do with William Fox's murder. No, I'll make it stronger—they almost certainly do. But what they also would definitely do, with no doubt at all, is ruin the lives of half a dozen prominent people."

"I'm sure that Raab would agree to keep quiet about the pictures," I said.

"Of course he would. And he would mean it. And I trust him to do his best. But if the pictures are evidence, then he would have to log them in, and someone else would have to see them—probably several somebodies. Certainly his bosses would take a look. And somewhere in that chain someone would take them aside just long enough to make copies, maybe to sell, maybe just to enjoy in private—although I'd lay five to one that they'd be for sale. And probably within two days. Remember how I get a lot of those exclusives that keep me and you and Gloria off the breadlines."

"I didn't think of that," I told him. "But couldn't you have just refused to tell him anything?"

"I'd like to have just turned the photographs over to Raab and washed my hands of the business," Brass said. "But I can't. If I refuse to give him information that he knows I have, he'll keep after it. He might even get a search warrant for my office safe. I don't know how those gentlemen, and that lady, managed to get themselves photographed in their sporting attire, but I should make some effort to find out before I blithely ruin their lives."

"You've got a point," I said. "So what are we going to do?"

"For the moment," Brass said, "we're going to eat breakfast."

For the next half hour I reaffirmed my discovery that a breakfast of smoked salmon, which the local intelligentsia calls "lox," and eggs is, in itself, a sufficient reason to leave Ohio. Over our second cup of coffee I remembered something else. "Tell me about the moxie girl," I said.

"The—oh, yes." Brass stared thoughtfully into the sugar bowl. "It must have been five or six years ago. Jack Diamond, who was not called 'Legs' to his face by anyone who wanted to see the sun rise, owned the Hotsy Totsy Club on Fifty-fourth Street, off Broadway, and one of the hatcheck girls was Cathy Wild, whose real name was, if I remember correctly, Karen Welikof, and who wanted to be a singer. Jack put the make on Cathy; told her that he could help her singing career, maybe find her a nice rent-paid apartment. And all he wanted was what you think he wanted. He put the proposition to her one night at his usual table in the corner next to the bandstand. And there, right in front of God and everybody, including an assortment of his gangster buddies, she slapped his face. Hard.

"The place froze. Even the waiters, trays in hand, remained motionless. It was like a set piece in a Broadway farce. Jack

Diamond slowly rose to his feet and glared at Cathy for an eternity—maybe ten seconds—and then he said, 'Sister, you've got moxie.' Everyone started to breathe again. Then Jack continued, 'I got no use for moxie.' Again everyone froze."

Brass looked up from the sugar bowl, but he was seeing the showroom of the Hotsy Totsy Club five years ago. "What happened?" I asked.

"The damnedest thing. The girl started to laugh. Not hysterical, but as though someone had just said something funny. And then Jack started to laugh. And then everyone started to laugh. I put it in my column the next day, and Cathy became the moxie girl."

"I guess she really did have moxie," I said.

Brass nodded. "I hope she still does," he said. "She's going to need it." He fished a nickel out of his pocket and slapped it on the table. "There's a pay phone in the corner," he said. "Call the city room and get Fox's address."

I did so and returned. "You're lucky," I told Brass. "He lives—lived—in Manhattan. Two-thirty-five East Fifty-fourth. No phone."

We took a cab uptown. Brass stopped briefly at the Manhattan Bank on way. He banked there, he had once explained to me, because it was founded by Aaron Burr, a true American hero. It was statements like this which made me think that we must have used a different history book in Ohio. It was only eleven-thirty in the morning when we knocked on Cathy Fox's door. I could have sworn that at least three days had passed since Brass had picked me up, but it had been less than four hours.

The apartment was on the second floor of a well-kept-up brownstone; there was a fairly new carpet runner on the floor of the hallway and the stairs, and the apartment doors had been freshly painted in that color that is known throughout New York City as landlord green.

At first our knocking produced no response. Then, finally, we heard some banging noises from inside, as though someone had dropped something or knocked something over. And then a girl's voice yelling, "Go away! Can't you let a girl sleep?" It was a sweet voice, a singer's voice, even yelling through a door. It sounded like it belonged to the sort of girl I would like to know. Fox was a lucky man. Had been…

Suddenly I wanted to be anywhere in the world except standing outside that freshly painted green door waiting to tell the girl with that voice that she was now what in my hometown would be known as "the Widow Fox."

Brass knocked again. "Mrs. Fox?" he called. "This is Alexander Brass, from the *World*. I'd like to speak to you for a minute."

There was a profound silence from inside the apartment. Then all at once we heard the chain being taken off the door, and the door swung open. She was young and blond and slender and beautiful, and her eyes were full of sleep. She wore a sheer nightgown of some sort, over which she had wrapped a man's terry cloth bathrobe. She stared at both of us, and we said nothing. Then, with no inflection in her voice, as though she were discussing the weather, she said, "It's Bill. He's dead, isn't he?"

Even Brass was startled, something I had seldom seen before. "Has someone been here before us, Mrs. Fox?" he asked.

"Call me Cathy. I've been asleep all morning. It's just—when I heard your voice... Then, he is dead? Not just in the hospital or something?"

"I'm sorry," Brass said. "He is dead. Murdered. William was. doing a job for me, and he was killed. I am so very sorry."

Cathy wrapped the bathrobe more tightly around her and stepped back from the door, and we entered the apartment. "He appreciated that, you know," Cathy said, closing the door and walking ahead of us down the short hallway to the living room.

"What?"

"Being called 'William.' Everyone insisted on calling him 'Billy.' He thought nobody took him seriously. He was pleased that you called him 'William,' but no one else would, so he was willing to settle for 'Bill.' We had long talks about it. It seemed so very important."

Her voice remained quite calm, almost flat, but when she turned around we could see two lines of tears running down her face. "Please sit down," she said. "Tell me what happened."

I settled into an ancient, well-worn brown couch that took up much of one wall of the small living room. Brass sat on a straight-back wooden chair under a framed front page of the *New York World* that was hung on the opposite wall. "This is my associate

Morgan DeWitt," he said, waving his hat in my direction. "We don't exactly know what happened. Yesterday I asked William to follow a man for me. I didn't know who the man was, which was why I wanted him followed, but I had no reason to think that the request was dangerous. This morning your husband was found dead in an apartment in Yorkville. He had been hit on the head and his throat had been cut. The police have no idea why. Neither do I. He was unconscious when he died, so he didn't suffer."

That last line was pure hokum. Brass had no way of knowing whether Fox was conscious or not when he died. But I was not going to correct him.

Cathy looked from one to the other of us. "Whose apartment?" she asked.

"It was rented by some sort of commercial organization," I told her. "The police are checking on that now."

"I see," she said. "Who was he following?"

I left that one for Brass. "A fat man who had some strange photographs," he said. "I don't know who he is. That's why I had Fox following him."

Cathy didn't say anything for a long time. She was staring out the window, but I doubt if she knew that. "You were one of his heroes," she said, turning to look at Brass. "You and Franklin Roosevelt and Babe Ruth and George Gershwin."

Brass took an envelope from inside his jacket and handed it to Cathy. "I never paid him for all the work he did for me," he said. "Here, please take this."

"I thought the newspaper paid him for all that," she said.

"Not entirely," Brass said. "I employed him to do some freelance work for me: legwork, writing, that sort of thing. And I owed him some back salary. This is it."

Cathy weighed the envelope in her hand. "This is very nice of you, but he would have told me," she said. "Except for that last day. You don't have to—"

"I do," Brass said. "I have to. If you need anything—*anything*—call me."

Cathy put the envelope on the coffee table. "Where do I go to see about his body and… whatever?"

"I'll take care of that," Brass told her. "You won't have to do anything until there are decisions to be made, then I'll consult with you. Is there anyone out of town who should be notified?"

"Oh my God!" Cathy said, sitting up and putting her fist in her mouth. When she took it out a few seconds later I could see the tooth marks on her knuckles. "His parents," she said. "I'll have to call them. How awful for them."

"They'll get whoever did this," Brass said.

Cathy stared at Brass for a minute. "I'll tell him," she said. "When they catch his murderer, I'll go out to his grave, and I'll be sure to tell him."

6

A chilling rain was falling when we left Cathy Fox's apartment and, as usual in New York, those who didn't want to get wet outnumbered the available taxicabs. We tried to flag down an empty cab for a few minutes, and then Brass and I buttoned our overcoats, pulled down our hats, turned up our collars, and started across town on foot. Silently we crossed the avenues together. There was nothing to say.

It was after one o'clock when we arrived at the office. Gloria was eating lunch at her desk: an egg salad on rye with a cup of tea from Danny's on the corner. She waved a note at Brass as we came in. "You're wanted," she said.

"By whom at the moment?" he asked, unbuttoning his coat and hanging it carefully on a wooden hanger, which he then took into the small storeroom, where it could drip harmlessly. I fished up another hanger and did likewise, not to be outdone in neatness by the boss. My hat was a sodden mess, but I put it on a shelf in the firm expectation that it would reblock itself as it dried.

"Mr. Sanders has called four times," Gloria said. "He wants to see you as soon as you come in."

"King Winston called himself?" I asked. "Personally?" Winston Sanders was the publisher of the *World,* known as "the King" by those who owed their weekly paychecks to him, and in my five years working for Brass in the *World* building I had seen him only twice, both times in the lobby as he strode toward his private elevator.

"The first two times his secretary called, the last two times it was he," Gloria said.

"Well," Brass said. "Most intriguing. I guess I'd better go upstairs and see what he wants." Brass, as he had told Inspector Raab, did not work for the *New York World,* but the World Features Syndicate, of which Sanders was the president, carried both of Brass's columns.

"While I'm gone I have work for both of you," Brass said. He turned to Gloria. "You heard what happened?"

"Yes," Gloria said. "People have been popping in here all morning keeping me up to date."

"We have just returned from visiting Mrs. Fox," Brass told her. "You know, it's odd the way things come around. I once did a column on her."

"I know," Gloria said. "Cathy Wild, née Karen Welikof. The moxie girl. She's singing at a club in the Village called The Stable. Mostly show stuff: Gershwin, Cole Porter, some Noel Coward. She's supposed to be very good."

"Yes," Brass said.

"I see that we're reserving those pictures for now," Gloria said.

"That's so," Brass agreed. "How did you know?"

"None of my informants knew about them, so I assumed that you hadn't mentioned them to the police."

Brass nodded. "You're worth every penny I'm paying you," he said.

"Oh," Gloria said, "considerably more than that." She took a dainty bite of her sandwich.

Brass removed the list of names of those people whose naked bodies had graced our collection of photographs from an inner pocket, uncreased it carefully, and laid it on Gloria's desk. "The folders for these people are on my desk," he said. "Find out where each of them has been for, say, the past two weeks. Make sure to tell whomever you talk to that you're from the *World*; we'll see if that provokes any reaction. Divide the names between you as you like. Also, see if Schiff identified those last two names."

"He did," Gloria said. "Their folders are on top of the others on your desk. The photographs were quite, ah, instructive."

"You looked?" Brass asked.

"Of course. I look at everything that comes into this office. It's my job. I am a newsman, after all."

"You are," Brass agreed. "And better than most. I'm glad you're so unflappable," he added. "Perhaps I should show you the rest of the photos when I get back. Your feminine eye might see something that our masculine ones overlooked." She smiled the smile of an ice princess. "I'm sure I will find different areas of interest, she said. "You men are so easily distracted by the sight of naked flesh."

"Some naked flesh is more distracting than others," Brass told her. "I look at myself in the mirror in the morning, and it does nothing for me." With that Brass went off to his meeting.

Gloria and I stared at the list of names. I went into Brass's office and retrieved the folders, including the two new ones. To the original six names we now added Homer Seinbrenner and Fletcher van Geuip.

Seinbrenner was the boss of B&S Distilleries, a company that did very little distilling, but imported much of the booze that thirsty New Yorkers sloshed about. When a Gothamite obeys Noel Coward's injunction to put his scotch or rye down and lie down, it is probably a scotch or rye supplied by B&S in the glass. The company had retreated to Canada during Prohibition and restricted itself to selling to rumrunners (or, presumably, scotch or rye runners) and letting them break the law. Or so Seinbrenner claimed.

Van Geuip—pronounced "gee-whip" with a soft *g*—was a writer of books about his own adventurous life. He traveled everywhere there was a track wide enough for a mule to carry him, and when he arrived he shot anything that moved. His books were full of passages like: "Ubo, my native bearer, handed me my elephant gun and I calmly took a bead on the elephant and brought him down. 'You brave man, *pemba,*' Ubo gushed, the awe showing in his expressive brown eyes." When I read things like that I can't help wondering what *pemba* translates to, and what the elephant thought about it.

"How do you want to split the list up?" I asked Gloria.

"I'll take Suzie Frienard," she said. "Aside from that, it doesn't matter; take whom you want."

"That's okay with me," I told her, "but just for my information, why do you want Suzie? Don't you think I can handle a woman?"

"Do *you* think you can handle a woman?" Gloria enquired sweetly. "But that's not it. If I call her, it's an item for the society page. If a man calls her, or asks about her, her husband is liable to think the paper is trying to investigate him, and we'll get no cooperation."

"When you're right, you're right," I said, knowing when to beat a graceful retreat. I took the first four names and went to my little cubical with them.

Bertram Childers
Gerald Garbin
Ephraim L. Wackersan II
Pass Helbine

Definitely names to conjure with. I got busy with my conjuring. Senator Childers was a snap. His Trenton office was happy to tell me that he had been in Washington for the past two weeks, but would be back in New Jersey, at his estate in Deal, tomorrow, and would be pleased to be interviewed by someone from the *World* if I would just call them to set it up first.

Judge Garbin didn't give interviews, his clerk told me. But when I asked him for the judge's schedule for the past two weeks, the clerk read it off to me out of his desk diary without pausing to inquire why. I guess they're used to odd requests from the press. The judge had been presiding over a complex civil case involving airplane parts for the past week. The week before that he had sat in judgment on the Florence Maybelle murder case. I had almost gone to sit in on that one myself. Mrs. Maybelle, twenty-nine, had been accused of murdering her husband, Roy, sixty-seven, a boating tycoon, for his money. She claimed that she thought he was a burglar. When called to the stand she had shed a lot of tears and shown a lot of leg, and been acquitted by the all-male jury, one of whom proposed marriage to her before she left the courtroom.

Ephraim Wackersan was more of a problem. He didn't believe in telephones, so the only one in his Sixth Avenue store was in the order department. The chief order-taker, a grimly efficient-sounding woman, assured me that he was there, that he arrived every day well before the store opened at 8 a.m. and remained until well after the store closed at 6 p.m. But could she really know that? He could have snuck out without his order department knowing a thing about it, or so I had to assume. I would reserve that one and go inspect the premises in person if Brass deemed it necessary. Onward to number four.

Pass Helbine proved difficult to find, and even more difficult to pin down. He wasn't in his New York office, and his secretary was vague about when he had been in. He wasn't at his Long Island estate, and his housekeeper said that he and the third Mrs. Helbine were in and out regularly, and she really couldn't keep track.

I started calling the Helbine Houses—the six flophouses that Helbine had painted and refurbished to give the bums a clean place to sleep at a dime a flop. The desk clerk at the first one I called suggested that I call another one, which I did. Helbine was there, serving dinner in the dining room. He came to the phone and yelled "Hello!" into the mouthpiece.

"Mr. Helbine? My name is Morgan DeWitt. I'm with the *New York World*. Could I have a minute of your time?"

"Now?"

"If it's convenient." I shifted the earpiece to my other hand. I really hate talking on the telephone.

"It isn't convenient, but then it never is," his voice boomed. "What do you want?"

"My paper wants to do a piece on you. 'Two Weeks in the Life of a Philanthropist.'"

"You want to follow me around for two weeks?"

"No. We feel that it wouldn't be spontaneous if we were with you. We'll just go with your last two weeks—whatever you did for the last two weeks. That is, unless there's something you'd rather not have us write about. We'll just interview you and whoever you've been with for the last two weeks. And we'll have to take pictures of the places you've been, of course."

I could hear that strange telephone sound that I always thought of as the static between the stars while he thought this over. "My life is an open book," he said finally. "I am essentially a public man."

"That's a wonderful attitude, Mr. Helbine," I said. "If you could just tell me where you've been the past two weeks—what places you visited, who you talked to."

"Well now," he said. "I'll have to make a list. I couldn't even tell you, right off, where I had lunch yesterday. Give me a day or so; I'll have my secretary type it up for you. Sort of a reverse itinerary, you might call it."

"You haven't been to any place especially exotic, have you?" I asked him. "I mean, if you took a flying trip to Europe or South America, I don't know if the *World* would spring for sending me and a photographer in your footsteps."

He laughed, a hearty haw-haw, us-boys-around-the-campfire-together sort of laugh. "No, nothing like that. Just dull old New York City and my Long Island estate, if I remember correctly. Call my secretary tomorrow. I'll have it typed for you."

"On behalf of the *New York World* and our two million readers, I thank you," I told him.

"Of course," he said. We both hung up. One thing about dealing with very rich people, particularly when they consider themselves philanthropists or industrialists or art collectors or have some other hobby that the rest of us can't afford: they expect other people to be interested in their lives. I understand that the Kings Louis of France, from number thirteen onward, used to have people come into their bedrooms in the morning and sit in a sort of gallery to watch them get up and go to the bathroom. It was considered a great honor to be invited, or you had to buy a ticket, I forget which. Maybe both.

Someone was crying; the sound came clearly into my small cubicle. I got up and went to the outer office. Cathy Wild Fox née Karen Welikof was standing in the middle of the floor in front of Gloria's desk clutching in one hand a cloth coat with some sort of fur collar, and in the other the white envelope that Brass had given her. She was holding the envelope out to Gloria, who had stood up on her side of the desk, and was trying to say something, but only incoherent sobs were coming out.

Gloria and I helped Cathy to the leather couch that stretched along one wall of the office, and I took the coat and envelope from her hands and stuffed the oversized white handkerchief from the breast pocket of my jacket into them. Gloria knelt on the couch next to Cathy and took her head in her arms like a mother holding a child. "There, there," she said. "You'd better stop that sobbing. Your mascara is running, and you'll get the hiccups."

Cathy buried her head in the handkerchief and took many deep breaths and then blew her nose three or four times, wiped her face, and looked up. Her mascara was all over her face, her lipstick was smeared, and her eyes were red and puffy, and she looked beautiful.

"My God," she said. "I'm sorry; I couldn't help it. How do I look?"

"Like a chipmunk who's trying to disguise herself as a raccoon," Gloria told her. "Come with me; I'll fix you up."

The two girls disappeared down the hallway into Brass's private washroom. I hung up Cathy's coat and put the white envelope down on the table and sat on the couch. The coat smelled of face powder and perfume, and I found myself thinking of all that Fox had lost.

I suddenly found myself very upset. I was sniffling. Luckily I had another handkerchief. I blew my nose just as Cathy and Gloria emerged from the bathroom. I was glad that they hadn't seen me. A man should never be seen crying.

The puffy redness was still evident on Cathy's face, but the mascara and other externals had been repaired. She came over to me and put out her hand. "I'm sorry," she said. "I didn't intend to make a scene. I'll have your handkerchief cleaned."

I took her hand. "That's okay," I said. "I'll just give it to the woman who does my washing. My laundry is usually so dull that she's been feeling sorry for me. A lipstick-smeared handkerchief will cheer her up." I was still holding Cathy's hand, and I quickly let it go before anyone else noticed.

Cathy smiled, which was quite an achievement, all things considered. "I wanted to see Mr. Brass," she said. She indicated the envelope on the table with a wide, expressive gesture using both arms, as though the envelope had suddenly become a hippopotamus. "I can't take that."

"What's the matter with it?" I asked.

Gloria picked it up. "What is it?" she asked.

"It's some money that Brass left Mrs. Fox to pay for some work Billy did, ah, a few days ago," I improvised. I restrained myself from saying what I thought: that Brass had stuck fifty or a hundred dollars in the envelope to help assuage the guilt he felt because Fox had died while working for him. Hell, I didn't blame him. *I* felt guilty myself, and I hadn't done anything.

"It's not, you know," Cathy said.

"How's that?"

"It's a gesture. Bill never earned that. It's a wonderful gesture, but I can't let him do it. I can't take that."

Gloria slipped open the envelope and took out the bills inside. "Some gesture," she said, fanning them like a bridge hand. "So that's what McKinley looks like."

I took a look and then got up and leaned toward them, drawn to the bills like I might be drawn to a precious stone: How often does one get to see such a magnificent sight? There were twelve bills in the fan: 2 five-hundred-dollar bills and 10 hundred-dollar bills. "That's two thousand dollars," I said cleverly.

Gloria looked at me. "Very good!" she said. "Next week we'll start you on simple fractions."

Cathy reached out and touched the fan of money, and then drew her hand away. "You know, I get five dollars a night for singing at the club," she said. "I sing three nights a week. That's fifteen dollars a week. And dinners; they feed me on the nights I work."

Gloria stuffed the money back into the envelope and laid it gently on the table. "That's not so bad, kid," she said.

"I know," Cathy said. "A lot of people get by on less. It's what I want to do, and I'm lucky to be doing it. Now that Bill is dead, the men are going to start—touching—me again, but I guess I can handle that."

"Touching you?" I asked. "The customers?"

"No, the bosses. Wherever I work there always seems to be at least one boss who thinks he has the right to touch me. Bill put a stop to that. But now he's gone."

"I know what you mean," Gloria said. "All men are wolves." She gave me a dirty look because I was the only available man.

"Isn't that a good reason to take the money?" I asked her. "It will mean you won't have to work any place where they don't treat you with respect. It will mean you can take voice lessons. Not that I think you need them," I added, realizing how that might sound. "But I've heard that all singers always want to take voice lessons."

"You think I should take the money?" Cathy asked. "Even though Bill did nothing to earn it except get killed? And I'm sure he wasn't planning to do that."

"I think Mr. Brass wants you to have the money," I told her. "I think he can afford it. I think he will be offended if you turn it down. I think he regrets that there is nothing else he can do to pay Fox for what happened except to give you money."

"But that's almost two years' salary!" Cathy said.

"Not for Mr. Brass," I said. "The amount he gives you has to be meaningful to him, even if it seems overwhelming to you. Otherwise there's no point to it."

"That makes a certain amount of sense," Gloria said. "Listen, kid, keep the money. If you try to give it back to Brass, he'll probably burn it."

"Oh, no!" Cathy said. "That would be horrible!"

7

We worked hard and long to convince Cathy to keep the money. She felt, as best she could express it, that having a husband get murdered was a hell of a way to earn two thousand dollars. If Brass was really going to burn it, then she would take it and give it to charity. I told her that Brass already gave enough to charity, which was true, although some of his charities wouldn't have made the Bishop's List. Finally we convinced her that Billy—William—would certainly want her to keep it, and that Mr. Brass wanted her to keep it, and so she should keep it. Gloria stuffed the bills back into the envelope and pressed it into her hands, and she clutched it to her bosom and started to sob quietly. Gloria kept talking, ignoring the tears, and I figured that Gloria must know what she was doing, so I joined in. We were deciding for her just how and where to do the keeping.

She shouldn't walk around with that much money, we decided; she might be robbed. And she'd better not leave it at home; she might be burglarized. And she couldn't trust banks, which could close, or move to Albania, and what could you do about that? Gloria and I came up with some esoteric solutions. I suggested that she fill her kitchen and living room with cans of tuna fish, spinach, and condensed milk; then at least she could always eat. Gloria held out for buying the biggest, best damned diamond ring she could for the money. "And don't mind the imperfections, as long as you can only see them under a microscope," Gloria said. "Imperfections are between you and your jeweler; as far as the world is concerned, it's the size that counts." We had Cathy giggling, and her tears had just about dried up when Brass came through the door, and in an instant all our good work flew out the window.

Cathy turned to face Brass and the tear ducts opened. She thrust the envelope full of cash out in front of her. "Oh, Mr. Brass," she wailed, "I can't take this!"

Brass took a second to focus on her, and another second to think about what she'd said. Then he reached out and took the envelope from her hands. "All right," he said. He patted her on the shoulder, and then walked through the room and down the short hall to his own office.

When I was eight years old I was knocked out of a rowboat by a medium-sized bass that I was trying to land. That was the last time I was quite this startled. At least this time I wasn't wet. The three of us formed a tableau for a minute: Cathy standing as she was and sobbing, and Gloria and I too stunned to move. At least I was; the expression on Gloria's face was hard to read. I have never actually seen Gloria surprised at anything, and a lot of surprising things have happened in that office.

The intercom buzzed twice, the signal for Gloria to go into Brass's office instead of answering, and so she did. Cathy turned to look at me, and then suddenly burst into fresh sobs and threw herself on the couch. I sat beside her and patted her on the shoulder and tried to think of something clever to say.

After a couple of minutes Gloria came out of Brass's office and went to Cathy. "Stop bawling," she told her sharply. "Mr. Brass wants to see you in his office, but not while you're crying; so stop!"

Cathy looked up, stifling a sob. She worked at wiping her tears away with the back of her hand. "It's not—it's not—"

"Sure it is," Gloria told her. "Come on, let's go back into the bathroom and I'll fix your face."

The two of them left the room. About ten minutes later Gloria poked her head in the doorway. "You too," she said, crooking a finger at me.

I entered Brass's office behind the two girls and we ranged ourselves in front of his desk. He glared at us. "Sit," he said. We did.

Brass leaned back in his chair. "First, the money," he said. "Gloria, you will escort Mrs. Fox to the Manhattan Bank branch on the corner tomorrow morning and open an account for her." He transferred his gaze to Cathy. "Unless you already have a bank account."

"What would I do with a bank account?" she asked.

"They are very useful," he told her, "now that Mr. Roosevelt has given us some assurance that they have to keep to some of the same standards that they demand of their customers. A savings account, I think. Gloria will help you. The process will be painless; Mr. Mergantaler, the branch manager, owes me a favor. Actually, several favors. Being a journalist has certain advantages."

"I guess everyone likes to have their name in the paper," Cathy said.

"In this case I kept his name out of the paper," Brass told her. "Don't be alarmed; it had nothing to do with his handling of the bank's affairs."

Brass leaned back in his chair. "Now," he said. "I have something to discuss about the recent events."

Cathy jumped to her feet. "About William?" she asked in one explosive breath.

"No," Brass said. "Not directly. But it does concern you. Please sit down."

She lowered herself onto the edge of the chair. It was a close approximation of sitting.

"I've just come from a meeting with the Big Three," Brass told us. "The publisher, the managing editor, and the city editor. All of whom were convinced, for some reason, that I had information about William Fox's murder that I was withholding from the police."

He stared at Cathy for a minute, and then transferred his gaze to me. "They said I would not have had Fox tailing someone on mere speculation. They had discussed it. They all agreed. They intimated that I would not have spent my own money unless I was sure of results, hinting at a reputation for penuriousness that I didn't know I had. They asked—they *demanded*—to know what that information was."

"What did you tell them?" Gloria asked.

"I told them that they didn't want to know. I said what I knew couldn't be used by the *World*. That if it leaked out it would ruin the lives of many important people. They said that surely they could be trusted."

Cathy returned to her feet. "Then you do know something more about William's death!" she said, her voice rising.

"Please, sit down," Brass said testily. "If you keep jumping up and down, it will make me nervous."

She perched herself on the edge of the chair like a bird that was ready to take flight at the next loud sound.

"But you didn't tell them anything," Gloria said. "You wouldn't."

"I don't know whether I wouldn't," Brass said, "but I didn't.

"What do you know about Bill's death?" Cathy asked. "Whatever it is, I have a right to know." She clenched and unclenched her fists. "Migod—I can't not know!"

Brass looked thoughtfully at her for a moment and then sighed.

"I will tell you if you ask. Would it help if I say that you can be actively involved in the search for your husband's killer, if you wish?"

Cathy regarded him suspiciously. "What do you mean?"

"I mean that the *World* will hire you, at a salary of twenty-five dollars a week, as a researcher."

"Twenty-five dollars!" Cathy sat down. "Thank you," she said. "I know you did this for me, and I appreciate it. But I'm not a researcher, I'm a singer."

"I did this for both of us," Brass said. "I know it's a lot to ask, but if you can put your singing career on hold for a little while, I would appreciate it. I am going to need some assistants who I can trust completely, who owe no allegiance to the paper, or the police department, or the people of the State of New York. At least as far as this matter is concerned."

Cathy pursed her lips and thought it over. "I will certainly stop singing for a while if I can truly be of help in catching Bill's killer," she said. "But surely there are many people more qualified. If you're just trying to find a way to give me even more money—I'd rather sing."

Brass leaned forward, his hands flat on the desk. "If I was merely assuaging my own guilt, which I admit I feel, I would call in a few markers and get you a singing gig at one of the big clubs—the Copacabana or the Sky Room. I know you can handle it; I've heard you sing. Indeed, if you choose not to work for me, I will do that. But this is a delicate and difficult problem we are facing, for reasons you don't as yet know. The qualities I need are intelligence and loyalty." Brass raised his right hand, palm out. "Honest."

"But if the newspaper is paying my salary…"

Brass nodded. "You have a well-developed moral sense," he said. "Most people would not let a small detail like that bother them. The *World* will be paying your salary with the understanding that you are to be working for me. If you doubt me, you can ask Mr. Sanders; he's the publisher."

"No," she said. "I believe you." She stared intently at Brass for a minute as though the answer to some dark riddle were written in the lines of his face—not that there are many lines on his face; I'm just being poetic—and then nodded. "Okay," she said.

Brass turned to Gloria. "Will you get those pictures out of the wall safe and give them to Mrs. Fox, please?" he said.

Gloria opened the wall safe, took out the packet of pictures, and handed them to Cathy. I tried to look casual while she examined them, but I think I was blushing. Hell of a thing for a grown man, but there you have it. If she had looked up at me while she was looking at the pictures, I'm sure she would have seen a pair of beet-red ears.

When she did look up, after several minutes spent examining the pictures one at a time, she was gazing calmly across the desk at Brass. "Well?" she said.

"I trust the subject matter didn't offend you," Brass said.

"I work in a cabaret in Greenwich Village," Cathy said. "Before that I worked in a mob night club. You'd have to go some to shock me. Tell me about the pictures."

"The man who gave us those photographs is the man Fox was following when he left here," Brass told her. "We assume that the man, and possibly—no, quite probably—the photographs, had something to do with his death."

"Who was the man?"

"We don't know. That's what Fox was trying to find out."

"Who are these people in the pictures?"

"That we do know. In each photograph one of the couple is a prominent man—or woman. We have no reason to assume that they had anything to do with the murder, but release of the pictures would harm them greatly. It's the reason we are keeping this from the authorities. Gloria will give you a briefing on who they all are."

"But you don't know for sure that they had nothing to do with it?"

"No. You will help us find out."

"Oh." She put the pictures on the desk and sat with her hands folded in her lap, thinking. "What do you want me to do?" she asked.

Brass smiled. "You've got moxie," he told her. "We could use some more moxie around here."

Pushing himself up from his chair, Brass went to the small closet which held, among other things, the office booze, and took out a bottle of cognac and four narrow-stemmed glasses.

The office booze collection consists mostly of bottles of various cognacs, Armagnacs, and wines. The only thing I know is that the booze Brass buys is very good and varies from impressively expensive to impressively inexpensive. We also keep a bottle of cheap rye for visiting newsies. Not that Brass would be hesitant to share his quality booze; newspaper men as a class seem to think it's unmanly to drink anything but cheap rye.

Brass poured the amber liquid into the glasses and passed them around. "I think we need this," he said.

Cathy sniffed cautiously at her glass, ran a few drops over her tongue, and nodded. "This is good," she said. "A lot better than the firewater they serve in the clubs."

"It better be," Brass told her. "It's forty dollars a bottle."

She looked up at Brass like he'd gone crazy, but then sort of sighed and took another sip.

Gloria was slowly going through the pictures as she sipped her booze. I saw her stop at one picture, examine it closely, and nod to herself. I wondered exactly what she was agreeing with, but I didn't ask.

Brass asked Gloria and me whether we thought we'd learned

anything useful from our phone calls, and we assured him that we had not. He told us to type up our notes anyway, you can never tell. "When you have finished you can go home," he told Gloria. "I'll need you here early tomorrow morning, because God knows I won't be. I expect it to be a long night."

"What of me?" Cathy asked.

"Why don't you go home and get a good night's sleep," Brass said. "You probably need it."

"I probably do," Cathy agreed, "but I don't want to go home. Not just yet. I don't think I want to be alone tonight."

Gloria reached over and patted her on the arm. "I have a couch, honey," she said. "It's not the most comfortable thing in the world, but I've slept on worse."

"Thank you," Cathy said.

Brass turned to me. "If you have the energy," he said, "I'd like you to come with me."

"I have the energy," I said. The man was at least fifteen years older than I. If he had the energy, I had the energy. I hoped.

Gloria put the pictures back down on the desk and Brass reached over and picked them up. "See anything interesting?" he asked her, snapping a rubber band around the packet and sticking it in his pocket.

She gave a tired smile. "Nothing I'd cross the street for," she said. "Some of those men should go on diets and try to get regular exercise."

8

The apartment Fox's body was found in had been rented by a I German expatriate group called the Verein für Wahrheit und Freiheit, which translates as the "Truth and Freedom Society." What had brought them together was a shared distaste for the social policies of Adolf Hitler. They used the mimeograph machine in the apartment to put out pamphlets with titles like "The Truth About National Socialism," "What Hitler Intends," and "Europe—Wake Up!" in six different languages, which they distributed to anyone who would read them. Since the members had little else in common, and their politics ranged from monarchist to communist, their meetings often dissolved into shouting contests, enlivened with occasional fisticuffs. Apparently, no one ever got seriously hurt, and the meetings broke up with everyone joining in the beer of forgiveness at the corner bierstube and agreeing that fighting Hitler was more important than fighting one another. Their ages ranged from the early twenties to the late seventies, with those years over fifty predominating. None of them looked like they had ever done any heavy lifting.

A gaggle of them were gathered in that apartment, spilling out into the hallway and the apartment across the hall, when Brass and I returned to the scene of the crime at about nine that evening. They were busily and noisily engaged in a meaningful discussion, but since it was in German, the topic of the evening eluded me. A rotund man with a red face yelled an emphatic German phrase at Brass as we came up the stairs. When Brass failed to respond, he grabbed him by the sleeve and pulled him down the hallway to an area that was relatively free of babble. I followed close behind. "You are not more police, yes?" he asked in a deep, gravelly voice. "You are too goddamn well dressed."

"I am not more police, no," Brass agreed. "I am a newspaper-man."

"That is good," the man said, bobbing his head up and down. "You will write about us, yes? You will tell what the Gestapo are doing to us, yes?"

"Now come on," I said from behind him. "The New York police aren't that bad."

He wheeled and jumped back, as though I had just prodded him with a hot needle.

"I'm with him," I said, indicating Brass. "I didn't mean to startle you."

He relaxed a little. "I am not speaking of the New York police," he said. "I am speaking of the *Geheime Staatspolizei*—the Gestapo. Heinrich Himmler's own revenge apparatus." He lowered his voice. "You are United States of America citizens, yes? Also you are New York City newspapermen, yes?"

Brass took the leather case holding his press pass from his pocket and showed it to the red-faced man. "Yes," he said. "We are."

I pulled out mine for emphasis and held it before his face. He seemed duly impressed. Considering that the passes were made up in the *World*'s composing room, and had no official status, they had served us well over the years.

"Ah, truly," the man said, peering closely at Brass's card. "You are the renowned Alexander Brass. I, myself, was a writer for a monthly journal of political opinion in München—Munich—until the day last July when our editor was removed to a concentration camp for his health. He was suffering from that contagious disease known as socialism. For my health—although I am not, you understand, a socialist—I was on the next train to Geneva, leaving behind my job, my dachshund, and my mistress; all of whom, I'm sure, were goddamn better off without me." He bowed slightly from the neck. "Willi Grosfeder at your service."

"What's happening?" Brass asked, indicating the fracas before us with a wave of his hand.

Grosfeder filled us in on the *Verein,* and then explained, "They are trying to decide whether they should hire a lawyer for Max or deny any connection with him. Some of them say one, some the other; some say neither, some say both; several are arguing over what Karl Marx would have done; Gumple, over there, is explaining something about Martin Buber, and Hollberger—that tall man in the doorway—is going to burst into tears at any minute and tell anyone who will listen that this is all pointless, and we are all ineffectual intellectuals, a phrase he is overly fond of. He's right, of course, but it changes nothing to say so."

"Who is Max, and why does he need a lawyer?" Brass asked.

"Ah! I assumed you knew. Max von Pilath is the head of our little group. That is his apartment across from where the body was found. About an hour ago he was arrested for the murder of that poor reporter."

"Is this Max von Pilath a very large man?" Brass asked, spreading his arms out from his waist to indicate in which dimension he meant this largeness. "And not very kempt?"

"Not very… *Ach,* so—I see! What you Americans do to your language; it is to be admired. On the contrary, Max is slender, ascetic-looking, and unnaturally well groomed. Also he speaks with a pronounced stutter except when he is standing on a podium addressing an audience, which fact I have always found of the utmost fascination."

"Why did they arrest him? Why do they think he murdered Fox?" Brass asked.

"They didn't say," Grosfeder said.

"Well, perhaps we should go find out," Brass said. "Thank you, Mr. Grosfeder. Come, DeWitt."

We shouldered our way through the nattering crowd and out onto Eighty-second Street. It was nine-thirty in the evening, but the street had not retired for the night. There were people on the stoops and in doorways and standing in little groups in shadowed areas along the sidewalk. No one ventured out into the pools of yellow light cast by the streetlamps except a few passersby like us, who had business elsewhere.

We caught a cab on First Avenue, and Brass directed it to Seventy-seventh and Lexington and sat impassively, staring, as far as I could tell, at the back of the driver's head for the five minutes it took us to make the trip.

There are two homicide squads in Manhattan: Homicide South and Homicide North. Homicide South is in the Police Headquarters Building downtown on Centre Street, and Homicide North takes up most of the third floor of the 23rd Precinct building on Seventy-seventh between Lexington and Third. Fifty-seventh Street is the dividing line for their jurisdiction. There is a possibly apocryphal story about a man who was found dead on an uptown bus. The investigation into his demise was delayed for a week while the two squads squabbled over whether he died above or below Fifty-seventh Street.

The desk sergeant at the 23rd Precinct—or the two-three, as the cops call it—beamed at us as we came in. "Mr. Brass," he said. "Good to see you."

"And you, Kelly," Brass said.

"You'll be wanting to go upstairs. You know the way."

"Indeed I do," Brass agreed. We took the wide staircase up to the second floor, and then the narrower staircase up to the third. The homicide squad room was empty, except for Alan Shine, who was sitting on a wooden bench that ran along the wall and absently folding his hat into a variety of shapes it had never been intended to assume. He looked up when we came in. "You got here quick," he said. "I just called it in."

I took his hat out of his hand, punched some shape into it, and stuck it on his head. "Called what in?"

"They've got someone for the Fox killing. They're in there talking to him now."

"What have they got on him?" Brass asked.

"They haven't told me," Shine said. "Say, you hear the one about the guy at the soup kitchen who says, 'Waiter, there's a fly in my soup,' and the waiter leans forward and says, 'Keep it quiet, we don't have enough flies to go around'?"

"They don't have waiters in soup kitchens," I said.

"Shaddup," Shine explained, grinning at me. He took his hat off and twisted it into a shape that looked like what a butterfly would look like if a butterfly looked like a hat.

Brass sat on the bench next to the *World*'s ace crime reporter. "What's been happening?"

"You tell me," Shine said. "They brought this guy in about—what?—two hours ago. I just found out from a source that he's being held for Billy's murder. But they won't release so much as his name, and they won't let me talk to him.

"What source?" I asked.

Shine rubbed his thumb and forefinger together. "A five-dollar source," he said. That meant it was one of the patrolmen. A sergeant or one of the detectives would be a ten-dollar source. "None of the other boys have it yet, so with any luck I'll have an exclusive. If any of the homicide dicks will come out here to talk to me."

"I have a little for you," Brass told him. "His name is Max von Pilath. He's the president, or whatever, of the Verein fiir Wahrheit und Freiheit, which is the group renting the room William's body was found in."

A notebook and pencil appeared in Shine's hand. "Spell that," he said. Brass did so, and translated it. "Also, he lives in the apartment across the hall," he added. "Why the police think he killed Fox, I don't know."

Shine jumped up. "Thanks," he said. "I'll phone this in." He trotted over to one of the empty desks and picked up the phone.

Inspector Raab and two of his flunkies came out of an office across the room. They started toward the interrogation rooms, but when Raab saw us he turned and headed straight for Brass. "Well, well," he said, stopping two feet short of Brass and glaring at him. "What brings you here?"

"Max von Pilath," Brass said.

"And just how the hell did you know that? Can't they keep anything secret for at least an hour or two around here?"

"DeWitt and I went to Eighty-second Street. A group of German pamphlet-writers are there trying to decide whether to hire an attorney for von Pilath, who is their titular head, or disown him."

"Yeah?" Raab pulled a pack of cigarettes from his pocket, muttered, "I gotta quit smoking!" and stuffed it back. "If I were them," he told Brass, "I'd go for the disowning. Either that or see if Darrow is still taking cases."

"So he did it?" Brass asked.

"His fingerprints are all over the room—"

"He worked there," I said before I could stop myself.

Raab glared at me. "His fingerprints, as I was saying, are all over the room. They are also on the murder weapon. And, we have an eyewitness. If that isn't enough to get a conviction, I'll retire to Connecticut and raise sheep."

"What kind of sheep?" Brass asked.

"How should I know?" Raab took the pack of cigarettes back out, glared at it, and thrust it back into his pocket. "Small ones."

"Why did he do it?"

Raab sighed. "So far we got no idea," he said. "He won't talk. He says we can beat him all we want to, but we'll get no information from him. He's very adamant. I have a feeling that if we did beat him, he'd clam up even tighter. We don't beat up people anymore. We use kindness. It often startles them into confessing. Back in the days when we did beat people, it wasn't his sort we beat anyway."

"What sort did you beat?" I asked.

Raab stared at me for a moment. "I'll tell you," he said. "When I first joined the force, a while before you were born, I had occasion to apprehend a lad who had been hitting his mother with a baseball bat. When I brought him into the station house, the desk sergeant listened to the charge and then said—it was a sort of accusation—'There's not a mark on him. He didn't resist arrest?'

"'No, Sarge,' I said.

"'Well, take him out back and have him resist arrest for a while,' the sergeant told me. 'I don't want to see nobody that beats their mother in here before they've resisted a lot of arrest.' And I did that. And I've never been sorry for it."

"That's a good story," Brass said. "I haven't heard that one before."

Raab thrust his hands deeply into his jacket pockets. "I'm saving it for my memoirs," he said. "So don't use it."

"Scout's honor," Brass said.

"Somehow the image of you as a Boy Scout is frightening," Raab said.

"Then you're safe," Brass said. "I never was. Who is the eyewitness?"

"A Spaniard named Velo who runs a travel agency across the street. He saw Fox enter the building and this von Pilath go in right behind him. And about ten minutes later he saw von Pilath leave with a brown paper bag, which he tossed into a trash can. The Spaniard pointed it out to one of my men, and they searched the can and found the bag. Inside it was a knife with an eight-inch blade, covered with blood."

Shine looked up from his telephone. "How do you spell that name, Inspector?"

Raab sighed a deep and heartfelt sigh. "I didn't see you sitting there," he said. "The city didn't buy that desk for your use."

"Come on, be a sport," Shine said.

Raab transferred his glare to Brass, and then briefly to me, and then back to Shine, as though trying to decide how to apportion guilt. "*V-E-L-O,*" he said. "Now get off the phone."

"Sure thing," Shine agreed, "whatever you say. I believe in working with the authorities. Say, did you hear the one—"

"Out!" Raab bellowed. "Up from the desk and downstairs to that little, airless room that we provide for the working press."

"Sure thing," Shine repeated. He murmured into the phone for a last second, and then hung it up and sprung to his feet. "I'll be downstairs if you want me," he said to the room at large, and headed out the door.

After he was gone, Brass asked Raab, "Did Señor Velo see the fat man that Fox was following?"

"He says nobody else went in or out around the same time. We didn't ask him specifically about a fat man. We don't want to go putting ideas into his head."

"What an original concept," Brass said. "Any chance of my seeing the prisoner?"

Raab thought it over. "He won't talk to us," he said. "Who knows? Maybe he'll talk to you. If he says anything useful, can you keep it to yourself until we have a chance to look at it?"

"Scout's honor," Brass said.

Raab snorted. "Come this way."

He led us down a corridor to the interrogation rooms and pushed the first door open. A thin, dapper man was sitting behind a small table with his hands together on the tabletop. One detective was standing over him, while another was leaning back on a rickety chair across the room. Nobody was saying anything as the door opened. "This is Alexander Brass," Raab said to the dapper man. "He wants to talk to you. He's a newspaperman. I'll give you ten minutes." He gestured to the two detectives, and they joined us outside the room as Brass entered. Raab closed the door and we continued down the hall to the next room. "Let's keep it quiet in here," Inspector Raab said as we entered the room. "Sound goes right through the wall." One of the detectives closed the door and turned the light off, and Inspector Raab slid open a panel in the wall, and a large one-way glass gave us a full view of the interrogation room.

I found it a curious feeling, watching someone I knew couldn't see me. Even though he wasn't doing anything but sitting at the table and staring stolidly at the mirror on the far wall, behind which I was staring back at him. Brass stood beside the table and silently examined the prisoner. Max von Pilath returned the silence, but not the examination. He didn't so much as turn his head enough to see what Brass looked like.

The silence stretched out.

Brass straddled the old wooden chair by the side of the table and leaned forward until his face was scant inches from von Pilath's. "The knife has your fingerprints on it," he said softly. "Did you use it to cut bratwurst?"

For a minute von Pilath stayed mute, staring rigidly ahead. Then he turned his head slowly until he was looking at Brass. "You can b-b-beat me," he said. "I will not t-t-talk."

"I can't beat you," Brass told him. "The police union won't let me. It's a jurisdictional thing: If I beat you, local 104 will go on strike. All I'm allowed to do is pop flashbulbs in your face and ask you annoying questions."

"I will not t-t-t-talk!" von Pilath stubbornly repeated.

"That's okay," Brass said encouragingly. "You stick with that. It'll look good in the paper. 'Arrested for the murder of *New York World* star reporter William Fox, Max von Pilath, head of a mysterious German organization in whose offices Fox's body was found, stands mute in the face of intensive police questioning.' Actually you're sitting mute, but that's not a trite enough phrase to clear rewrite."

Von Pilath shrunk away from Brass slightly. Then something of what Brass had said seemed to sink in. "You are t-t-truly a j-journalist?" he asked. For the rest of the conversation I will leave out the repeated consonants. Von Pilath's stutter was actually fairly soft and unobtrusive, and it looks worse on the printed page than it was. Just keep in mind that a fair bit of gentle stuttering was going on from von Pilath's side of the table.

Brass took out his all-purpose press card and displayed it to von Pilath. "Really," he said.

Von Pilath took several deep breaths and then leaned back and relaxed. Then he stiffened again. "Why are they letting you speak with me?" he demanded.

"The freedom of the press," Brass told him. "It's the First Amendment to the Constitution of the United States of America," he explained, the syllables rolling off his tongue like a Fourth of July speech. "They have to."

"Ah!" von Pilath said. "I have heard of this."

"Did you kill William Fox?"

"No, of course not."

"Then why don't you tell the police that you're innocent?"

"I will say nothing to the police. It would not matter what I said. They work with the Gestapo; it is a clearly established fact."

On my side of the wall Inspector Raab made a soft muttering sound, and then shut up.

Brass said, "They do? Are you sure?"

Von Pilath moved his head up and down slightly in what was probably a nod. "Through ICPB," he said.

"Did you leave the building carrying a brown paper bag?" Brass asked.

"I was not there all day," von Pilath said, "until this evening when I was arrested. I have been in—no, I cannot say where. But elsewhere."

"If you won't tell me where you were, was anyone else with you?"

"I will not—I cannot—say."

Brass leaned back and stared at von Pilath. "Your friends at the *Verein* are thinking of hiring an attorney for you."

Von Pilath thought this over for a second. "They should not bother," he Said. "Either I cannot be convicted for something I did not do, or I can. If I can, it will be because of circumstances over which a lawyer will have little control."

"You think you'll be railroaded?"

Von Pilath looked puzzled. "Railroaded?"

"You believe there is a conspiracy to convict you of a crime you did not commit?"

"I am convinced of it. Regard the evidence which has already been manufactured. The question is, are the New York City police a part of it or are they not?"

"I think you'll find that they are not. They have their problems, but railroading the innocent is not among them."

"I hope you are right, and that it does not occur that you are the innocent and not I," von Pilath said.

Brass thought this over for a moment, then stood up. "Are there any photographers in your group?" he asked.

"Photographers? No. I don't think so. No."

"Thank you," Brass said. "I may return later." He walked to the door, and knocked to be let out.

Raab slid the panel closed and we exited from our spy room. One of the detectives opened the door for Brass and went in as Brass came out.

"That was not much help," Raab said as we walked down the corridor. "Although you certainly got more out of him than we did. Someday I'll have to have a discussion with you about just what problems the police department has. What was that about photographers? You trying to locate your chubby picture purveyor?"

"It might be a good idea," Brass said.

"Well, maybe. But we've got the murderer."

"He didn't do it," Brass said.

"So he says," Raab said. "And you believe him. Why?"

"I can't explain it. Just a gut reaction."

"Well, you keep your gut reaction, and I'll keep my bloody knife with his fingerprints on it, and we'll see which one impresses the jury," Raab said.

"What's ICPB?" I asked.

"The International Criminal Police Bureau," Raab told me. "It mainly exists to simplify the exchange of information among police departments around the world."

"Is there any truth to what von Whosis said about it?"

Raab shrugged. "It's a story that's going around among the anti-Nazi emigré groups," he said. "My guess is that Nazi sympathizers here started it themselves to make their enemies afraid to go to the police. The fact is that we are members of ICPB, as are the German national police. Which means that if they request police information about anyone, we are obliged to share it with them—up to a point. But they don't tell us who to charge with a crime, and we don't tell them who to beat up."

"A succinct way to put it," Brass said. "Well, it's heading toward eleven o'clock, and I have a column to write. I think I'll head off to the Stork Club."

"A hard life you lead," Raab said. "An endless round of gaiety and free booze."

Brass put his hand on Raab's shoulder. "Have you ever noticed," he said, "that people who work at soda fountains soon lose their taste for ice cream?"

9

Brass went to the Stork Club and I headed home to get what was left of a good night's sleep. My alarm went off at six-thirty, as usual, and I was wide awake before my hand hit the shutoff button. I sat up and swung my legs over the side of the bed. I felt like running in place and doing a set of sit-ups, push-ups, and jumping jacks. Perhaps even attempting something that required coordination. Resisting this impulse to do violent physical exercise, I shaved, showered, started the coffee perking, dressed, made my bed and pushed it up into its hiding place in the wall, poured a cup of coffee, and sat down at my typewriter for my morning bout with the saga of Percival. I rolled a fresh sheet of paper into the machine and poised my fingers above the keys.

I might be awake and alert, but this morning I was not creative. Words would not come. I got up and poured myself another cup of coffee. I sharpened a pencil. I adjusted the window to just the right height. I sat down. I got up and closed the window. I sat down. I opened the window again and stuck my head out to examine the street below. The morning was mild, with a feeling in the air that spring was about to thrust itself upon the city. A chubby man in a tuxedo, top hat, and black tie askew was doing a drunken pavane down the sidewalk below me; he was being extravagantly ignored by the fifteen or so people scurrying to early morning jobs. Gotham.

Suddenly the events of yesterday came back to me. All of them, all at once, and I knew why I was wide awake. My unconscious must have been pondering them all night. Now, with the coming of day, my unconscious handed the memories back to me. William Fox. The Widow Fox. Max von Pilath. I felt overwhelmed and in need of answers.

I was not going to work on my book this morning. I would take a long walk, heading for the office in some roundabout way, and try to think things out as I walked. It worked for Brass, it should work for me. I put on my jacket, decided that spring had indeed arrived and I didn't need an overcoat, grabbed my hat, and went downstairs. I went over to Central Park West and turned downtown, walking on the park side of the street. Before I could think of the answers, I would have to formulate the questions. But, aside from the obvious ones of who killed William Fox and who took the dirty pictures, none came to mind. And neither of those presented obvious solutions.

I stopped for a hot dog and an orange drink at the Seventy-second Street entrance to the park, where a vendor had set up his cart in hopes of catching the early morning hot dog crowd. My alfresco breakfast warmed and cheered me, but my thoughts kept spiraling around the questions I was trying to analyze. Aside from realizing within the first few blocks that I should have taken an overcoat, I came to no conclusions. Half an hour later, when I reached the *World* building, I had several ideas, but none reasonable enough to suggest to Brass. I won't embarrass myself by going over them, but if I say that one of them involved a hot-air balloon, you see what I mean. My only fairly respectable notion was to go to the various subjects of our collection of dirty pictures and ask them if they had any idea of who had been taking snapshots of them while they were otherwise engaged. But Brass would not approve. Fine. Then let him think of something.

It was ten after eight when I pushed through the door to the office. Gloria was already at her desk. She was wearing a dress that I would call tan, but I guess she would call beige, and a necklace of some sort of thick beads, and had managed her usual trick of looking simultaneously desirable and untouchable. The sound of typing was coming from the inner hall.

Gloria looked up. "You're here early," she said. "Let me guess. You hocked your overcoat to pay your gambling debts and your landlady kicked you out when you couldn't make the rent. Right?"

"Very good," I said. "And now, for the grand prize: If the plural of *goose* is *geese,* what's the plural of *gooseberry*?"

"Jam," she said.

"Congratulations! You've won a one-way trip on the day boat to Albany, steerage class, bring your own lunch." I tossed my hat on the peg. "You're a bit early yourself. What's happening?"

"Cathy couldn't sleep, so we came to work," she told me.

The typewriter in the hall stopped banging, and a few seconds later a somber-looking Cathy Fox appeared in the inner doorway. She was wearing a black skirt and jacket and a little black cloche hat with her hair tucked up inside it or around it or however women do these things. "Good morning, Mr. DeWitt," she said. "Where do you keep your typewriter ribbons?"

"In the closet," I said. "On one of the shelves in back. How are you feeling this morning?"

"I'm not feeling this morning," she said. "I'm keeping busy so that I won't feel. Gloria said I should stay at her place today, but I didn't want to be alone. I hope Mr. Brass has a lot for me to do. I hope it has something to do with—with..." She stopped speaking and moving and stared at me, unable to finish the sentence.

I wanted to offer some word of comfort, but nothing came to mind that wouldn't have sounded trite or patronizing or just stupid. "I hope so too," I said, and sort of patted her on the shoulder as I walked by, headed for my office.

Brass came in around ten-thirty and greeted each of his minions as he made his way to his office. I gave him a couple of minutes to get settled and then went in after him. He was standing behind his desk staring out the window at the Hudson River. "There must be something in the air," I said. "Gloria and Cathy were here before me, and I was here two hours early. And now you're an hour ahead of your usual time."

"I'll try not to make a habit of it," Brass said. "I stopped at the medical examiner's on my way here. They'll release Fox's body today. I'll have to find out what Mrs. Fox wants done with it."

"How quickly a person becomes an it," I said.

Brass sat on the edge of his desk. "Momentary emotion, no matter how sincere, is not a good basis for a philosophy," he told me. "It also creates lousy legislation." He pointed a finger toward the door. "Get her. I'll do it now."

I went to the little alcove that contained the spare typewriter and Cathy Fox, and told her that the boss wanted to see her. She straightened her jacket, touched her hat to make sure it hadn't disappeared, and went through into his office. I followed.

Brass motioned her to a seat. "I've made arrangements for the Campbell Funeral Home to pick up William's body," he told her. "If you approve."

Cathy nodded. "They did Rudolph Valentino," she said. "I was thirteen. I stood in line for three hours to see him." She took a deep breath. "Do you suppose anyone will stand in line to see William?" She was fighting down some powerful emotion, but she was fighting it successfully.

"He had a lot of friends," I said.

Cathy looked at me, and then turned back to Brass. "Do you think there's a heaven?" she asked him.

Brass took Cathy's hand. "Whether or not there is a heaven," he told her, "we live on in the memory of those who love us. As long as you are alive, William Fox is immortal."

I thought she'd burst out crying, and so did she for a second, but she gulped twice and nodded.

Gloria appeared in the doorway. "Sorry to interrupt, but the bund is here to see you," she told Brass.

"What bund?" Brass asked.

"I don't know," Gloria said. "There are four Germans out front who want in. They seem agitated, but not dangerous."

"What do they want?"

"They want to see you about Max von Pilath," Gloria said. "They said you'd know who he is. Who is Max von Pilath?"

"The police arrested him last night for the murder of William Fox—"

Cathy jumped to her feet.

"—but I don't think he did it." Brass patted Cathy on the shoulder. "I'm sorry. It isn't going to be that easy."

Cathy sat back down.

Brass moved to his desk and lowered himself gingerly into his chair. "Bring them in," he said.

The four men came in and ranged themselves in front of Brass's desk. Gloria introduced them from left to right. "Mr. Schulman, Mr. Grosfeder, Mr. Eisen, Mr. Keis—Mr. Brass."

Brass nodded. "My associates," he said, waving an arm in our direction. "Mr. DeWitt and Mrs. Fox. You know Miss Adams."

Gloria and I pulled some chairs from the far wall to the front of the desk, but our guests remained standing. Grosfeder, the erstwhile German journalist, we'd met earlier. Schulman was a small man in a tweed suit with leather patch pockets, leather patches at the elbows, and leather trim. He had a spade beard and eyes that protruded slightly from his head and never stayed still. Eisen was tall, dressed in an ill-fitting black suit, white shirt, and black bow tie, and seemed to be leaning forward even when he was standing still. He gave the impression that whatever he put on would look ill-fitting after he had been wearing it for an hour. Keis—pronounced to rhyme with *ice*—was a portly man wearing a shiny blue suit and black shoes that were either patent leather or very well shined. He looked as though any second he was going to try to sell you something.

Grosfeder turned to look at Cathy. "Mrs. Fox?" he asked. "You are a relation of the poor man who was murdered in our offices, yes? His wife, perhaps?"

Cathy nodded without speaking.

"You have our most deep sympathies, I assure you," Grosfeder told her. He turned back to Brass. "We, my associates and I, are here as supplicants. We wish you to aid us, to advise us, and we can offer little in return."

"You can start by sitting down," Brass told him. "All of you. It makes me nervous to have people looming over me while we talk."

They sat down.

"Grosfeder told us of meeting you last evening," Keis said, "and so we decided to come see you."

Schulman leaned forward. "I've read your column, Mr. Brass," he said. "You use your superior writing skills to write pap for the bourgeoisie, and parade for them tales of people they cannot be and places they cannot go and things they cannot do. Do you consider this socially relevant? Do you not agree that the writer's only important function is to educate the masses?"

"Schulman!" Grosfeder leaned over and put his hand on Schulman's arm. "Don't start! You agreed—"

"That's all right," Brass said, leaning back in his chair and fixing his gaze on the little man in the tweed suit. "Those who refer to other people as 'the masses' usually have small regard for them as individuals. Those who write to polemicize rather than entertain usually succeed in doing neither." He looked around at the rest of the German contingent. "Now, did you want to discuss something with me?"

The four looked at one another and began talking German. The conversation began quietly enough, but hand gestures were quickly added, and it grew louder by the second. Brass waited patiently for about a minute, and then opened the side drawer in his desk, took out a silver whistle, and blew one piercing blow.

Silence.

Brass jiggled the whistle between his hands. "This was given to me by FDR when he was governor of New York," he said. "For helping to blow the whistle on organized crime. It was quite a ceremony. There were, I believe, five whistles given out. I haven't noticed any reduction in organized crime, but I suppose it's the symbolism that counts." He tossed the whistle back into the drawer. "It's the first time I've used it."

"You will forgive us," Grosfeder said, doing his best to bow an apology from a sitting position. "We are not used to working together on anything. It is why we accomplish so little." This threatened to set off another round of German vocal exercise, but Grosfeder managed to squelch it before it got out of hand. When silence again reigned, he nodded to the man on his left. "You will speak what is necessary for us, Professor Eisen, yes?"

Eisen nodded and stood up. "I apologize for our uncivility," he said. "It is an honor to meet you, Mr. Brass. You, through your writings, have done much to teach we poor, confused émigrés what it means to live in America."

Brass looked up with his "don't kid a kidder" expression, his hands wide apart on the desk, a broad smile on his face. "Yes, valuable lessons about American life," he said. "Gangsters, bootleggers, chorus girls, crooked politicians, nightclubs—"

"That is not the lesson," Professor Eisen said, jumping in as Brass paused to take a breath. "You write also about the good things of America: about people of different nationalities working together, about a policeman who climbs a tree to rescue a kitten for a little girl."

"Oh yes, the kitten story," Brass said. "I got more letters about that—But the point of the story was that the cop got stuck up the tree himself, and they had to call the fire department to get him down."

"Your point, perhaps," Professor Eisen said. "But a policeman who rescues kittens is not a policeman who breaks windows and beats people up because they are socialists or communists or Jews." Eisen sat down as though he were suddenly very tired.

Keis buttoned the top button of his blue suit jacket, sat up straight, and took a deep breath. "The truth is, Mr. Brass, that we are afraid of asking your help," he said. "But then, we are afraid of everything. We have learned to live with fear, as others learned to live with a toothache or a wooden leg. But constant fear is a debilitating disease, and its primary symptoms are indecision and uncertainty. And so we go around even more indecisive and ineffectual than usual, and bicker among ourselves because there is a certain amount of pleasure in being able to yell at someone and a certain amount of safety in not agreeing on any course of action."

"What are you afraid of," Brass asked, "and in what way do you think I can help?"

"That is two separate questions," Grosfeder broke in. "What we want you to do is investigate the murder of William Fox, and show—prove—that Max von Pilath had nothing to do with it. In which fact, I assure you, there is nothing but truth."

"It is that the police are holding von Pilath under the suspicion of murdering William Fox," Professor Eisen said. "And it is that Max von Pilath is not capable of killing anyone, and besides had absolutely no reason to wish this *New York World* reporter harm. But it is also that we would not be useful in speaking to the police. They will put his name on the ICPB, and the Berlin police—Max is from Berlin—will discover several crimes for which he is suspected, or even possibly convicted. And if we try to help directly, the results will be the same. I will become a bank robber in Frankfurt. My friend Keis here will be a man who molests small children in Munich. Perhaps the German police will even demand that we be exported."

"Deported," Grosfeder said.

"The German police would make up lies about you?" Brass asked, looking around at his guests. "I have always heard that the German police are among the most competent and efficient in the world."

"The German police will do what the German government tells them to," Grosfeder said. "Obedience to authority is one of their finest traits. And the government of Herr Hitler and his cronies does not encourage dissent."

"So I have heard. You want me to intercede for you with the police in their investigation of Max von Pilath?"

"Yes," Grosfeder said. "That is it."

"We want you to tell the investigators that Max could not have done this," Schulman said, his protruding eyes round with the earnestness of his words. "And further, that Sebastian Velo is a Fascist." With each of these assertions Schulman stabbed the desk repeatedly with his ring finger, causing an impressive staccato of thumps.

"Sebastian Velo?"

"The man who runs the Madrid Travel Agency, which is located in the building across the street from our office," Eisen said. "The man who swears to having seen Max and Mr. Fox together. The man who found the knife. He is a Spanish Fascist. And the Fascists and the Nazis have been known to do each other favors. For thirty years there was a dry-cleaning establishment in that shop. Then, eight months ago the Verein für Wahrheit und Freiheit rented an apartment to use as an office, and six months ago the dry cleaner went out of business and this Fascist moved in."

"And on occasion," Keis added, "a man is sitting in the window of the shop with a very expensive Leica camera, taking pictures of everyone who goes in or out of our building."

"This is what we know," Grosfeder said. "We do not know who killed Mr. Fox, but we believe that the Nazis are using the opportunity of his death to discredit us. They would rather kill us, and may get around to that, but this will suffice for the moment.

In the process, of course, the truth of the death of Mr. Fox will be lost."

"Von Pilath refuses to say where he was when Fox was killed," Brass said. "Do you know?"

They all looked at one another. Professor Eisen leaned forward. "If the information is essential, we must share it. We have an apartment some blocks away that is our"—he searched for the word—"safety house. Most of the members know we have it, but only a few know where it is. Max was there."

"Alone?"

"He was helping a family get settled into it, which is where they will be for the next few weeks."

"Then why don't they come forward and say so?"

"They are not in this country legally. They would be sent back to Germany. Besides, who would believe them? They would obviously say anything for the man who saved their lives."

"Excuse me," I said. "Their lives?"

Keis turned to look at me. "They are wanted by the Gestapo."

"The whole family?" I asked.

"The Gestapo does not make fine distinctions," Keis said.

"Did you get von Pilath a lawyer?" Brass asked.

"Not yet," Grosfeder said.

"Well, you'd better do that next." He stood up. "Thank you for coming," he said. "I'll see what I can do."

They accepted dismissal gracefully and, after a few final words, they all stood up, put their hats and coats on, and filed out of the office. I followed them to see them out the door. They began a conversation in German while waiting for the elevator, and by the time it arrived their voices were raised and their hand gestures had become emphatic.

I returned to Brass's office. Gloria and Cathy were putting the extra chairs back against the wall, and Brass was staring out the window. "They're as nutty as fruitcakes," I said.

Brass turned. "You think so?"

"Sure. What else? I don't think they had anything to do with Bill's murder, but they're not making much sense about it. You're spying against them, I'm spying against them. The police are in league with the Gestapo. The guy in the travel agency is sneaking pictures of them through the window." I dropped into my chair. "Paranoid."

"All of them?" Brass asked.

"Why not?" I asked. "Maybe they attract each other."

"I thought they were very sincere," Cathy said. "And they didn't seem crazy, just frightened."

Brass turned to Gloria. "What did you think?"

"They convinced me," she said. "They're afraid of something, and it's very real to them. I think we ought to tread carefully."

"I think I'll tread downstairs and get a little lunch," I said. "Unless you need me for something?"

"A good idea," Brass said. "Go to Danny's and bring back sandwiches and coffee for everyone. Put everything on my tab."

Being the amanuensis of a world-famous columnist offers a wide variety of exciting job experiences. I took out my notebook. A pastrami on rye with a side of potato salad for Brass, egg salad on white for Cathy, a cup of naked tuna fish and a tomato for Gloria. I left.

10

Danny's Waterfront Café occupies the southwest corner of Tenth Avenue and Fifty-ninth Street, two blocks from the water. It moved two years ago from its original location fronting the water, but Danny decided not to change the name. The café was opened in 1901, which makes it thirty-four years old. Danny was born in 1902. Manny, her father, opened the café during his wife's pregnancy and named it after his impending son. When his son turned out to be a daughter, he shrugged, smiled, and named her Danette. Manny still works there occasionally, but Danny runs the place, and he's gradually turning over the ownership to her. She now owns, as she puts it, all of the chairs and most of the tables. The place is open until at least two in the morning every day but Sunday, and many a night Brass and I have grabbed a late-night meal before Brass went off to some early morning cabaret and I went down to one of the Greenwich Village coffeehouses I sometimes hang out in, or, more often, home to bed.

I straddled a stool by the cash register and yelled my order to Danny, who was balancing five or six plates of food on her way over to one of the tables. The rule in the place was that everyone did whatever had to be done, and that included the owner. There were no separate waiters or busboys. Everyone waited tables, bussed tables, cleaned, mopped, and insulted the customers equally.

Danny nodded, mouthed a kiss in my direction, juggled the

plates onto the table, and disappeared back into the kitchen. About five minutes later she emerged with a large brown bag and handed it to me. "Give my love to your boss," she said. "I don't see him much anymore. He talks about the Copa and the Sky Room in his columns, but he doesn't come here."

"You want a mention?" I asked her.

She shook her head. "No way," she said. "I'm happy with the customers I got, and I don't think that the ones who would come because of a mention in 'Brass Tacks' would do anything but crowd the place. But I like talking to Mr. Brass. He's got an interesting head. Why don't you and him come in some evening, late, so I've got time to sit down and argue with Mr. Brass. I'll fry you a couple of steaks."

"I'll drag him down myself," I promised her. "But you'll have to forgive him the nightclubs. They're a dreadful duty that he must perform to do his job. Just ask him."

I told Danny to put the bill on Brass's tab and ran back across the street clutching the paper bag. Gloria and Cathy were not in the office when I got back, having run over to the bank to deposit Cathy's fortune, and Brass was staring at his typewriter in a splendid imitation of work, so I set the bag down and retreated to my own office. I hadn't sharpened more than half a dozen pencils when the girls returned.

We all gathered in Brass's office to eat. Brass, as usual, read tear sheets from one of the news wires while he ate—he had an insatiable curiosity about what was happening everywhere else. Gloria was reading a book: *The Good Earth* by Pearl S. Buck. I asked her what it was about, and she said, "China," so I went back to my sandwich. Anyone who doesn't recognize a conversational ploy when it is waved in front of her nose is not worth talking to. Cathy ate her egg salad and drank her orange juice staring into space, but she did eat, and that was a good sign.

After a minute Gloria closed her book. "What's 'Tacks' going to be about today?" she asked.

"Celebrities," Brass told her. "I talked with a couple at the Stork Club last night, and they gave me enough material to write a few thousand words without serious thought. Which is good, because I'm not sure I'm capable of serious thought today."

"Who'd you see?" Gloria asked.

"Jimmy Durante and Mae West."

"Together?" Cathy asked.

"No. Durante was at a table with a few of his cronies, telling bad jokes at the top of his voice—well, considering his voice, it was probably somewhere around the middle—to an ever-increasing circle of diners who looked thrilled to have their meals interrupted by a precocious, middle-aged, loud-mouthed imp."

"Don't be malicious," Gloria said. "Be satirical. Remember, you're the word slinger who skewers his victims with barbs of satire rather than cleaving them with the meat ax of malice."

She was quoting a recent *Time* magazine profile that Brass had found more than usually offensive.

Brass grinned. "I like Jimmy," he said. "I will neither skewer him nor cleave him. As a person. He's friendly, loyal, reasonably honest. It's as an entertainer that I can't stand him, but that's not his fault. And I am obviously in the minority."

"I met him once when he played at the Hotsy Totsy Club," Cathy said. "He was a gentleman."

Gloria sniffed. "At the Hotsy Totsy Club a gentleman was any man who didn't molest the help."

"There is that," Cathy agreed.

Brass said, "Jimmy came by my table on his way back from 'taking a whiz.' His words. He asked me why I haven't mentioned 'Jimmy da man—Jimmy da Human Bean' in my column for the past six months and four days—not that he's counting. I told him to say something funny so I can quote him."

"Did he?" Cathy asked.

"He did his whole act for me right there. One of his sidemen wheeled a piano in and he plunked himself down at it. He sang two choruses of 'Jimmy the Well-Dressed Man,' and continued with half an hour of nonstop Durante. He said he figured there has to be something funny in it; people were laughing. And they were. Everyone in the place gathered around in a big circle, the center of which was Durante and his piano. And after a couple of minutes his manic energy transmitted itself to the crowd, and they were clapping and singing and stamping their feet along with him. I felt like I was watching Aristophanes, and I was the only one in the room who didn't speak Greek. They all got it; I didn't."

"That's a good story in itself," Gloria said.

"I know," Brass said. "After Durante left a silence seemed to settle on the room, like the aftermath of a hurricane, when everyone's too exhausted to talk just from having been close to this great force of nature."

Gloria turned to Cathy. "He's writing his column as he speaks," she said. "You can tell by the similes. Any second he's going to branch out into onomatopoeia."

"Tell us about Mae West," Gloria said.

"She was having dinner quietly in a corner with two very pretty young men."

"Good for Mae!" Gloria said.

"She told me she's writing a play."

Gloria nodded. "She writes a lot of her own material."

"She's going to produce it herself," Brass said.

"I can guess what it's about," I said.

"You'd be wrong," Brass told me. "Miss West thinks that love, in all its infinite varieties, is worthy of respect and public inspection. Her play is a love story about homosexual men."

"It's a *what?*"

Brass smiled at me. "But of course you knew that."

I was speechless. Brass broke my silence by saying, "I have to put out a column to support this ménage. I won't mention Miss West's proposed story line or it will never make it to opening night." He gathered the paperware detritus from lunch on the desk and tossed it in the wastebasket. "While I do that, I have jobs for the three of you."

I took out my notebook and put it on my lap and fished in my pocket for a pencil.

Brass considered for a moment. "Before I give you your assignments, I want to state a few ground rules. We are going to take this very seriously and proceed very carefully. You must at all times consider your own safety and the necessity of keeping the identities of our athletic friends in the photographs a secret."

"You're worried about our safety?" I asked him. "Are you buying what those krauts were saying?"

"No," Brass said. "I'm buying the death of a reporter who

thought he was just following a harmless fat man. And you would hone your writing skills more if you think of ways to insult people that do not involve racial or national epithets. How would you like it if someone called you—whatever the hell you are?"

"Sorry," I said.

"The pictures must not be discussed—must not be mentioned—outside of this office. We'll have to come up with consistent cover stories for whatever investigating we do. Gloria, you and Cathy will spend the next few days getting complete background workups on each of our subjects. Start with the files from the morgue and work outward from there. Talk to friends, business associates, the hired help, anyone who might know anything."

"What are we looking for?" Gloria asked.

"A good question. What we really want to know, we can't ask. I don't know what you can ask that will lead us where we want to go. Past or present lovers or mistresses or girlfriends, if you can find out without making any waves. Any place they go, any people they see, any signs that they're being blackmailed; although what those signs might be, I can't suggest."

"If any of them have accounts at the Manhattan Bank," Cathy suggested, "we could ask Mr. Mergantaler to look over their checks. From the way he treated me, I have the feeling that he would do just about anything you asked."

"A good idea," Brass said. "Start by making up a list of twenty names that include our eight, for a little protective coloration, and find out how many of them have accounts at Mergantaler's bank. Don't go further with it until I tell you."

Gloria nodded.

"You'll type up your reports daily, when you can, in this office. If you can't for any reason, you will wait until you can. Whatever you find out is to be kept here and nowhere else. We'll put everything we have about this case in the special file every night."

"The special file?" Cathy asked.

Brass got up and went to the closet, which held his liquor cabinet. "As I wander through the various levels of New York life," he said, opening the closet door, "picking up information here and there for my column, I find out many things that I can't print. Some items I don't have enough information on yet or can't yet prove, like grafting politicians, cops on the take, or other examples of city, state, or federal malfeasance. If stories like that ever come together, I will use them. Some of it, like husbands cheating on their wives or wives cheating on their husbands; or the criminous secrets of certain notorious hoodlums, told to me in confidence at a corner table in Momma Lenora's on Sullivan Street; or the drunken revelations of several famous poets and writers in the back room of The White Horse Tavern in the wee hours of a Sunday morning—these are secrets for the ages which should be recorded but not revealed for decades to come."

He fiddled with two of the shelves in the closet, and a section of the right-hand wall opened on silent hinges to reveal a four-drawer file cabinet set into the wall. "This file cabinet is supposed to be fireproof," he said. "But I hope we never have to make the experiment. It's not exactly burglarproof, but it is hard to find. The assumption is that a burglar would go for the safe, which should take a while to open, after which he'll be too anxious to get out of here to go banging on closet walls."

"It's like one of those movie serials," Cathy said. "'Radio Men From the Moon' or something. They leap out of windows yelling 'Into the air!' and fly off with this gadget strapped to their backs. They always have secret cupboards that conceal the controls."

"Controls to what?" Gloria asked.

"You know. Flying things that look like sausages and can see inside your house and blow up if you touch them. That sort of thing."

"I'm afraid I cannot reach the heights, of imagination to which the writers of those movies ascend," Brass said. "If I leap out of the window I will fall to my death, and you couldn't repeat what I'd be yelling in mixed company." He closed the closet wall and the closet door and returned to his desk.

"About our subjects," I said. "I think what we should look for is intersections. Things that they might have in common. Do they, for instance, all play golf at the same country club, or all use the same barber?"

"Another good thought," Brass said. "Okay. Gloria and Cathy, you two work up the files on each of our notables. Look for points of correlation between them, anything that will give us a handle."

"What about me?" I asked.

Brass fished the packet of pictures out of his pocket and tossed them across the desk to me. "There's a man named Southerland Mitchell," he said. "Used to work for the *Daily Graphic.* He invented the composite picture. Started 'recreating' crime scenes and 'love nests' by staging the scene and grafting the heads of those involved onto the bodies of his actors. They were very big on love nests. He left the *Graphic* and now has a studio on MacDougal Alley, where he takes pictures of loaves of bread and calls it art."

"What kind of bread?" I asked.

"Kosher rye," Brass told me. "He also knows more about the technical side of photography than anyone else in the city. Take the pictures to him and tell him I want to know everything there is to know about them. Withhold nothing from him of what we know about the pictures if he asks, but he won't. He is one of the most essentially uncurious people I have ever known."

I stuck the pictures in the inside pocket of my jacket and buttoned the little tab that I never button that closes the pocket.

"On your way back," Brass told me, "check in with Inspector Raab and see if there's anything new and look in on our German friends to see what they're up to. And, in your copious free time after that, check out any photographic studios within a couple of blocks of that house."

"What will I do with one if I find it?"

"See if our fat friend works there. If you find him, do your best not to alarm him."

"You think he works in a photo studio because he had those pictures?" I asked. "That's a long shot."

"It has a good chance of running in the money," Brass said. "Remember his hands?"

I pictured the fat man and remembered his hands. "Chubby," I said. "Ink-stained."

"Not ink," Brass told me. "The stain was heaviest on the little finger and ring finger of his right hand. Just where he'd get it if he was a little careless while developing trays of prints in a darkroom."

"Son of a—gun," I said.

11

I took the Sixth Avenue El to Eighth Street, trotted down the stairs, and walked a few blocks south to MacDougal Alley.

Greenwich Village has been a hangout for those folk that the bourgeoisie are pleased to call "bohemians" for the past fifty or sixty years. A hundred years before that it was the habitation of the city's free Negroes, another distrusted minority. These days the Village is a mix of aspiring artists, actors, poets, writers, musicians, models, and, in the evenings, tourists. Men and women of all ages, classes, and previous conditions of servitude—who can't afford to go directly to Paris—come to Greenwich Village from all over the country to carve out for themselves a career in the arts. And the tourists come from all over the country to gawk at their cousins who have settled here and been debauched by their arty brethren.

The Village, an essentially communal place, welcomes deviants of all flavors, and judges people only on their manners, not their mores; but there's actually very little debauching. There are, in the little clubs along Bleeker Street that the ordinary tourists never get to see, men who dress like women and men who act like women, women who dress and act like men, and more variations on the theme than most people believe possible. But almost all of them knew what they were before they left Kansas or Texas to find a place that allowed them to be who they were despite what they were.

Since I arrived in New York I have spent many evenings in the

Village, listening to jazz in small, smoky nightclubs or arguing about world affairs or the state of the theater in small, overheated coffeehouses.

MacDougal Alley is two blocks long and neither intersects nor parallels MacDougal Street, which terminates two blocks away. Located in the heart, or perhaps the liver, of Greenwich Village, MacDougal Alley is a street of mostly two-story houses that was actually once merely an alley, providing the back entrances to the buildings that front the streets on either side. The houses along MacDougal Alley were the carriage houses and stables for those buildings. Now, although not nearly as fine looking as they were when they sheltered horses, they provide inexpensive lodging and studio space for artists and writers.

Southerland Mitchell had his entire two-story house to himself: the downstairs for living and the upstairs one large and very cluttered studio. When I pushed the doorbell, I could hear a loud clanging noise from somewhere in the back of the house. It must have been two minutes before Mitchell opened the door and peered out suspiciously at me. He was a tall, angular, extremely thin man with unkempt hair, rumpled clothes, and a large head, on which rested a pair of oversized tortoiseshell glasses. "What are you selling?" he asked.

"Mr. Mitchell? I'm not selling anything—"

"What religion are you espousing?"

"No, I'm not doing that either. I've come—"

"Then why are you bothering me?"

I sighed. "I'm trying to tell you. I've come from Alexander Brass. He wants you to do something for him."

He stepped aside. "Come in. I've very little time and much to do, but that seems to be my usual condition. If Brass has something important—did you say this was important?"

"It is, very," I assured him.

"Come this way." Mitchell led the way past his bedroom, living room, and kitchen to a back stairs leading up to the studio. The room took up the whole floor, but as the building wasn't very large, neither was the studio. But it was full of so many things that the first impression was of overwhelming space and clutter. The first objects I noticed as I entered were a plaster horse's head;

a three-foot-high model of the Eiffel Tower; a papier-mâché duck the size of a person; five or six doors set into frames, with no walls, going nowhere; and a model of the zeppelin *Hindenburg,* six feet long, suspended from the ceiling.

Across the room was a comparatively clear space under a skylight, on which was a wrought-iron bench of a design that looked as ethereal as wrought iron is capable of looking. On the bench, wrapped in some sort of diaphanous gauze, sat a slender, long-legged, dark-haired girl. When she saw that Mitchell had not returned alone, she jumped up and rushed to get her robe from a chair by the window.

"Molly," Mitchell said, "this is..." He turned to me. "Who are you?"

"Morgan DeWitt," I told him.

"Morgan DeWitt," he repeated. "He claims to work for Alexander Brass, but I haven't asked to see his credentials."

Molly crossed the room, her right hand extended, her left holding the robe closed. "Mr. DeWitt," she said. "I'm Molly Masker."

"My pleasure," I said, taking her hand.

"Excuse Southy's rudeness," she said. "It's his defense against an onrushing world. He doesn't mean it."

"I do so." Mitchell pushed aside a box of grapefruit-sized marbles, three light stands, and a giant cardboard cutout of a bottle of cheap domestic wine to reveal a car seat. "Sit down." he said. "Do you want some tea?"

"Ah..." I said.

"We have a variety of excellent teas from far and distant places," Mitchell said. "Molly thinks that coffee is bad for me, so she is introducing me to the delights of tea. We scour the docks for incoming ships from the Orient and ask for exotic teas. Sometimes we have a hard time convincing them that it is really tea we want, but occasionally we acquire packets of tea seldom seen east of Suez. Or would that be west of Suez? Where exactly is Suez, anyway?"

"Egypt," I said.

"Ah," Mitchell replied, nodding.

"He drank, I'd say, twenty cups of coffee a day," Molly said. "And he'd forget to eat for days at a time. Look at him!"

“I am naturally slender,” Mitchell said.

“I’d like some tea,” I said.

“If I hadn’t come along they could have used him for a course in anatomy without bothering to dissect him,” Molly said. “I’ll make tea. Is Darjeeling okay?” She clattered down the stairs when I assured her that Darjeeling was fine.

Mitchell looked fondly after her. “She became my model about six months ago,” he said. “And now she is my life.” He transferred his gaze to me. “You wouldn’t believe this, but I used to be a surly and unhappy man.”

I shook my head sadly to indicate the quality of my disbelief.

Mitchell smiled to show me how completely he had become the new, nonsurly Mitchell. “What can I do for Alexander Brass?” he asked.

“I have some photos to show you,” I told him. “Mr. Brass wants to know everything about them.”

“What sort of everything?”

“Everything you can find out about how and where the pictures were taken. He says that you can tell whether or not they are composites, but aside from that I don’t know what information it’s possible to get from a picture.”

“That depends on the photograph,” he said. “Let me see them.”

I unbuttoned my inner jacket pocket and handed him the packet of pictures. He leafed through them. “Good lighting for indoors,” he said. “It looks diffuse, but with most of it coming from directly above the subjects. Let’s get a better look.”

He threaded his way across the room to a table that had a strong light mounted above it and a six-inch magnifying glass on a sort of swivel arrangement to the side. I tried to follow in his footsteps but I had to work my way around a five-foot stuffed panda that miraculously appeared in my path. When I arrived at his side, he had the light on and was peering through the glass at one of the photographs. He spent a couple of minutes on it before progressing to the next one. By the time he was on the fourth photo, Molly was clomping back up the stairs with an oversized China teapot and three white mugs.

“We should let it steep for a couple of minutes,” she said, clearing a place for the teapot on top of an old iron safe that was standing ajar in the middle of the room. "What have you there?"

"Photographs of men and women with no clothes on doing what men and women tend to do when they have no clothes on," Mitchell said without looking up.

"When I have no clothes on, I tend to strike a pose," Molly said, promptly striking a pose that would have been very interesting if she had no clothes on.

Mitchell worked his way through the photos, while Molly poured the tea and passed us each a mug. I picked up a stack of oversized prints from a stuffed yak's back and looked through them while I was waiting. They were shots of Molly Masker in a variety of unusual locations. In many of them she had no clothes on, and she did indeed look very interesting.

"What do you think?"

I almost jumped. Molly had come up behind me without my noticing, and was peering over my shoulder. "Very nice," I said. "I think you've got a lot of nerve, posing nude in Wall Street, and at—is this the Parthenon?"

She giggled. "Yes," she said. "And—" She flipped through some of the prints. "This is the Taj Mahal; and this is the Eighty-sixth Street subway platform—downtown; and this is the Empire State Building observation deck."

I stared at the photos. "Don't you ever get arrested?" I asked.

Southy Mitchell called me back across the room. The photos were spread out across the table like leaves on the strand. "Here's what I think," he said.

I took out my notebook and turned to a blank page and wrote "dirty pictures" across the top.

"First, they're not composites. There has been no cutting and pasting of body parts to achieve an unnatural whole. All the shadows are right, and that's where even the best composite gives itself away. I don't say nobody could have done it. I could have. But they wouldn't look just like this; they'd have to be subtly different. *These* pictures are not composites. Now, what else? They were all taken in the same location, but I guess you've noticed that. The lighting comes from above, and not from a point source. I'd guess a fairly good-sized skylight. The camera was, probably, a four-by-five with a fast lens. The depth of field is impressive. It must have been one of the faster films, because there couldn't have been that much light, but it's a very fine-grain film. The developing was done by someone who knows his business, and knows what he's after. Here, look—" He grabbed one of the pictures and held it out to me. "The guy is sort of sitting up, so nothing is in shadow, and the whole picture is clear and of even density."

"I see," I said.

"Now look at this one. The face was in shadow, so the plate was developed longer to bring it out. See how the rest of the room is slightly overdeveloped?"

"I see what you mean," I said.

"That's about it," Mitchell said. "The paper is a fine-grain stock. German. Don't see much of it over here."

"German?"

"If I wanted to repeat myself," Mitchell said fiercely. "I would have bought a monkey!"

"Sorry," I said.

Molly wrapped her arms around Mitchell's neck. "Southy, what on earth does that mean, you would have bought a monkey?"

"I have no idea," Mitchell said. "I say what comes into my head. I figure my subconscious knows what it's doing, and doesn't need any help from me."

"I worry about you," Molly told him. "If you weren't a genius, you'd be a nut."

"Maybe I'm both," Mitchell suggested, reaching up and taking her hands in his.

I felt that I was in the way, or would be shortly, so I gathered up the pictures. "Thank you, Mr. Mitchell," I said.

"Call me Southy," he said, working his right hand free of Molly and thrusting it out. "All my friends do."

"You have no friends," Molly said.

"Shut up," he demurred.

I shook his hand and left his house, waving good-bye to Molly as I headed for the stairs. I walked over to the east side, took the subway up to Seventy-seventh Street and Lexington Avenue, and walked the half block to the 23rd Precinct.

Inspector Raab was not in his office, and the hired help had nothing of interest to tell me. Von Pilath was still being held on suspicion, and none of the detectives on the case had any other suspicions they were willing to share with me. From there I walked over to the Eighty-second Street home of the Verein für Wahrheit und Freiheit, and couldn't get through the front door. Nobody answered the ring at the *Verein* apartment, so I rang some bells at random, but nobody buzzed me in or yelled at me. I decided that the bell system was out of order, and was debating throwing pebbles up to the third-story window, if I could find any pebbles to throw, if I could reach the third floor, if I could figure out which window belonged to the *Verein,* when a window to my left was pushed open with a hearty shove and a heavily muscled young man with close cropped blond hair leaned out. "Yes?" he asked. "What you want?"

"I would like to speak to someone from the Verein für Wahrheit und Freiheit," I told him, giving the German pronunciation my best shot.

"They are not here," he said. "They are all left."

I almost said, "How far left?" but realized that would take me down linguistic paths that I did not wish to travel. "Thank you," I said instead. "When do you think one of them will be around?"

"It is hard to say," he said. "Come back then!" And he slammed down the window.

I can take a hint.

It was only about ten after five but I was hungry, so I decided that the next stop was dinner. I went into Bavaria Haus Restaurant on Eighty-sixth Street and was served bratwurst and kraut by a fat man in leather shorts. While I was eating I borrowed a Manhattan phone book and looked up photographic studios. There were six within ten blocks. I jotted the addresses down in my notebook and decided that I could probably handle the strudel for dessert.

It was a little after six when I left the restaurant. Most of the stores along Eighty-sixth Street seemed to be still open, so I thought I'd try scouting out a few of the photo studios. There were four movie theaters farther along Eighty-sixth Street, so maybe the stores stayed open late to catch the after-theater crowd. "Wasn't that W.C. Fields just irresistibly funny, dear? Let's buy a pot to go with the dishes we got at the theater." Could be.

The closest photo studio, on Lexington Avenue just off Eighty-sixth, had a window full of wedding pictures that did nothing to encourage thoughts of marriage in passersby. In one the bride was smiling, but the groom looked trapped; in another the groom was grinning, but the bride looked like she was in shock. In several both bride and groom were smiling at the camera as though it were a painful duty.

The door dinged when I opened it to go in, and donged when I closed it behind me. For a while it seemed as though the ding-dong had attracted no one, but then a man pushed aside a curtain leading to a room in back and came up to the counter. He was thin, with a thin face, dressed in a black suit and white shirt with a black bow tie around a high collar of the sort that I thought had gone out of style twenty years ago. "Yes?" the man said.

"Are you the owner?" I asked.

"I'm the only," the man said. "I'm the owner and all the help wrapped into one package. What can I do for you? I should warn you that if you're selling anything, you're wasting your time in here."

"I'm not selling anything," I told him. "I'm looking for a photographer that took some pictures of my kid. We want to get some prints made, my wife and I, but I don't remember the man's name or address. My wife thinks that his studio was somewhere here in Yorkville."

"Look on the back of the picture," the man said. "The studio's name and address will be rubber-stamped on the back." He turned to go back behind the curtain.

"We lost the pictures," I told him. "There was a fire. My son died. Five years old. My wife would really like to see if we can find that photographer."

That stopped him. He turned around. "I'd like to help you, but what can I do if you don't know the name or address?"

"The photographer was heavy," I told him. "You might almost say fat. He was about this tall—" I indicated the height with my hand "—and balding, with his hair, you know, combed over the bald spot. He wore a double-breasted blue suit that seemed a bit too small for him."

"That sounds like Hermann," the man said. "But he does not do baby pictures. Most decidedly he does not."

"My wife talked him into it," I said. "We met him at a party."

"Well," the man said. "It may be Hermann."

"Hermann who?" I asked. "And where is he?"

"A few blocks from here. His studio is on Eighty-third Street and First Avenue. Third-floor walkup; he has no street trade. I don't know the address, but it's the second or third building east of Second on the south side of the street. Hermann Dworkyn." He spelled it for me.

I thanked him and left, feeling exhilarated. I can understand the rush thieves and confidence men get doing their job. I had fooled this man—okay, I had lied to this man—and felt very good about it. I hoped it was because the lying had accomplished a necessary and worthwhile goal, and not because I enjoyed sin for its own sake. I thought of De Quincey's essay on murder, where he decried it as leading to lying and Sabbath-breaking. Could the reverse be true?

The hallway of 428 East Eighty-third Street, the third building in from the corner of Second Avenue, was the entrance to a building that had seen better days, but not recently. The front door closed but didn't lock. The inner door had so many coats of paint on it that it didn't quite close, and several of the outer coats were peeling so that a motley of colors showed, mostly shades of green, except for one layer of dark brown. There was a separate, large mailbox, with Dworkyn Studios neatly calligraphed on its face, screwed into the wall next to the regular mailboxes.

I went up two flights to the door that had similar calligraphy on the front. I could hear voices, faintly, from inside. There was a small sign pasted above the door buzzer that said RING, so I did. After a minute I rang again. In case the buzzer was broken, I knocked. Nothing. I put my ear to the door. I heard a man speaking and, after a second, a woman answering. There was something familiar about the voices, but I couldn't pin it down. I knocked again.

A woman came up the stairs and headed down the hall toward me. She was somewhere in her late twenties or early thirties, wearing a black, tight-fitting dress that was a bit shorter than most and heels a bit higher than I would have expected. She wore no jewelry around her neck or pinned to the dress, but her arms were covered with silver bracelets that jangled when she walked.

In face, form, and dress she was much better looking than the building deserved. "You want to see Herm?" she asked.

"I would very much like to see Mr. Dworkyn," I told her.

"That's Herm. The bell don't work; it broke a couple of weeks ago and the landlord—" She shrugged to say everything necessary about landlords. "And if he's in the darkroom, he can't hear you knock."

"I thought I heard someone inside," I said, "but maybe I was wrong. Maybe he's gone home. It's getting kind of late."

"This is his home," she said. "He got some prints for you?" She took a key from her little black-with-a-diamond-studded-catch clutch purse and inserted it in the lock. "Come on in. My name is Bobbi—with an *i*. Who are you?"

She pushed the door open and I told her my name and followed her into what once was a fairly large living room. There didn't seem to be anyone in the room, but I could hear the voices much clearer now, and I recognized them: Lamont Cranston and Margot Lane. It was the voice of the Invisible Shadow, narrating one of his half-hour adventures over the console radio in the far corner. The room was full of lights and props, including a king-sized bed, a sofa, a love seat, an ottoman, and a portable wall with two portholes in it. The various articles of furniture were all shoved against the far wall, except for the bed, which was in the middle of the floor. Behind the bed were a couple of flats painted to look like the corner of an elegant bedroom, the sort you'd find in a château in France. An ornate dressing table was against one of the flats, and the whole area was full of artfully arranged drapes and casually distributed puffy pillows.

"Hey, Herm, it's Bobbi—I'm back!" the lady in black yelled. "Put your pants on; we have a customer!"

She saw my expression and chuckled deep in her throat. "It's not what you think," she said, "whatever that may be. It gets very hot in the darkroom when Herm's working in there, so sometimes he works in his shorts."

"I didn't—" I said.

"Maybe not," she said. "But most people would. Guy who makes his living taking art pictures, working in his underwear. He doesn't do that when any of the girls are here. He's very proper.

But very relaxed-like. Otherwise the girls would get uptight." She went over to turn off the radio. "No wonder he couldn't hear us, with this thing blaring."

"Art pictures?" I asked.

"You know, it's funny," Bobbi said. "Usually the guys get more uptight about taking their clothes off than the girls." She turned and yelled, "Herm! You okay in there? Come on out!" Then she turned back to me. "Yeah, art pictures. You know—like those." She pointed to the near wall, which was full of thumbtacked-up photos. I walked over to examine them.

"Herm!" she yelled again. "I got two suitcases downstairs. I left them with Selma. You want to bring them up for me? Or should I give the Harris kid a quarter?"

The pictures were the sort found in girlie magazines; ladies in various stages of undress, reacting to the camera as though it were an intruder or a Peeping Tom. Some of the girls looked coy, some looked shocked, and some looked inviting. The people who publish these sort of pictures like to refer to them as "art studies." They were mildly erotic without being actively pornographic, and no illegal or illicit activity was shown, although several were suggested. In the pictures with men in them, the men were not even touching the women, although they were posed to look as though they might at any second. The magazines that used this sort of photography were sold under the counter in drugstores across the country, and at least half of the titillation was in the act of buying them.

Bobbi jangled across the room and opened a door which led to a short hallway and several other doors. "Shit!" she said. "He ain't here. If he was in the darkroom," she indicated the right-hand door, "the little red light would be on."

"Maybe I should go," I said.

"Nah!" Bobbi said, recrossing the room. "Sit tight. He's probably out stuffing his face. And he has a lot of face to stuff. He won't be long." She went out the front door and a few seconds later I heard her knocking on a door down the hall and calling: "Mrs. Harris, is your son Larry at home?" She negotiated with the son, who sounded like he was about fourteen, to retrieve her suitcases, and returned to the apartment-studio.

"I just got back from Philadelphia," she confided to me, sitting on the bed and kicking her shoes off. "I was working a club date. Well, it was more like what you call a 'smoker.' A lot of husbands who'd left their wives at home, sitting around in this small room watching me take my clothes off."

I moved away from the wall of photos and sat in a straight-back chair near the bed. "Is that what you do?" I asked.

"Sure," she said. "I'm an exotic dancer. When I'm working the circuit I'm billed as "Celeste the VaVoom Girl," or as "Celeste with her Mystical Dance of Love," depending on which routine I'm doing. I'm a headliner. But when I'm working club dates I don't use that name, 'cause it would lower my price if it became known that a headliner was working club dates."

"I see," I said.

"Sure," she said. "What do you want to see Herm about? He take some pictures for you?"

"Actually," I told her, "I'm not sure. I have some photographs that he might have taken, and I want to talk to him about them."

"Let's see them," Bobbi said. "I can probably tell you. I know his style. He's a perfectionist, you know. Everything has to be just right: costume, lighting, makeup—everything."

"I'm sure," I said. "I don't have the pictures with me."

She looked at me as though I'd said something odd, which I suppose I had. I decided on an explanation that was as close to honest as I could manage. After all, if Herm was our man, he'd know about the pictures.

"A man whom we think may have been Mr. Dworkyn showed my boss some pictures," I said. "We'd like to talk to that man, so I'm waiting to see if Mr. Dworkyn is him."

"I like men who say 'whom,'" Bobbi said, shifting over in the bed. She patted the blanket. "Come sit next to me."

Here was the invitation I'd been waiting for for years. An attractive woman—a *very* attractive woman—wanted me to sit next to her. On a bed. "Ahhh," I said. I didn't move. I tried, but I seemed to be incapable of motion.

"What's the matter?" Bobbi asked. "Don't you like girls? I can usually tell, but sometimes I misjudge. It's all right, nothing to be ashamed of. I'm just disappointed, is all."

"No, no," I said. "It's not that. It's just, well... what if Herm comes home?"

"For Christ's sake," she said. "He's my brother, not my husband. The only thing he'd do is maybe take pictures."

I thought of the photographs in my breast pocket. "Really?" I asked.

She thought about it for a second. "Nah, not really. Not unless there was a market for them. Besides, he knows I'd kill him."

"Has he ever taken pictures like that—you know, with two people mutually engaged?"

"Mutually engaged? I like that. You talk good." She shook her head. "Not so far as I know, and I'd know. He loves to show off his pictures, talk about them. He's proud of his art. Sometimes one of the magazines will want pictures that show more skin, or more action, and he won't do it."

An adolescent boy with more than his share of acne pushed his way through the door lugging two suitcases. Larry dropped the suitcases on the floor inside the door. "Here you are, Miss Starr," he said.

"Thank you, Larry," she said, hunting for a quarter in her purse and tossing it to him.

"Thank you, Miss Starr," he said, raising his hand in an undefinable gesture and exiting.

"Miss Star?" I asked.

"It's my stage name," she said. "Celeste Starr, with two r's."

"Oh," I said.

"'Roberta Dworkyn' wouldn't pull in the customers," she said. "I'd better put the suitcases inside." She got up.

"Let me help." I retrieved the two suitcases, and realized that Larry was stronger than he looked. Celeste Starr did not pack light for an overnight smoker in Philadelphia.

"This way," she said, leading me toward the back. "I'm just staying with Herm temporarily until I can get another place. The last place I was in, over on Thirty-seventh and Lexington, had a fire. It wasn't bad, but I moved out the next day. I have a thing about fires." She entered the little hallway and opened the door on the left, opposite the darkroom. I was a couple of steps behind her, trying to maneuver the suitcases around some furniture.

"This is the room I'm—oh shit!" she said. "What the hell happened in here?"

I put the suitcases down and peered over her shoulder into the room. There was a single bed in one corner, and a bureau next to it, and three wooden five-drawer file cabinets across the room. The bed had one of those large comforters on it. On the comforter was a great pile of papers, envelopes, and glossy photographs. Similar detritus was distributed about the floor. Every drawer in the file cabinets and the bureau had been pulled open. On the bureau was a pile of lady's undergarments—stockings, brassieres, panties—all stirred into one large, colorful, exotic mess.

Bobbi walked gingerly into the room. "Someone's been pawing through my underwear," she said. "While I was stripping for those perverts in Philadelphia, some perverted asshole in New York has been fondling my brassieres. And those are my working bras; they cost eight bucks apiece!" She sounded as if she was close to tears.

I put my hand on her shoulder. "I don't think so," I said.

She turned to me and put her arms around me with a sort of convulsive motion. Her nose was pushed against my shoulder, and various parts of her body were snug against various parts of my body. "You don't think what?" she asked.

The proximity of her body did strange things to my thought processes. It took me a moment to remember what I hadn't thought. "I don't think whoever did this was particularly interested in your undergarments," I told her. "They've put more effort into messing up the pictures. My guess is they were looking for something."

She clung to me for another long moment, and then let go and turned around. She considered the mess in front of her. "You're right," she said. "These are Hermann's files. He's going to be pissed when he sees this." She tiptoed across the floor, doing her best to avoid the pictures, and started putting her underwear away. "I'll bet it's that kid from across the street. What's his name? Grossberg—something like that. Herm caught the kid sneaking onto the fire escape so's he could watch the girls during shoots. He even brought his friends up. I think he was charging them a nickel a peep. Herm painted the windows black. Maybe the kid was taking his revenge for loss of income."

I didn't think it was the Grossberg kid. I had a horrible feeling that I didn't want to share with Bobbi just yet. If I was wrong, there was no point in frightening her. I hoped I was wrong. "Maybe we should check the other rooms," I said.

"Oh, yeah," she said. "Take a look, will you? I want to finish cleaning up this mess."

There were three other doors along the hallway. The first was Hermann's bedroom. There was a large, unmade four-poster bed against the wall, and two dressers against the other wall beneath the two windows, which looked out on the building across the courtyard. There were two separate piles of clothing on the floor, and several piles of various camera accessories on the dressers and the floor between them. Two suits were hanging in the closet, the door of which was standing open, and several pairs of shoes had been tossed onto the closet floor. It was a mess, but a mess that had been created by its occupant. On the near dresser was a framed snapshot of a man and woman at the beach, holding hands and smiling at the camera. The woman was Bobbi, and the man, presumably Hermann, was the gentleman who had given Brass the dirty pictures. Well. That, at least, was settled.

The middle door was the bathroom, a spotless and sanitary refuge. After having seen Hermann's bedroom, I assumed that his sister was responsible for cleaning the bathroom. Or maybe they had a housekeeper. Photostudiokeeper?

I opened the door to the darkroom. It was a dark room. The spill from the hall light revealed little. I felt around the inside wall near the door for a light switch, and finally found it higher on the wall than I had expected. I flipped it on.

The room was large, it had probably been the master bedroom, and there were cabinets and sinks along the walls. The windows had been painted over and covered by black drapes. There were two enlargers and several pieces of equipment I didn't recognize placed strategically about.

Hermann was there. He had been there for some time. He was tied to a chair in the middle of the floor, naked, with one of his sister's black silk stockings stuffed into his mouth. He was dead, but judging by the gouges and slashes on his face and body and the blood on the floor, he had been a long time dying. His knees had been tied to the sides of the chair, forcing his legs apart, and it looked as if a good bit of his torment had been aimed at his genitals. Blood flowing from the various wounds had formed a clotted sheet of red, purple, and black down his body. In some places patches of skin had been removed; in others the skin was partially cut away, and hung grotesquely from his body, leaving blotchy views of interior things that should be seen only by surgeons.

I managed to make it to the bathroom before I threw up.

12

I haven't had much practice puking, so I don't do it very well. I was fascinated to find that, even as an involuntary act, it required effort and concentration to do it right. It was a couple of minutes, perhaps longer, before I realized that Bobbi was standing in the bathroom doorway watching me with a critical eye.

I moved my head from over the toilet bowl to the sink and grabbed a couple of towels to clean myself up. "Sorry," I mumbled. I was desperately trying to remember whether I had closed the door to the darkroom before stumbling into the bathroom.

"Here," she said. "Let me do that. I've had a lot of practice." She soaked a towel in hot water and briskly rubbed my face with it with the professionalism of a mother cleaning up a three-year-old. "You didn't eat anything since you got here," she commented. "Been drinking? You faked me out."

"No," I said.

She turned me around. "Here's a comb. What the hell happened?"

"You do this a lot?" I asked, waving my hand vaguely at the sink.

"Sure," she said. "The johns at the clubs I work. The ones that wait for the girls after the show. They drink too much, they grope you, they promise you a night of fun, then they upchuck on you. It's a sort of ritual."

I took a couple of deep breaths and stood up to look in the mirror and comb my hair. "Is there a telephone in the apartment?"

"In the front room. The fancy French-looking phone by the bed doesn't work—it's a prop—but there's a pay phone by the window."

"A pay phone?"

"Yeah. The models spend their lives on the phone, and Herm got tired of paying for it. You need a nickel?"

"No, I think I've got change." I took her hand and led her out of the bathroom. The darkroom door was closed, thank God. We went through into the front room. "Bobbi," I said, "sit down. There's something I've got to tell you."

She dropped onto the bed. "Why, Mr. DeWitt," she said, "this is so sudden. Shall we have the honeymoon before or after the marriage? Or perhaps instead of?"

"Bobbi—"

"Paris, Vienna, Hoboken; the choice is yours."

If there was world enough and time… "Bobbi, listen to me! Your brother is dead. I have to call the police."

She stared at me as though I were speaking a foreign language that she could almost understand. The words were there, but the content—"My brother… Herm… where…?" She started toward the rear door, but I stopped her and held her. "He's in the darkroom. You don't want to go in there."

She struggled against me for a moment and then stopped and clung to me. "The slob," she said, "the poor fat slob. What happened; his heart?"

"He was murdered," I told her. "It's not pretty."

"Ohmigod!" she said, backing away from me, her eyes wide. "I told him! I warned him!" She backed into the edge of the bed and her knees buckled and she half fell, half sat down.

"Warned him about what?"

"The bookies." She started crying softly. I decided she wasn't going to make a mad dash for the darkroom, so I went over to the window and dropped a nickel in the phone and dialed my boss; the private line that doesn't go through the *World* switchboard. It was after eight and he might not be there, but he'd be displeased if I didn't try him before calling the police. Explanations about the bookies would have to wait.

"Mr. Brass's office." The voice that sank a thousand ships.

"Gloria, it's me. What are you doing there this late?"

"Woman's work is never done. What's up?"

"Is the boss in?"

"He is. And so is Inspector Raab. They're debating whether Mr. Brass is withholding some information of importance to an ongoing murder investigation. Neither of them has actually struck the other yet."

"Put me through to Brass."

"I don't think—"

"Trust me on this one."

There was a click, and that strange lack-of-noise that sounds like you've been connected to the center of the earth, and then Brass came on. "Hello, DeWitt?"

"I've found the fat man," I told him. "He's dead. He was sliced up pretty badly. I think he was tortured." There was a gasp from behind me, and I realized that Bobbi was listening to my side of the conversation.

"Ah! And his profession?"

"Photographer."

"Are there any pertinent examples of his art about?"

I thought that one over for a second. "If you mean are there any dirty pictures, yes, sort of, but only minor-league stuff, the kind of stuff you find in girlie magazines. Professional models in lacy lingerie. I haven't seen any like the ones he brought to you, but I'll check. But I have to call the police."

"Inspector Raab is in the office," Brass said. "I will inform him, which will take care of your obligation, and we'll be right over. You might concern yourself with that question before we arrive. What's the address?"

I told him and hung up.

"Bobbi," I said, returning to the bed and sitting beside her. "There isn't much time; the police will be here soon. If there's anything we should dispose of before they get here, we'd better get busy."

She was lying on her back staring at the bleak white ceiling, with her feet dangling on the floor. At my words she pushed herself to a sitting position. "What are you talking about?"

"Well, any photographs of your brother's that are significantly racier than the ones on the walls. Anything you wouldn't want the police to see."

"There isn't anything like that, I told you," she said. "Why are you so convinced that there is?"

"Your brother showed me some photographs that were truly pornographic," I told her. "I don't think he took them, but he had them. There may be copies of them here. If so, and the police find them, they will certainly get the wrong idea about Hermann's activities."

"You're lying," she said flatly. "Herm would never do anything like that." She pointed a finger at me, but her heart wasn't in it.

"You said something about bookies," I said. "Was your brother a heavy gambler? Could he have been into the bookies for a lot of money?"

"Nah!" She pushed herself to her feet. "I kept after him about his gambling, but it really wasn't much. Not like some I know. He was never down more than a nickel." I looked at her, and she explained. "That's five hundred bucks. Not a lot as gamblers go, and I know some big-time sports. Herm wasn't a big-time gambler. Hell, he wasn't a big-time anything." She shook her head sadly. "I think I'll go look at him before the police get here."

"I wouldn't," I said; "it'll give you bad dreams."

She paused in the doorway and turned to look at me. "Bad?"

"Very," I said. "It wasn't bookies. For a nickel they might send someone around to bust an arm, but they wouldn't do anything like that. For no amount of money would they do anything like that."

"Could it have something to do with those pictures?"

"I don't know. It could."

She thought for a few seconds. "I don't think I want to see Hermann all beat up, or whatever," she decided. "I might remember him that way when I think of him, and I wouldn't want that. Maybe we should look for those pictures."

"Good idea," I said, restraining an impulse to kiss her.

Hermann's files were actually eight-by-ten white envelopes, each holding the negatives from a photo shoot, and sometimes the prints. They were numbered chronologically. This year's, which had been in the top drawer of the right-hand file cabinet but were now strewn about the bedroom floor, began with 351, for the first shoot in 1935, and ended, as far as we could tell, with 35102, for the hundred and second shoot. There was also a date stamp showing that envelope 351 had been filed, or shot, or processed, or whatever on 01-04-1935, and envelope 35102 only two days ago. Which would seem to indicate that Hermann had been alive then, at least long enough to do his filing. This was no great surprise; it was only three days ago that Hermann had appeared in Brass's office.

Most of the photos seemed to be from shoots that Hermann had done; I could tell by the props and location. Bobbi claimed to be able to recognize her brother's style, and perhaps she could. Some were clearly shot by others, and had been given to Hermann for processing. He usually kept the negatives, Bobbi explained, so he could make more prints on demand. We gathered and sorted the envelopes, and found two missing: numbers 3588 and 3597.

We continued looking through the negatives just to be sure, but I would have been willing to bet a nickel that we wouldn't find anything. I would have paid a dime for a look at numbers 3588 and 3597.

It was about half an hour before Brass and Inspector Raab walked in together, with three detectives close behind. Brass and Raab headed for the darkroom with two of the detectives following. Bobbi and I, for lack of anything better to do, remained sitting on the edge of the bed.

A couple of minutes later Raab strode out of the back hallway and stood in front of me, his hands on his hips. The remaining detective, a wistful-looking young man whom I had never seen before, came up next to him and whipped out a notebook and flipped it open. It was the sort that flips open from the top. I noticed that the wistful detective's navy-blue suit and white shirt were both well ironed, his red and blue striped tie had been carefully knotted, and his brown brogans wore an exuberant coat of polish. We novelists train ourselves to notice details like that.

"Tell me about it," Raab said.

"As you've noticed, there's a dead man in the darkroom," I said. "It was probably designed as the master bedroom, but it's been converted, with a couple of enlargers and a row of sinks and that sort of thing. The dead man's name is Hermann—with two *n*'s—Dworkyn. This lady is his sister."

"You found him," Raab said accusingly.

"That's right," I said. "Miss Starr was just arriving home when I got here."

"Who's Miss Starr?" asked the wistful detective, looking up from his notebook.

"I am," Bobbi said. "It's my nom de burlesque. I'm a headliner with the Ardbaum circuit."

Raab switched his attention to Bobbi. "Where were you getting home from?" he asked.

"Philadelphia," she said.

"When did you arrive?"

"It must have been about seven-thirty. The train came into Penn Station around seven, and I took a cab."

"How long were you in Philadelphia?"

"Three days. We did a couple of smokers and spent one day looking at all the historical monuments which the city is noted for. It was very pleasant."

"Anyone who can verify that you were in Philadelphia?" Raab asked.

"The mayor, the chief of police, two aldermen, and a municipal court judge," she said. "Also, I traveled with two fellow artistes: Wanda the Whip and Kandy Kane—with two K's."

"I see," Raab said. "Thank you." He turned to me. "Can you identify him?"

"The corpse?" I thought for a second. "He is the man who came to our office. I don't know him as Hermann Dworkyn because he didn't give us his name. There is a picture of him in his bedroom holding hands with Miss Starr...."

Bobbi nodded. "That's Herm," she said. "We went to Coney Island last year. Bickey took the picture."

"Who's Bickey?" Raab asked.

"He's a comic with whom I was formerly going out," Bobbi said. "I haven't seen him in a while. We will not speak further of him."

Alan Shine came into the apartment, hat in hand, and glanced around the room. "Hi, all," he said.

"Wait outside, Shine," Raab barked. "We're not done with the crime scene yet."

"Yeah, sure," Shine said, continuing into the room. "What are you planning to do with it, set it in bronze?"

Inspector Raab sighed. "Don't touch anything!" he said.

"Yeah," Shine said. "Say, you hear the one about the chorus girl who would do anything for a fur coat—and then when she got it, she couldn't button it?"

Raab glared at him. Shine shrugged and went over to inspect the wall full of Hermann's artwork.

Brass returned from the darkroom and stood in the doorway. "I don't like this," he said.

"*You* don't like it!" Bobbi said, her voice rising into a minor screech. "He's my brother!"

Brass came over. "You have my sympathies, Miss, ah—"

I introduced them. Bobbi offered her hand, and Brass shook it firmly. "Do you have a place to stay tonight, Miss Starr?" he asked.

"Oh," she said. "What a thought. I can't stay here. I mean, I wouldn't even if I could." She shuddered.

Brass took out a card and scribbled something on the back of it. "Take this," he said, holding it out. "Go downstairs and get a cab and take it to the Park South Hotel. Give the card to the manager, and he will give you a room, a very nice room."

"What's the rates?" she asked, staring at the card and trying to decipher Brass's handwriting.

"No charge," Brass told her. "I have an arrangement with the hotel."

"I see," she said, standing up. "And I suppose you live there, is that part of the arrangement?"

Brass shook his head. "I live down the block," he said.

"Just as I thought," Bobbi said. "Take your card back; I'll bed down at Mrs. Adamson's on Sixty-seventh: four bucks a week and no strings."

Brass chuckled. "I see," he said. "There are no strings here either. I want to talk to you."

"Sure; talk!" Bobbi said, making it sound like a dirty word.

"Talk," Brass repeated. "Over breakfast. Tomorrow. At Lindner's on the corner of Sixth Avenue, around ten-thirty."

There was a long pause. "Oh," Bobbi said. Another pause. "Well, how was I to know you were a gentleman? Let me get my suitcases."

Brass turned to me. "Why don't you help Miss Starr downstairs with her luggage and then go home yourself?" he said. "I'd like you to join us for breakfast."

And so, after pausing to make sure Inspector Raab was through with us for the evening, I did.

13

It was just seven o'clock the next morning when I left my room to stagger down the hall to the bathroom for my morning ablutions. My next-door neighbor Pinky was doing push-ups in the hall, wearing an ancient white terry-cloth bathrobe that exposed a pair of skinny, bony legs. Why he was using the hall was understandable: a retired circus clown, Pinky lived in two small rooms, both so filled with a lifetime of circus and carnival artifacts that there wasn't enough room to swing a slapstick. Each separate playbill, broadsheet, tent peg, and fright wig had its own story of romance, of pathos, of gaiety, or of ribald humor that Pinky delighted in telling at the drop of a scrapbook. The question was why a man in his early seventies, who had never evidenced the slightest interest in exercising in the year I'd known him, would be doing push-ups at all.

I didn't feel awake enough to ask anyone anything until after I'd showered and shaved and had a cup of coffee in my hand, so I carefully stepped around Pinky and enclosed myself in the bathroom. When I came out Pinky was doing sit-ups.

I retreated to my room and poured two cups of coffee. A minute later I opened the door and found Pinky leaning against the wall, breathing hard. "Come in, Pinky," I said. "Have a cup of coffee and tell me whom to call when you collapse."

He staggered into my room and took the cup from my hands. "Sugar," he said. "Lots of sugar!"

I passed him the jar full of cube sugar, which I steal from various restaurants around town. I started to get dressed while Pinky contemplated the sugar.

"Age creeps up on a fellow," he said. "You feel the same day after day, but then comes the day you find you get out of breath after doing fifty sit-ups. I used to do a warm-up every day before breakfast—sit-ups, push-ups, pull-ups, walking a tight wire—like that. It's a hell of a thing to suddenly discover you're old." Pinky dropped six cubes in his cup and watched them dissolve. "You know, there's a good bar trick you can do with sugar cubes in a cup of coffee."

"How does it work?" I asked.

"Too late now, I've already put the sugar in. Next time I'll show you." He stirred the coffee with the spoon that I had thoughtfully placed in the cup for him. Then he took the spoon out and examined it. "Horn and Hardart," he said. "The Automat must supply half the silverware in New York."

"A fine institution," I agreed. "I'd give them all my business but their sugar doesn't come in cubes."

"I'll speak to Mr. Horn about it," Pinky said.

"Why the sudden renewed interest in exercise?" I asked him. "You clip one of those Charles Atlas coupons from the back of a men's magazine?"

"Just trying to get into some sort of shape," he said. "I got talked into doing some clowning for a bunch of kids, and I want to make sure the muscles are all working. Clowning takes a fair amount of physical exertion, you know."

"I'm sure it does." I picked out a light blue tie with a recurring pattern of yellow sunbursts, a gift from a friend who works on the *Sun*. It's the usual Christmas present of his boss, and he had four of them. Peering into the mirror above my bureau I carefully worked on getting the knot right the first time. "Who are you working for, some kiddie birthday party?"

"No, it's a Catholic children's hospital up in the Bronx. A few of the boys are going up on Sunday and do a few routines on the lawn, I guess it is. Then we'll visit the kids who can't get out of bed. That reminds me, I've got to pick up a gross of balloons; I'll be making balloon animals all day."

"A Catholic hospital? I thought you were Jewish."

He looked at me. "Shhh!" he said. "Don't tell the children!"

I ripped the knot out; first attempt a failure. "I guess that was a stupid thing to say," I said, readjusting the tie around my neck.

"Let me tell you," he said. "Aside from the fact that children is children, whatever their labels, there's the fact that clowns is clowns. I've worked with Irish clowns, French clowns, Italian clowns, German clowns, Mexican clowns, and, let's see, a few Baptist clowns—they like to do what they call 'Bible clowning'—and a Chinese clown or two. I've worked with giants and fat ladies and little people—they like to be called little people—and people born with monstrous deformities who make their livings being stared at. I've worked with a lady clown or two, and a couple of Negro clowns. When we play the south, we put them in blackface and the locals don't notice. And in all of the forty years I was with it, nobody I worked with ever gave a damn about my race, religion, sex, nationality, or any other damn thing except my act."

"The circus seems to be ahead of the rest of the country," I said.

"Damn right," Pinky agreed. "Except for the trapeze artists. If you can't do at least one somersault in mid-air, you can't sit at their table. You want me to tie that for you?"

"I don't think so," I said.

"Come on," Pinky said. "I know this great knot." He stretched his hands apart: "Big!"

"I'm sure," I told him. I looped the knot around, and this time it came out right.

"Mine would've looked better," Pinky said. He got up. "I gotta pack. See you later."

I left the house and walked into the park. It was windy and overcast, but it wasn't raining. I put on my raincoat anyway, because I like the coat and will wear it at any excuse. It's a war surplus officer's trench coat, and I like to think it makes me look worldly and sophisticated. Perhaps it does.

I sat on a bench and stared at the skyline. A flock of pigeons settled in front of me and waited expectantly. I found a piece of tissue paper in the pocket of the trench coat, so I ripped it into small pieces and tossed them amid the pigeons. They pecked at the bits of paper for a while, but then started looking at me out of the corners of their eyes and muttering to each other, so I got up and moved on.

I arrived at Lindner's at about ten-fifteen. Brass came in at about ten-thirty-five and sat opposite me. "Good morning, DeWitt," he said. "Did you settle our princess in last night?"

"I saw her register, but I didn't go upstairs with her," I said. "I assume she made it all right. She didn't show any signs of wanting to skip."

Our conversation paused while Brass ordered poached eggs with two slices of bacon and a glass of what the waitress swore was indeed fresh-squeezed orange juice, and I ordered pancakes and ham.

"Have you ever noticed that breakfast is the most idiosyncratic meal of the day?" Brass asked me as the waitress pulled away. "Most people, however adventurous they are at lunch or dinner, eat the breakfast of their youth."

"Really?" I asked. "I always ate cornflakes for breakfast at home."

"While others," Brass continued, pouring cream in his coffee with studied concentration, "of the sort who go on the stage, write novels, or swindle widows and orphans for a living, will change their eating habits entirely. It's one of the sure signs of the degenerate personality."

"And everything I have become I owe to your splendid example," I told him.

"I warned you when you took the job," Brass said. "Do you have the pictures?" he asked.

I touched my jacket, over my heart. "Securely buttoned down."

"Keep them so until we get back to the office. Did Mitchell have anything interesting to say about them?"

"They're not composites," I said. "Aside from that, nothing that seemed particularly helpful." I told him what Mitchell had suggested.

"Write it up and stick it in the file," Brass said. "You never know."

"You never know," I agreed. "What happened last night after we left?"

"More reporters showed up. A sharp-eyed detective spotted MacArthur of the *Mirror* taking down a couple of photos that were pinned up in the front room, so the police took them all down and are holding them as evidence. The police are working on the theory that the killer was a jealous husband or boyfriend, or possibly a father that didn't like what his daughter was doing for a living."

Our food came, and I thoughtfully poured syrup over my pancakes. "Do they really believe that?" I asked.

"I doubt if they really believe anything," Brass said. "But it is a possibility that they have to check out. I did discover one thing of interest before I left."

I started to say, "What's that?" and got as far as "Wha—" when Bobbi appeared at the booth. She was not as flamboyantly dressed as when I met her last evening, but she didn't need flamboyance to make an effect. She was wearing a green wool skirt and sweater that made me want to compliment the sheep. I didn't stare.

"Hello," she said. "Sorry I'm late." She tucked her handbag, a black contraption large enough to hold King Kong and all the little Kongs, under the seat and slid in next to me. "I'm glad you ordered breakfast without waiting. I've been up at Herm's apartment."

"You went back?" I did stare. "Why?"

"I had an idea," she told me. She turned to the waitress and said that Brass's poached eggs looked good, which they didn't after the way he'd been poking at them, and she'd like some sausage and potatoes with the eggs. Then she turned to Brass. "Good morning," she said.

"What sort of idea? And good morning to you," Brass said. "Did you sleep well?"

"What a bed!" she said with a wide smile and a joyous wriggle. "And what a bathtub! You could swim in it. I *did* swim in it. Can I stay there tonight?"

"I told the manager you'd be there two weeks," Brass said. "You don't have to rush off."

"Two weeks! Say, that's great! I leave for Pittsburgh in two weeks, first stop on a four-month tour of Ardbaum's red circuit." She looked thoughtful for a second, and then leaned forward. "Say," she said to Brass, "you planning to visit during these two weeks?"

Brass wiped his mouth with his napkin and took a drink of coffee. He leaned forward. "Let me make something clear, Miss Starr. If I want to proposition a girl, I do it before I rent the hotel room, not after."

"Okay, okay," Bobbi said. "It wasn't such a dumb idea. Not all men are knights in shining armor, you know."

"From my reading of history," Brass said, "even the knights in shining armor weren't. But my ego won't let me try to attract women with anything beyond my native wit and charm. No baubles, no limousines, no suites in fancy hotels. I rent the room you're staying in by the year in case of need. It's much cheaper by the year. The last person before you to stay in it was a writer named Scott Fitzgerald, who was in from the coast for a week. He drank, and talked about his wife, Zelda, who's somewhere out West, and complained about the size of the advance his publisher was offering him for his next book. I did not make a pass at him."

"Say, don't get upset," she said. "Men not making passes is something new to my experience, and I have to get used to it, is all. It's okay. I like it."

"Fair enough," Brass said.

"What's the red circuit?" I asked her.

"The Ardbaums run two circuits, the red and the blue," she said. "Different cities, is all. And maybe for the red circuit a girl can get away with wearing a few less garments in her act. Not all the way down to pasties and a G-string—the Ardbaums don't go for that—but pretty close."

"I see," I said. Life presents an endless vista of educational opportunities.

She reached into her purse and took out a file card. "Here," she said, extending it across the table to Brass.

"What's this?"

"It's what I went uptown for." She turned to me. "I got to thinking last night about how we searched the room and everything, looking for those pictures that I kept telling you Herm wouldn't have taken..."

"Yes," I said.

"And those two numbers that were missing."

"Yes?" I asked.

"What two numbers?" Brass asked.

I explained about Dworkyn's dating system and the two files that were gone.

"Ah!" Brass said. "The police missed that—at least while I was there."

"Well, I got to thinking," Bobbi said, "and I remembered that Herm keeps cards on his clients—the ones he does darkroom work for as well as the magazines—so he knows what number file the negatives are in. And this—" she waved the card in her hand like a tiny flag "—is the file card with those numbers on it."

Brass took the card and looked at it reverently, and then passed it to me. It was a three-by-five file card, of the sort you can buy in stationery stores for a nickel a pack. On the upper left was printed in big block letters in a neat hand—Herm's, I assumed—BIRD. Under it, neatly under one another, slightly indented from the name, were the entries 3526, 3588, and 3597, and on the right side of the card, across from the other numbers, one more entry: C516.

"Do you know who Bird is?" Brass asked.

"No idea," Bobbi said. "I don't know any of Herm's clients, except that I'd see them around, you know."

"I understand," Brass said.

"The two files that were missing were 3588 and 3597," I said. "I wonder what 3526 was, and what C516 means."

"Oh, I brought them along," Bobbi said. "I thought you might want to see them." She reached into her handbag with both hands and pulled out a folder. "They're not very exciting," she said, passing it to Brass. "The *C* stands for contact sheet. When Herm develops—" she paused to gulp twice "—developed thirty-five-millimeter-roll film he would print a contact sheet, which is like all the pictures are fitted onto one eight-by-ten sheet and the client can pick the ones he wants enlarged from that."

"Yes, I am familiar with the concept," Brass said. He opened the folder, pulled out the contact sheet, and squinted at it. "A girl who seems to have no clothes on," he said. "Not unfamiliar subject matter. But she seems to be alone, which is original."

"Herm sometimes did nature studies," Bobbi said. "But he doesn't even have a thirty-five-millimeter camera, so these aren't his."

"I can't make out much detail; I'll have to have the pictures blown up," Brass said. "Let's look at the rest of this stuff." He dumped the rest of the folder's contents onto the table and we stared down at a selection of glassine envelopes holding four-by-five-inch negatives. Brass counted them. "Eight negatives," he said. He held one of them up to the light. "People," he said, "with their clothes on. Standing, looking at the camera. Not art, just a snapshot. Probably someone's family."

"The rest of them are all like that," Bobbi said. "I would have printed them for you, but it would take too long. Are they any good to you?"

Brass passed them to me, and I held one up. There's something very strange about looking at negatives; it's like you're looking at people and things inside out. It makes it very hard for me to tell what I'm seeing.

"I can't tell what information they have for us until I have them printed," Brass said. "I can have that done at the newspaper. I don't think you should go back to that apartment for anything else."

"I wasn't going to," Bobbi said. "It gives me the creeps."

Breakfast continued, and we talked about various things. No more about her brother or our other problems, but mostly about life in what Bobbi called "the show-all business." Brass got Bobbi talking, and kept her going. He was gathering material, although much of what she told us couldn't be printed in any of his current markets. She told us stories about life on the road that made me feel that I knew nothing whatever about life or how it is lived. I would have to tear up my manuscript and start again, and write about real people: dancers and strippers and singers and comics and jugglers and magicians—real people.

Brass had an acquisitive look in his eyes as he listened to Bobbi's stories. Occasionally he would throw in a story himself, just to keep the ball rolling, but mostly he listened. Some of Bobbi's stories meandered and had no proper end, and some jumped from here to there with abandon, but that's what life is like. Bobbi didn't know she was telling stories, she was just relating her life to us. She sat there with her post-breakfast pastry and coffee ("One thing about being a dancer, a girl doesn't have to watch her weight.") and talked.

"It's true what they say about company managers," she said, chewing her Danish and staring at the picture of Whistler's mother-in-law on the wall as she talked. "One time in Cleveland—this would have been May or June a couple of years ago, I guess... No, wait a minute—it was thirty-three, June of thirty-three—we are playing the Alhambra Theater and not doing too well. June is always slow, and besides, nobody has any money, not even fifteen cents to get into the show.

"The company manager, Benny—no, Bernie—comes backstage one evening right before the late show and tells the girls it might be a good idea if they show a little more skin during the specialty numbers. Just a little, and just for this one show, he says, so he can see if he likes it."

She took a sip of coffee. "Well, there's always girls who are eager to show it all, if they got any excuse, so Bernie gets what he asked for. The audience likes it, except for one guy in the front row who is sitting there with his arms crossed and an expression on his face like he has just sucked a lemon. Right next to him is sitting Bernie, who is deadpan, and one cannot tell what he is thinking. It turns out that the guy next to Bernie is the head of the Ohio Legion of Morality and Decency, or some such, and Bernie has invited him to come to the show, in the fond hope that he'll find it immoral and indecent. There is a passel of reporters waiting in the lobby to hear what this guy has to say. If he pans the show loud enough, we'll be playing to packed houses for the rest of the run."

"And did he?" Brass asked.

"Oh, my, yes. And the chief of police threatens to close us down if we don't clean up the show, which we have already done because the skin show was for one night only. It costs Bemie a twenty to get the chief to make this threat, but he comes through like a gentleman and the box office does not suffer. But then the morality guy comes back the next evening, and this time there's no Bernie and no reporters. The day after that he is there for all four shows. And the day after that. It turns out he has developed a crush on Princess Alice, which is not her stage name, which is Fifi Delite, but is what we call her because she is so high-falutin' she dislikes having to breathe the same air as the rest of the girls.

"Anyway, this gent, whose name turns out to be Lester, and who is a bank manager when he isn't being moral and decent, can't take his eyes off Alice when she does her number. I mean, there are a good number of men who can't take their eyes off Alice, but not like Lester. Alice's turn consists of coming out in an evening gown and slowly singing "My Heart Belongs to Daddy" while removing the gown and getting ready for bed—her set is a bed and a dressing table. When she is bereft of her gown and most of her undies, she slips into this nothing of a nightie, slides into bed, and blows the lights out."

"Sounds like a provocative act," Brass commented.

"It sure provokes Lester," Bobbi said. "He works up his nerve to ask her out after the last show on the third night, and proposes to her that night. A week later he marries her. The good people of Cleveland, at least those good people who Lester is accustomed to associating with, are not amused. Lester loses his job at the bank, and his mother, with whom he is living, gives him the boot. So he and Alice move to New York and Mrs. Ardbaum gives him a job as accountant for the red circuit, which, incidentally, pays more than he was getting at the bank. The princess gives up burlesque and goes into radio. She does specialty voices for the daytime dramas. Mostly little children and dogs."

We finished our coffee and left the restaurant, Bobbi heading for Seventh Avenue to shop for working clothes, and Brass and I office-bound.

14

Inspector Raab was stretched out on the couch in Brass's inner office when we arrived, his head on one armrest, his feet sticking out past the other. Gloria put her finger to her lips as we came through the front door and led us in to look at the sleeping beauty. Then she gestured us back out to the outer office, closing the door behind her. "Poor man needs his sleep," she said.

Brass glared at his closed office door. "Presumably he has a home," he griped. "Why can't he sleep there? I need my office."

Gloria smiled sweetly at him. "You used to be able to write anywhere," she said.

"I can still write anywhere," Brass told her. "That's not the point. You can't just let every Tom, Dick, and Harry wander into my office and sack out on the couch. He didn't even take his shoes off!"

"Well, I'm sorry!" Gloria said. "It was my idea. He came in here looking for you, and I didn't know how long you'd be, and he said he'd wait, and the poor man looked like he hadn't slept since Groveley Day, so I told him to take a nap on the couch until you got here."

I carefully hung my raincoat on a wooden hanger. "Groveley Day?" I asked.

"Just never mind," Gloria said. "Sit here," she told Brass, swinging the typewriter up from its compartment in her desk. "Write your column. Let the man sleep."

Brass transferred his glare to Gloria, and then sighed a long-suffering sigh and sat behind the desk and rolled a sheet of paper into the typewriter. He stared into space for a minute and then poised his hands above the keyboard. A determined look came into his eye. He was going to prove to us that he was no sissy, that he didn't need his overstuffed chair, his large desk, his shelves of reference books, his river view to write his column: He could write it anywhere. He typed a word. He paused for thought. He typed another word. He stared at the closet door. A smile formed on his lips and he began to type in earnest.

Gloria sat on the couch, a steno notebook in her lap, writing something. I worked my way around to the back of the desk, subtly, so as not to disturb Brass, to see what he was typing. It was:

> *I am writing these words on the typing machine in my reception room, as my office is in use at the moment. But that's O.K. As master novelist Charles Dickens once said, "It is a far, far better thing I do..." Lying on my office couch as I write these words, fast asleep at a quarter to noon, is a detective inspector of the New York City Police Department, Homicide Squad. He is taking a short nap, and he deserves it. He has been up all night. He may have been up for several nights, I'm not sure. Homicide Squad detectives do not punch time clocks when they're working on a murder, and neither does their boss.*

Brass might have to suffer, but not silently. Twenty million people were going to know of his stoic heroism tomorrow morning over breakfast. I tiptoed away to my tiny office and sat down.

I worked on answering letters for about twenty minutes, when I heard the inner office door open, and Inspector Raab bellow, "Why the hell didn't somebody wake me!"

Brass came into the hall. "Oh, have you finished your nap?" he enquired. "We didn't want to disturb you."

"How thoughtful," Raab said. "Come in here, I want to talk to you."

Brass returned to his office, and I was about two steps behind him. Raab was adjusting his tie, using the window as a mirror. "Coffee?" Brass asked Raab.

"Nah, it puts me to sleep."

Brass settled in behind his desk and gave his chair a couple of easy twists from side to side. He leaned back. "I assume you came here for something other than to use my couch," he said. "Not that you're not perfectly welcome to sack out here any time you feel the need."

Raab pulled a chair up to the desk and settled into it. "Perfectly friendly," he said.

"What?"

"I want to keep this perfectly friendly. You and I have known each other for a long time. You've said nice things about me in your column. I've given you tips, when I could."

"True," Brass agreed. "And I you."

"And now you're hiding something from me, and I want to know what it is."

Brass shook his head. "We've been through this, Inspector. If there was anything I could tell you, I would."

Gloria came in and closed the door behind her. She stood there by the door, clearly prepared to referee if it came to a slugging match.

"Did you know," Raab said, "that the back of Dworkyn's building is connected by an alley to the back of the building that Billy Fox's body was found in?"

"Yes. I figured that out last night." Brass swiveled to face me. "I started to tell you at breakfast, but we got sidetracked. Oh, yes; that's when Miss Starr sat down."

"So you had breakfast with the stripper, eh?" Raab asked. "Both of you?"

"We met her at Lindner's," Brass said, sounding annoyed.

"Sure you did," Raab said. "But that's none of my business, what you do. Did you know that Fox was killed in Dworkyn's studio and his body was carried through the alley to where we found it?"

"That was certainly one of the possibilities," Brass commented.

"Well, it's no longer a possibility, it's what happened."

"You're sure?"

"There's a trail of blood, sparse but followable. There are some footprints. There is a slight bit of fabric from his coat caught on a fence nail by the other building. I could probably dream up a scenario where this is all a coincidence, if you like, but I don't think I could sell it."

I noticed that Gloria had her steno pad out and was unobtrusively taking notes. Brass ran his hand through his hair and, as always, seemed annoyed that there wasn't more of it. "Perhaps you should speak to Señor Velo, the oh-so-helpful travel agent," Brass suggested. "His version of the event seems unlikely."

"We thought of that," Raab said. "The travel agency is closed, and Velo is nowhere to be found."

"Perhaps he's on his honeymoon," Brass said. "Have you released von Pilath yet?"

"Not yet," Raab said. At Brass's look, he continued defensively, "Well, he might have done it, after all. Besides, we got a report through ICPB that he is wanted by the Berlin police for burglary."

"And reeling and writhing and fainting in coils," Brass said. "I was told that the Nazis might try something like this. Does he look like a burglar to you?"

"What does a burglar look like?" Raab asked sensibly. "And who told you?"

"Several of his associates in the Verein für Whosis."

"Why didn't they tell me?" Raab demanded.

"It should be obvious," Brass said, leaning back. "You'll inquire about them over ICPB and get back that they're wanted for mopery or barratry or using a bratwurst for immoral purposes. According to them the present German government uses the police as an instrument of policy; a situation in which truth is not highly regarded."

"Well, I'm not convinced that that's true," Raab said. "The Berlin police department has always had high standards, and I don't think that they'd go along with any hanky-panky."

"I hope you're right," Brass said.

"In any case," Raab continued, "I don't have to take notice of the ICPB filing unless someone formally asks for von Pilath's extradition, which so far they have not done."

"I don't see where any of this is going to take us," Brass said, "but I suppose information is always useful."

"My point," Raab said, waving his index finger at Brass. "That's why I want you to tell me what you're holding back." He pulled a pack of cigarettes from his pocket, shook one out, and stuck it between his lips. Then he glared at the pack in his hand, as though wondering how it had got there, jammed it back in his pocket, took the cigarette out of his mouth, and crumpled it and threw it in the wastebasket.

He turned back to Brass. "Now look, we've been friends, of a sort, for a long time. I know you. The story you told about that fat man was bullshit when you told it and it's still bullshit." He turned to Gloria. "Excuse my French."

"That's okay," she told him. "I work on a newspaper; I'm used to bullshit."

Raab nodded. "The way I figure it," he told Brass, "is the fat man came up here and showed you some pictures he wanted to sell. Either you bought them or you didn't; if they were any good you bought them. That's none of my business. But he wouldn't tell you who he was, so you asked Fox to follow him. And Fox got killed. So now it is my business. I want to know what was in those pictures that a man—two men—would get killed for them."

"You don't want to know," Brass told him. "Trust me."

"When did you take charge of the New York City Police Department?" Raab asked, not quite shouting. "It's not your decision! The First Amendment does not give you the right to withhold evidence, and you damn well know it!"

The two men stared at each other for a minute or so. Then Brass let out a long breath of air. "Let's suppose—"

"Suppose nothing!" Raab snapped. "I want to know what was in those pictures!"

Brass contemplated the little Chinese god on the corner of his desk, his fingers drumming on the desktop while he considered. Then he contemplated Raab, who just stood there impassively waiting for Brass's response. Brass sighed. "First I want to assure you that the next ten minutes are, as Mr. Roosevelt is so fond of saying, strictly off the record."

Raab slammed his hand down on the desk. "Goddamn it," he yelled. "I'll decide what's on or off the record, not you! I'm not going to promise to withhold evidence in a murder case, whatever it is!"

"You misunderstand me," Brass said. He leaned forward. "The

decision is yours." He turned to me. "DeWitt, will you please hand Inspector Raab the packet of photographs?"

I unbuttoned the flap on my jacket pocket and pulled out the pictures. "Here you are," I said, handing them to Raab.

"Hmph!" Raab said. He moved his chair over and turned on the floor lamp by the side of the desk. "So you bought them? How much?"

"Actually, he gave them to me," Brass told him.

"Yeah? Then what the..."

Inspector Raab must have seen something interesting in the picture he was looking at; he stopped talking and peered closely down at the photographs, going slowly from one to the next. Brass and Gloria and I maintained the silence, which stretched out for a while.

"Shit!" Raab said after a while, with feeling. He looked up at Brass. "I recognize the senator and Judge Garbin. Are the rest of them—"

"DeWitt," Brass said, "read Inspector Raab the list of names."

I pulled out my little notebook. "Senator Bertram Childers," I said. "Judge Gerald Garbin. Ephraim L. Wackersan, of the department store of the same name. Pass Helbine, friend of the poor, and of every politician in the city. Suzie Frienard; you may know her husband, Dominic, who builds things. Stepney Partcher, of Partcher, Meedle and Coster—he's a lawyer. Homer Seinbrenner, he sells booze. Fletcher van Geuip, he writes books."

"That's it?"

"That's it."

"Shit!" Raab repeated.

Gloria appeared at Raab's side and handed him a glass. "Cognac," she said.

Raab stared at it, drank it down, and put the glass on the desk. "Damn," he said. "Why'd you show those to me?"

"Inspector!" Brass protested.

"Yeah, yeah. It's my own damn fault. You warned me. You think it's blackmail? You think one of them killed Dworkyn and Fox?"

"I have no idea," Brass said, "but I rather think not. It may well be blackmail, but I don't think Dworkyn was the blackmailer. He claimed to be trying to find out who had taken the pictures."

Raab got up and looked around the room. I didn't know what he was looking at, or for. "If I take these," he said, "there's no way—I can't even—Goddamn it!"

"Sorry," Brass said.

"Yeah," Raab said. He gathered the photos up and tossed the packet across the desk. "Put those away. This conversation never happened. I swallowed your cock-and-bull story about Dworkyn, and you never showed me the pictures. Right?"

"Right."

Raab sat back down. "I don't like looking like an idiot," he said, "but I want to stay on the force long enough to collect my pension. I'll go at it another way, although I'm damned if I see what way that is at this moment."

"If I get anything, I'll pass it on to you," Brass assured him.

"Yeah," Raab said. "And ain't that a hell of a note? When I figure out which of them did it—if one of them did it—I'll indict the son of a bitch, political pull or no. But if I try investigating all of them, the seven of them who didn't do it will have my ass, not to mention my badge. Except for the writer; writers don't have any political clout. Unless they all did it together. You think they all did it?"

"No," Brass said.

"Yeah. Me too." Raab hauled out his pack of cigarettes again, and tapped it against his hand, but no cigarette emerged. He stared balefully at the pack for a moment, then crumpled it and tossed it in the wastebasket. "Does anyone else know about those pictures?"

"The four of us in this room," Brass told him, "and Cathy, William Fox's widow, who is now working for me, and an expert I had examine them. He won't talk; he never talks."

"What'd he think?"

"They're real."

"Yeah." Raab took a pad from his pocket and a fountain pen from another pocket and wrote down the eight names I had read to him. He didn't have to ask me to repeat any of them. I don't know whether that was a credit to his memory or the prominence of the names or the situation. "I can check these people to a certain extent," he said. "I can have their whereabouts at the time of the murders established. There are ways of doing that without raising anyone's hackles, or explaining just why we're asking. Beyond that I cannot go without telling my superiors about the pictures. And they are all very political, which means they'll be looking for someone to blame. Neither of us would like that."

"It's not a situation I'm particularly fond of either," Brass said. "When we catch whoever did this, we'll have to give him a stem talking-to."

"You planning on doing the catching?" Raab asked.

"I will certainly ask for your assistance when there is something for you to assist in," Brass told him.

"You do that," Raab said.

15

Inspector Raab was not a happy policeman as he left our office. I would not want to be a miscreant who fell into his clutches for the next few hours. As soon as Raab was gone, Brass pulled the page out of the reception desk typewriter and took it into his office to finish the story of the sleeping detective. I wondered how Raab would feel about that when he read it tomorrow.

I took the packet of pornographic photographs and put it in the special file in the closet behind the booze. He who steals our purse steals trash, but he who steals our dirty picture collection could make a lot of money blackmailing influential citizens. Then I retreated to my office with the day's mail and began opening the envelopes and sorting the contents into different piles. I am particularly fond of the nut mail; the letters you can't believe are real, but neither can you believe anyone made them up. A couple of milder examples from this morning's mail will show you what I mean:

Dear Mr Brass,
I rite you because of how you are always helping the littel people. I am a littel man & my wife to & I need your help. Could you send me about $80 woud be a grate help.

Sinserly George Wrantke

The letter was postmarked Chicago, but there was no return address. How he expected to get his money, I don't know.

And:

Alexander Brass
The World Building
New York

My Dear Mr. Alexander Brass:
In one of your recent columns you spoke of the plight of the jobless people who still roam the streets of our major cities looking for work, and of the good work the WPA and other "alphabet" organizations started by President Roosevelt has done in helping these "unfortunates."

I assume you mean well, but you have fallen prey to the propaganda of the Jew industrialists that are trying to turn our Republic into a Communistic state, as is written in the Protocols of the Elders of Zion, their own document, for all to see. There is no secret about this except in the blindness of the citizens of our great democracy to see what is before their very eyes before it is too late.

The Depression was created by the Hebrew bankers to throw this great country into chaos so they could further their diabolical schemes. These people on the streets don't even want to work. Go on and offer one of them a job, and see what happens. President Roosevelt, whose real name is Rosenfeld, it has been conclusively proven, is a conscious agent of this Jew-Freemason conspiracy.

I write you in the best of motivations, to remove the cloud from before your eyes. Don't be fooled before it is too late.

Most Sincerely, your friend,
Karl Swendele
Ayer, Mass.

Ps. If you send me an envelope with some postage on it, I will send you some books to read that will really open your eyes.

He did include his full address, or at least a post office box number, and I was tempted to send him an envelope with some postage on it, but I didn't.

I heard Cathy come upstairs from the morgue, where she had

been gathering material on our eight photo pals beyond what was in their folders. "You know Mr. Schiff is a really nice man," she said, "so helpful."

Brass appeared in his doorway. "Have you found anything that would connect any of them to each other?"

"Not yet," she said. "I'm making up a list of possibilities, but they'll have to be checked out. Like, two of them went to Harvard, but one of them went to Princeton, and I don't know where the others went. Stepney Partcher and Homer Seinbrenner are both members of the Thespian Club, but I don't know if any of the others are."

I had a stack of mail in my hand, which I continued to open while this conversation went on. I pulled a card out of its envelope and read it, and held it up in the air. "The princes of Serendip strike again!" I announced.

Brass smiled. "What stroke of serendipity have you stumbled upon?" he asked.

"You have here an invitation," I told him, "to a dinner party in honor of Charles A. Lindbergh."

"Well!" Brass said. "This, I think, will be Lindbergh's first outing since the trial."

He was referring, of course, to the trial of Bruno Hauptmann for the kidnaping and murder of Lindbergh's baby son, for those of you who have been on Mars for the past few years. Hauptmann was still sitting on death row at the New Jersey state prison at Trenton.

"What has this to do with our problem?" Brass asked me.

"The party is at the estate of Senator and Mrs. Bertram Childers, at Deal, New Jersey."

"Is it?" Brass took the card and read it, and then handed it to Gloria. "It is RSVP," he said. "Call the senator's social secretary and say there'll be four of us coming. I don't think they'll complain; in order to snag a celebrity guest, one has to put up with his entourage."

"I thought Lindbergh was the celebrity," I said.

Brass was not offended. "They can use all the celebrities they can get," he told me. "It's one of those two-hundred-dollar-a-plate Republican fund-raisers." He patted me on the shoulder. "Don't worry, we celebrities get to eat free. And we don't have to tell them how we're planning to vote."

"It's for Saturday," Gloria said.

"So?"

"You're speaking on Saturday," she flipped through the pages of the appointment book, "to the annual dinner of the Society of Radio Broadcasters."

"Call Winchell and ask him to go in my place; free food and an audience—he'll jump at it."

"All right."

Brass looked at his watch. "It's two o'clock, well past lunchtime," he said. "Let's go across the street to Danny's; I'm buying."

"What a prince!" I said.

"I'll just stay here and work," Cathy said. "I want to call the Harvard Club and see if any of our people are members. If they went to Harvard, they probably will be."

"A good idea," Brass said, "but you can do it after lunch."

"Come on, Cathy," Gloria said, "you've got to eat."

"Actually," she said, looking embarrassed, "I've eaten."

"Oh? When?"

"Mr. Schiff invited me to share his lunch. He was telling me stories, and it seemed impolite not to—"

"Ah!" Brass said. "The old Schiff magic. Candles and wine? Did he break out his balalaika and strum a few tunes?"

"Well, yes."

Brass patted her on the shoulder. "He's harmless, although he'd kill me if he heard me say that, and he's good for you. He really likes and respects women."

Danny's was not crowded; the last of the late-lunch crowd was just leaving as we arrived. There were a couple of *World* reporters taking a break at one table, and some men from the pressroom around another. They were not socializing; there is a strong pecking order in newspapers. Pressmen have a much higher status than reporters. They, after all, have a real union. We sat at the corner table near the kitchen that Brass always grabbed when it was otherwise unoccupied.

After a couple of minutes Danny appeared out of the kitchen. "Sorry," she said, "there was a slight crisis involving fish." She perched on the empty chair and poised her pencil before her order form. "Steak sandwich with mashed, pastrami on white with fries, and what would you like, my dear?" The last addressed to Gloria.

"Do you have any fish you're not having a problem with?" Gloria asked.

"Shad," Danny told her. "The man brought me some wonderful Hudson River shad; I'll broil you one. Mashed?"

"Rice?"

"Rice it is. And a salad." She disappeared into the kitchen.

Gloria turned her chair to face Brass. "Well?" she asked.

"Well what?"

"Are we making progress?"

"We're further along than we were yesterday," Brass replied, "but it feels more like we're being tossed ahead by the tide than like we're propelling ourselves forward."

"We know more about the pictures," Gloria said.

"True. We know they're not faked, or at least Mitchell thinks they're not; that they were all taken in the same location, and that someone named Bird is somehow involved. And we are quite sure that someone thinks they're worth killing for. But what's the common denominator?"

"I've been thinking," I said. "Our eight picture pals do have one thing in common, probably."

Brass turned to look at me. Gloria smiled encouragingly. I suddenly felt like a sixth-grader who is about to give a report before the whole class.

"What's that?" Brass asked.

"Well, they're probably all being blackmailed. That is, I can't think of anything else those pictures could be used for."

"They're certainly not art," Gloria agreed.

"Yes." Brass asked, "And what does that buy us?"

"Suppose we approach each of them as though we know they're being blackmailed, and we want to help."

"It's an interesting idea," Brass said. "The approach would have to be very delicately done; we don't want to frighten anyone, and we certainly don't want anyone thinking that we are the blackmailers. That's a comedy of errors we could live without."

"And there's always the chance that they aren't being blackmailed *yet*," Gloria added. "In which case they'd wonder what we're talking about and call the police."

Brass nodded. In a deep voice he intoned: "'Columnist Indicted for Extortion. "I was framed," screams noted syndicated columnist Alexander Brass. While not wishing to prejudge the case, this paper will no longer carry Mr. Brass's column so as not to offend the sensibilities of the unindicted.' By God, Winchell would have a field day. Heywood Broun would stick up for me and put me down in the same paragraph. Alexander Woollcott would make a pun. By God, it's almost worth it. Like Tom Sawyer coming to his own funeral."

Danny appeared at the table carrying plates of food. "*Tom Sawyer*?" she asked. "I thought *Huckleberry Finn* was a better book; more stuff in it." She put the plates down.

Danny stayed at the table and chatted with us while we ate. Which was a good thing: Besides being a welcome addition to any conversation on her own merits, she kept us from the topic that would have monopolized the meal. We discussed poetry and playwriting and fishing, with a few digressions into the meaning of life and the future of civilization. Aristotle was mentioned, and Anatole France; Nietzsche and nihilism. The only crimes we discussed were literary ones, and the only deaths, ones that had occurred years if not centuries before.

It was a little after three when we returned to the *World* building. We took the elevator to sixteen and were headed to the door of our office when a deep thump shook the corridor walls and floor ever so slightly. The vibrations quickly damped out, and an acrid, sort of burned smell filled the corridor. Brass suddenly shouted, "Damn!" and threw himself toward the office door. Gloria and I followed, perhaps a little more hesitantly. We made it through the door just in time to see three men emerge from the hallway to the inner office. When they saw us they charged, fullbacks breaking through the line to the open space of the hall beyond. Two of them were built like football flayers, and the third was thin and wiry, but he could move fast enough. They all wore blue knitted caps, which they pulled down past their chins as they charged us.

In an instant, the three were past us and down the hall to the stairway. Brass and I were knocked to the floor, and Gloria was shoved up against the door, from which she slid to the floor on her own. As we lay there, we could hear our assailants rapidly clattering down the stairs.

I was not in pain but a warm feeling was spreading over my face. I reached up to touch it, and my hand came away covered with blood.

Brass pushed himself to his feet, sort of doubled over with his hands wrapped tightly around his chest. "Damn!" he said.

"You said that," Gloria said. She stood up and took a few steps, and fell into her chair.

Brass staggered to the edge of the desk and supported himself against it. "Are you all right?" he asked Gloria.

"I think so," she said. "I need to catch my breath."

Brass turned to me. "Are you—" He stared at me. "Migod! What happened?"

"I have no idea," I said. "I think I'm bleeding."

"Take my word for it," he said, staggering over to me. He pulled a handkerchief from his pocket and dabbed at my face with it. "He was wearing knucks when he hit you," Brass said. "You're lucky; he could have broken your nose."

"It's not broken?" I asked.

"I don't think so."

Gloria was on the phone to the infirmary on the seventh floor before Brass finished dabbing at my face. "The nurse will be right up," she said.

"Damn!" Brass said again, and we looked at him.

"Cathy!" he called, and headed toward the inner hallway.

There are times when anxiety becomes a physical feeling, and a painful knot of anxiety grabbed at my chest with Brass's call. I pulled myself to my feet and followed Gloria, who was two steps in front of me. The two of them paused in the doorway to Brass's office, blocking my view.

Brass and Gloria went on into the office, and I started to follow, but instead I folded up and fell to the floor.

16

White. Shining white, brilliant white.

My closed eyes opened and, as through a glass brightly, I saw white: hazy, sparkling white. Slowly, gradually, my eyes focused and I saw that the white was not uniform, it was differenced, it was dirty and cracked in places. It was a ceiling.

I was staring at a ceiling. I must be lying on my back. Something throbbed and was in great pain. I searched through the possibilities and the realization grew, slowly, that it was my head. The white was the ceiling, the pain was my head; that was all of the universe that I knew, and all that was needful for me to know. I closed my eyes. It was black.

Time passed. I opened my eyes. They focused faster this time and I could make out more detail. But it was still a ceiling, essentially uninteresting. I moved my head. Now I could see a wall. It was white.

"How do you feel?"

It was a voice. It was a lovely voice. It was a familiar voice. I turned my head. Gloria was sitting by the side of the bed—I was in a bed, that was good to know—looking down at me with concern in her eyes.

"What happened?" I asked.

"The doctor says you got a mild concussion," Gloria said. "When that bruiser hit you with the brass knuckles it knocked your head back, and then he slammed into you with his shoulder to get through the door, and you went down, hitting your head on the floor. The brass knucks didn't do much damage, you lucked out there, but the floor did. That's how the doc figures it. Now it's your turn; how do you feel?"

"Like somebody slammed my head against the floor. What bruiser? What brass knuckles? What are you talking about? How did I get here? And just where is 'here'?"

"You're in a private room on the third floor of New York Hospital," Gloria told me. She patiently repeated to me the events concerning our recent misadventure, concluding with, "And we found Cathy tied to a chair in the office with a kind of weird beige cloth tape. She was all right when we got her untied, but very angry. She'd been frightened out of her mind, and she didn't like it. The intruders, whoever they were, went through the desk and the file cabinets like a cyclone, tossing everything on the floor and leaving an incredible mess."

As she talked my memory of the events had returned. "And the safe," I said. "They must have blown the safe; that was the boom we heard."

"That's right," Gloria agreed. "Brass thinks they were after the pictures, but they didn't get them; they were in the special file."

"How long have I been here?"

"It's tomorrow," Gloria told me. She looked at the watch on her wrist. She wore a large man's watch, with a black band, and I've always meant to ask her why. But not now. "It's a little after one in the morning."

"Is everyone else okay?" I asked.

"I'm fine. Alexander has had his ribs taped up. The doctor thinks they're bruised but not broken. Anyway, he's in pain, which we're going to be reminded of for the next couple of weeks. It's a good thing you were hurt worse, or he'd be insufferable. He's outside, probably downstairs in the cafeteria; I'll get him."

"Wait a minute," I said, and she paused in the doorway. "You both waited here?"

"All three, actually. Cathy is here too."

"I feel loved," I said. "I'll have to get a minor concussion more often."

"Well." Gloria looked down at the floor. "We didn't know it

was a minor concussion until you woke up."

"Oh," I said.

"If it was a major concussion, then you might not have awakened."

"For how long?"

"Ever, maybe," she said, and went out the door.

Two minutes later a short but distinguished-looking man in a spade beard and a dinner jacket walked in. "Hello, there, fellow," he said. "I'm Dr. Kaplan. What's your name?"

"Morgan DeWitt. Why?"

"I just want to make sure you know it. It's my job; I'm your doctor."

"Oh," I said.

He came over and peered into my eyes with a little light. "Do you remember what happened to you?"

"I didn't for the first couple of minutes after I came to, but I do now."

"Who is the president of the United States?"

"Eleanor Roosevelt."

Dr. Kaplan looked quizzically at me. "You're joking? Perhaps you shouldn't joke until we ascertain that your memory is functioning properly."

"Sorry."

Gloria brought Brass and Cathy in while the doctor was still poking, probing, and asking questions. I was pleased to be able to inform them that, since it was after midnight, today was Friday, March 15, 1935; that the doctor was holding up three fingers; that my mother's name was Edith; and that my mental processes were probably as good as they had ever been—this last from Dr. Kaplan.

The doctor stood up and buttoned his jacket. "We'll keep him until morning just to be sure, but he doesn't seem to have suffered any lasting damage."

"Thank you, Doctor," Brass said.

"No, no, thank you," Dr. Kaplan said. "You pulled me out of a particularly boring awards dinner and saved me from the only food in New York worse than what's served in the cafeteria here."

"Oh, yes," Brass said. "Your answering service said you were at an Astor Foundation dinner, wasn't it? Who was getting the award?"

"I was." Dr. Kaplan looked down at me. "Take care of yourself, young man," he said. "We don't really understand the workings of the brain that well yet, and I might have had to cut out some part you find useful. Well, good night; or, I should say, good morning." And he was out the door.

"I guess we should all get some sleep," Brass said. "There'll be a guard outside your door for the night. I called Bradford and had him send a man over." Michael Bradford, owner of Bradford's Detective Agency, was an old friend of Brass's and his agency was one of the best in the city.

"I appreciate the concern," I said, "but is it necessary?"

"I hope not," Brass said. "But since they didn't get what they were after, who knows what they'll do next?"

I tried sitting up, but my head throbbed a warning, so I lay back down. "Then you'd better look after yourselves as well," I said.

"Gloria and Cathy will stay in my spare bedroom for now," Brass told me, "and Garrett will be alerted to the situation."

Theodore Garrett, Brass's man of all things not associated with the office, was a large, burly veteran of the War to End All Wars with a twisted sense of humor and a propensity for puns; and if his job was to keep you safe, then you were safe. I nodded, which hurt my head, and I said, "Go away now," and they did. Sometime in the next twenty seconds I fell asleep.

When I awoke, dappled sunlight was streaming through the window, its myriad sparkling feet dancing joyously about the room in celebration of the morn. Sometimes I get the urge to write sentences like that, but I suppress the urge or crumple up the page and toss it. I left this one in to show you every writer's fear: that his subconscious has slipped a sentence like that by him unnoticed, and no one will tell him. We'll start again.

When I woke up it was morning, and a nurse in a starched white uniform was standing by the side of my bed holding a bedpan. "Oh, you're awake," she said. "Let me slide this under you."

"I can get up," I told her. "I don't need that. But thank you for thinking of me."

"You're sure?" she asked. "Don't let false pride result in a soiled bed."

I sat up gingerly and discovered that the throbbing was still present, but very slightly, and it didn't hurt too much to turn my head from side to side. "I'm sure," I told her. "Where is the bathroom, and where can I get a toothbrush?"

She pointed to a door. "That's the bathroom. I will go down the hall and get you a toothbrush and some toothpaste. Would you like a razor? Straight-edge or safety?"

"Safety, I think," I said. "I don't want to be like that man who accidentally shaved himself while he was trying to cut his throat."

She looked at me strangely and left the room.

I went to the bathroom and, with a certain amount of pride, proved that I could do without a bedpan. My head didn't hurt except that it throbbed when I moved it about too rapidly. I showered and used the tools the nurse brought me. I got dressed.

The Bradford op, who told me his name was Luther, came downstairs with me, but then went off on his own, his job done.

I took a cab to 33 Central Park South, figuring that there was no chance that Brass was out of his apartment yet. The doorman let me in and the elevator man took me up to the twenty-eighth floor without a word. I wanted to say something clever but nothing came to mind, so the silence was mutual.

Garrett opened the door. "Well, Mr. DeWitt," he said with a broad smile, "I hear your head isn't as hard as we both thought it was. You're just in time for breakfast." He turned around to precede me into the dining room, and I saw that he had an Army .45 automatic stuck in his belt. I felt protected.

The clan was assembled at the dining room table when I came in. This business of being threatened with death and mayhem would make early risers of us all. Brass, his mouth full, waved me to a seat and pointed to the food. I filled my plate.

Gloria and Cathy asked me how I felt, and I said, "Bowed but unbloodied," and fell to eating my eggs. Then I recollected that I wasn't the only one who had gone through trying times. "How are you doing?" I asked Cathy. "Was it horrible?"

"I've never been so mad in my life," she told me. "They burst in and trussed me up like a sack of potatoes, and I had to watch them paw their way through all the desk drawers and the file cabinets."

"All but one," Gloria said. "They didn't find the special file."

"Indeed," Brass agreed. "The wall safe is a splendid distraction. But there can be no doubt what they were after."

"I think it's a copy of that column you're writing on how movie stars keep their baby-soft complexions," I said between sips of juice. "'"I use Pond's cold cream in a daily regimen of facial care," says noted film star Harpo Marx, caught at home lounging in a teal-blue bathrobe of the sheerest silk lamé.' It's revelations like that that keep this country the great land that it is."

Brass poured himself a fresh cup of coffee. "The ladies and I are going to continue gathering and sorting information today," he said. "If you are sufficiently recovered, Morgan, I think you should begin interviewing some of the people on our list. Subtly—if you can manage that—determine their whereabouts at the times that interest us, as well as anything else that seems relevant."

"Great," I said. "Who should I see?"

Brass took a scrap of paper from his pocket and smoothed it on the table. He makes all his notes on random scraps of paper; if he carried a notebook, someone might mistake him for a reporter. "Why don't you begin with Mr. Wackersan, whom I understand is an early riser, and continue with Mr. Helbine, whom I understand is not. Try not to alarm them with your questions."

"Fine," I said. "Anything specific that I should ask them?"

"I rely on your native wit," Brass said, "but try not to be too witty."

"I'll do my best."

I stopped off at home to change my clothes and by ten o'clock I was up on the executive floor of Wackersan's Department Store, which takes up most of the block between Sixth and Seventh avenues from Thirty-first to Thirty-second streets.

The father of the present Wackersan had founded the department store bearing his name in the 1880s as a monument to modern marketing and sales methods. It remained a monument as the world and the city changed. Wackersan's still did a good business, even for these depressed times, but both the sales force and the customers got older every year.

Junior Wackersan kept me waiting for about half an hour,

which was long enough to impress upon me that he owned a department store, while I was just a working stiff, but not long enough to turn me into a Bolshevik.

Wackersan's office had not been changed since his father had furnished it forty years before, except that the oak-paneled walls were now covered with too many framed pictures of the Wackersans, Senior and Junior, shaking hands or rubbing elbows with the great and near great.

Wackersan, Jr. was a short, stocky man who fidgeted his way around the office while we talked. He was not so much nervous as blessed—or cursed—with a surplus of energy, which he constantly had to drain off or it would bubble out of him. He kept making a swinging gesture that I didn't understand until I pictured a tennis racket emerging from his right fist. "Yes, yes," he bubbled. "Always glad to make time for the working press. Always glad. Good public relations is at the heart of good customer relations, which was a dictum of my father, the late Ephraim L. Wackersan, Sr. But, as much as I like to chat, we'll have to make this brief. Time is money, and I am a busy man. A busy man. *Tempus fugit,* as they say. *Tempus fugit.* What magazine did you say you were from?"

"A newspaper, Mr. Wackersan. The *New York World.*"

"And you want to do a story about Wackersan's?"

I took out my notebook. "Not exactly, Mr. Wackersan. We would like to do a story about you."

"Me?" Junior tried not to look pleased. His father cast a long shadow from which he had yet to emerge. He bubbled over to his desk and sat down. "What do you want to—that is, what sort of thing are you doing?"

"My editor is thinking of running a series, 'Great Men of New York.' We'll cover important political figures like Mayor LaGuardia and Governor Lehman, and figures from the sporting world like Babe Ruth and Gene Tunney; but we feel that the world of commerce is too often overlooked. We want to include profiles on Mr. Macy, Mr. Gimbel, and yourself."

Wackersan leaned back in his chair and looked stern. He sank into deep thought for fifteen or twenty seconds and then nodded slowly. Wackersan's Department Store was not in the league of Macy's or Gimbel's, or even Wanamaker's or McCreery's, but

Wackersan was prepared to overlook that. "What would you like to know?" he asked me.

I flipped open the notebook to a blank page. "What is an average day like in the life of Ephraim Wackersan?"

It was over an hour later that I left Wackersan and Wackersan's, and five pages of my notebook had been filled with the angular scratchings that I call my shorthand. I actually used a form of Pitman that I learned in high school, but it was so erratic that if I didn't transcribe my notes within a day or so I would start to lose words. After a couple of weeks I would have no idea what I had written.

The notebook contained a lot of facts about the day-to-day life of Junior Wackersan, but whether I had inscribed anything of interest to Brass, I didn't know. It didn't much interest me. I found out that Wackersan, Jr. arrived at the office at precisely 7:45 in the morning and left no earlier than 6:30 in the evening every day but Saturday and Sunday. He worked only a half-day Saturday, and he took the Lord's Day off. It was this punctuality, more than anything else, to which he attributed his success. That was lucky because, as far as I could determine, he did nothing else of any value for the store.

Wackersan had the enlightened social and political outlook of Caligula or Phillip II of Spain. He was appalled at the creeping Bolshevism that was taking over the country. "Agents of foreign powers," he told me solemnly, "have infiltrated the work force. They are causing worker unrest throughout the country, demanding things like employee bathrooms and shorter work weeks. In my own store some employees have been heard to complain that twenty-five cents an hour is too low a wage!"

I wondered who heard them, and how much an hour he was getting, but I kept my mouth shut.

All Wackersan's female employees were single, and of good moral character. "Married women should not work!" Junior told me. "A married woman's place is in the hearth and home." But Wackersan was not unsympathetic to the needs of newlyweds. Any Wackersan female employee who got married got a five-dollar bonus as she got fired.

There's more, but I don't want to repeat it and you don't want to hear it. I typed it all up that evening for Brass to go over, and it's still in the file for future generations to see how big business thought in the fourth decade of the twentieth century.

Pass Helbine's secretary, a cute blonde named Charity with one of those fluffy hairdos that looked like a yellow cloud had descended around her ears, had a list prepared for me of all Helbine's activities for the past two weeks, which was what I'd asked him for over the phone. She didn't think jokes about her name were funny, and she had no idea where he was. I went from one Helbine House to another until I finally caught up with Helbine at the Helbine Gallery of Fine Art on Twenty-third Street. They were setting up for a one-man show of the work of a new young artist Helbine had discovered, and Helbine was overseeing the hanging of the pictures. A slender man with intense eyes stood by the door as I came in. He wore the tweed jacket with patch pockets that artists and writers are required to own and was puffing on the curved briar pipe that is one of the other guild regulations. "What do you think?" he asked, turning to me and waving his pipe toward the group hanging the pictures.

"About what?" I asked.

"Do you think they have any idea what they're doing?"

"I don't know," I said. "I have no idea what they're doing."

"They're hanging my paintings on the wall for the one-man show which Prince Helbine is giving me."

"Oh," I said. "You're the artist."

He stuck out his hand. "Aaron Berkman," he said. "Are you a friend of Helbine's? If so, I meant 'prince' in only the nicest way. As in, 'What a prince of a fellow he is.'"

"Morgan DeWitt," I said. "I've never met Helbine. I work for a newspaper."

"You're not an art critic," Berkman said. "I know all the art critics. Besides, you're not dressed for the part. That's Helbine over there." He waved at the wall upon which his paintings were being hung. Helbine was a slender man with an aristocratic nose who looked much better in his clothes than out of them. He was directing a trio of very well dressed men and one very expensively dressed woman who were doing the hanging. "Well, what do you think?" Berkman asked.

"I am not an art critic," I told him. "I know nothing about art, and I don't even know what I like."

"Good man," Berkman said. I looked at the wall, which stretched the length of the gallery, about thirty feet. Seven paintings had already been hung. Their subjects were men and women interacting in restaurants, bars, around a chess table in the park, and various street scenes, sketched out with blotches of color that brought them more vividly to life than if they had been meticulously rendered with tiny brush strokes. They were exciting and alive, caught in the act of living, and I liked them. I guess I did know what I liked.

Helbine was directing the hanging of painting number eight at about belly-button level, a contrast from the one before, which was about seven feet off the floor. The entire row of paintings zigzagged like that: some high, some low, a few somewhere in the middle. "Won't they be sort of hard to look at?" I asked Berkman.

"The point exactly!" he told me. "Helbine wants my paintings to be 'artistically arranged to demonstrate the ebb and flux of the universe.' I told him—I tried to tell him—that the paintings are the art, not the wall, and the paintings should be at eye level, easy to see."

"What did he say?"

"The prince? He said, 'Don't be silly.'" Berkman shook his head wryly. "So here I stand not being silly."

"They're your paintings," I said.

"It's Helbine's money," Berkman replied. "As he has pointed out to me at every opportunity."

I turned and studied the wall. "I like your work," I told Berkman. "What do you call this sort of art?"

Berkman thrust his hands into his jacket pockets. "I call them my paintings," he told me. "But if you want to sound like you know what you're talking about, say something like: 'The vibrant palette of primary colors slathered on canvas in oil creates an effect that leaps off the canvas and assaults the eyes like Basin Street jazz assaults the ears.' That's a quote, son."

"Thanks," I said. "I'll memorize it. What does it mean?"

Berkman shrugged.

Helbine stepped back to survey his wall, and I decided that

now was as good a time as any to speak to him. I stepped forward. "Mr. Helbine? I'm Morgan DeWitt from the *New York World*."

He swiveled on one heel and stared. I had the feeling that he was looking down at me from a height, even though he was a couple of inches shorter than I. Sometime I'd like to figure out how he managed that. He stared silently for long enough for me to start feeling nervous, like a rabbit in the eye of a circling hawk, and then he spoke. "Yes," he said. "On the telephone. I remember. You're the chap who wants to follow me around."

"Not exactly," I told him. "I want to talk about where you've been, not where you're going."

"Ah!" he said. "That's right. The last two weeks. I called up your publisher, you know. Personal friend. Asked him why he hadn't called himself to warn me of what you planned to do, find out if I had any objection, that sort of thing. He told me you don't even work for the paper. You work for that columnist fellow—what's his name?"

"Alexander Brass," I said.

"Him," Helbine agreed. "So you lied to me."

"No, sir," I told him. "I work for Mr. Brass, Mr. Brass works for the *World Syndicate,* his column is published in the *World.* Explaining that over the phone would have been an exceedingly roundabout way of getting to the same place."

"Hmph!" Helbine said. "I had Charity make you up a list of my peregrinations for the last two weeks. Did you get it?"

"I did, and I thank you. Since you didn't peregrinate to foreign shores, you have remained within our budget. Can you spare me a minute?"

Helbine sighed a mighty sigh. "It won't be just a minute, will it? It never is. Come over here."

He strode before me to the far corner of the large room, where there was a card table topped with bottles, glasses, and buckets of ice. "A little refreshment," he said. His right hand went out and hovered over various bottles, finally pouncing on one and bringing it forth. "Champagne," he said. "Duc de Richelieu Estates Reserve. Only twenty cases of this come into the country each year, and they go right from the ship to my wine cellar. I am a distant relative of the Duc."

"I see," I said.

He popped the cork with his thumbs and poured the effervescent grape juice into three slim glasses. "You don't," he said. "It takes years to develop a truly discriminating palette. And an extensive wine cellar." He turned. "Berkman!" he yelled. "Come over here, fellow, and join us in a libation." The seignior being chummy with his peasants.

"My aunt Pru," I told him, "to whom I am distantly related because she lives in Petaluma, California, makes very good grape jam. She wins awards at the state fair."

He looked at me, unsure whether I was kidding or not. "There is only one jar of it in New York," I continued. "It is in my cupboard. Would you like me to bring it over? We usually have it on white bread with peanut butter."

I took a glass of champagne from his hand before he had a chance to throw it at me and gulped it down. "Good stuff," I said. The conversation deteriorated from there, and I may not have made the sort of impression on him that I had intended to make.

17

I left Helbine before one of us annoyed the other beyond repair and returned to his business office, in which he kept his secretary. Charity needed to be coaxed into talking about her boss. But once I had assured her that a reporter never reveals his sources, she talked as though it were her sacred duty. An hour with her told me more than enough about Helbine's habits, intentions, pretensions, activities, philanthropies, eccentricities, likes, dislikes, and inanities, along with a master's thesis on the way he treated his employees. Except for confirming that this was not a man whom it was delightful to know, I spotted nothing helpful in the pages of shorthand notes; but I was merely the journeyman scribe. Interpreting was a job for a master newsy like Brass.

I stopped for an egg salad on rye and a Dr. Brown's ginger ale on the way uptown. When I got back to the office Gloria and Cathy were sitting across from Brass, who was scowling at them from over a stack of files he had spread out on his desk. He turned the scowl to me. "Well?" he said. "I hope you have something."

"Not that I know of," I told him. I took out my notebook and read from it all the points of possible interest in the recent lives and political philosophies of Messrs. Wackersan and Helbine. It took most of ten minutes. "I'll type it up for the file," I said, "but I don't see that any of that gets us anywhere."

"Nor do I," Brass said. "Cathy has assembled everything that is known about the eight people on our list." He waved a hand over the jumble of files. "And if you can find anything of value in them, I'll fry my hat and eat it."

"The straw hat, I hope," I said, pulling a chair over to join the group. "Felt is bloating."

"I tried," Cathy said. "I'm sorry. I'll keep looking."

"Nonsense," Brass said severely. "You found everything there is to find in the morgue and did some very clever follow-up. We now know that three of our subjects went to Harvard, but five did not. Two of them belong to the same club; two others go to the same clinic; two of them go boating on the Hudson, but they belong to different boat clubs. The only two that we've established know each other are Fletcher van Geuip and Judge Garbin; they were childhood friends. Van Geuip was in New York last week, back from an expedition to British East Africa, and he stayed with Garbin for three days. But then he left for Borneo."

"I've been to see Suzie Frienard," Gloria told me. "She is incapable of planning a murder. She is almost capable of planning a lunch. She is uncertain about things. She changes her mind. Her husband, on the other hand, is capable of murder in a very direct and immediate fashion. Had he found out about that picture he would have beaten poor Dworkyn's door down, beaten Dworkyn to a pulp, and broken all the furniture. If he suspected that we had copies of the pictures, he wouldn't hire anyone to blow the safe—he would stride in here and demand them, breaking everything in reach. Then he would calm down and apologize and pay for the damage.

"When I left her I went to see Stepney Partcher, but he has no interest in talking to the press. I had to settle for his secretary. Partcher, Meedle and Coster does not want any sort of publicity. Stepney Partcher turned down the job of corporation counsel in the Hoover administration because he wanted to stay out of the public eye."

"Wouldn't want to hog the limelight," I said.

"If Partcher were ever to decide to kill someone, he would take a year to plan it, and the method would be particularly precise and bloodless. He washes his hands twelve times a day. He makes luncheon appointments for twelve-oh-seven, and that's when he arrives."

Brass slapped his hand on the desk with a sharp crack, like a small firecracker going off. "We're getting nowhere," he said. "Let's hope the senator's gathering tomorrow gives us some sort of break."

"What sort?" I asked.

He glared at me and then turned his chair around to stare out the window. When he showed no sign of turning back, I left the office and headed down to the Blind Harlequin, a Greenwich Village restaurant, coffeehouse, and hangout, for dinner and a discussion of the state of the novel with two friends of mine who were real, full-time, professional writers.

Bill Welsch writes short stories for the war pulps and the detective pulps, and started selling regularly to *Black Mask* about a year ago, joining the exalted ranks of such as Dashiell Hammett, Erie Stanley Gardner, and Raymond Chandler.

Agnes Silverson produced hard-boiled detective stories under the pen name Charles D. Epp. Her series character, Dagger Dell, was "a private eye with a nose for mayhem," to quote the blurb on her latest opus in *All-Detective Story Magazine*. She had to use a man's name on the stories because the editors wouldn't buy hard-boiled tales under a woman's byline. She was in her late thirties, and had been married once, as she would admit if pressed. But she would speak no further about the experience, not even as to whether she was currently separated, divorced, or widowed, except to occasionally refer to her erstwhile husband as "that cornucopia of shit I was once married to."

Bill Welsch was maybe forty, and had done all of those things that writers use to pad out the author's biography on the flap of the book. He had been a captain in the Army Flying Corps, with three confirmed kills to his credit and a hand that had a great scar running across the back and would no longer close into a fist. He had been a starving writer in Paris in the twenties, when that was the thing to do; had been kept by an Italian countess in her villa outside of Florence (which didn't make the book jacket); had been a private detective in Chicago; and had written advertising copy for an agency in New York. One day he read an issue of *Air Aces* magazine and said, "It wasn't like that at all." So he wrote a story to tell what it really was like, and he's been doing it ever since.

The two of them were making a good living writing, and they were both very good at it. I liked their stuff. It wasn't highbrow literature, but they told fast-moving yarns that made the reader want to turn the page. I couldn't understand why they were wasting their talents writing for the pulps. That night, over a late-night slice of cheesecake and cold coffee, I asked them.

Welsch looked at me like I was crazy. "I'm not wasting my talent," he said. "Hell, that *is* my talent."

Silverson stared into her glass of amaretto, or whatever Italian soda she was drinking that night, and said, "I wrote a novel once—a real novel. Full of deep insights into the way people live and make love and hurt each other. I was nineteen. It was dreadful."

Welsch leaned across the table and waved his finger at my nose. "You should examine your literary prejudices," he said. "There are no better stylists working today than some of the *Black Mask* boys."

"And girls," Silverson added.

"And girls."

Agnes grabbed my arm. "For God's sake, Morgan," she said, "we have high hopes for you. Don't become one of those stuffed-shirt Establishment novelists!"

"I sometimes doubt," I told her, "whether I'll ever become any sort of novelist at all."

Bill smiled a sad smile. "That's the curse of the writer," he said. "The act of creating demands constant self-doubt, which never ends no matter how long you've been doing it. If you're not continually possessed of the feeling that your stuff is never as good as it should be, than you don't care enough to master your craft, and you'll never be a really good writer. On the other hand, a feeling that your stuff is no good is not a guarantee that it actually is good. You might be right, after all."

"Thanks," I said.

For a while we all stared morosely into our various drinks. "If you want a real reason to lose respect for me," I told them, "I'm going to a Republican fund-raiser tomorrow."

They shifted their stares to me. I felt impelled to explain this unnatural act, so I told them what I could of our impending visit to Senator Childers's parts.

"He's from a very old, very rich family," Welsch said. "His ancestors have been cheating and stealing and oppressing the proletariat for hundreds of years. He bought himself a senate seat, which I suppose is better than buying himself a string of polo ponies or a Rembrandt."

"Better how?" Agnes asked.

"It spreads the money around more. His son, Andrew Brisch Childers, has been kicked out of all the best schools for insobriety and general disdain, and is now getting a law degree in a school his father bought for him. His daughter, Bitsy 'the Brat' Childers, has had several husbands and boyfriends and suffers from unspecified behavior problems that are supporting a large part of the alienist population of northern New Jersey and New York. It isn't eugenic; they'd both probably be perfectly normal kids if their father was a shoe salesman making thirty-five bucks a week."

"You got something against the rich?" Agnes asked. "You wouldn't trade places with them in an instant; no, you wouldn't."

"Not if I had to stop writing for *Black Mask,* I wouldn't. My ambition is to starve for my art in the pulps." Welsch raised his thumb over a clenched fist and waggled it at me. "You know the difference between us and the rich?" he asked. "They have money!"

"May I sit at your feet," I said, "and eat the crumbs that fall from your beard, O Master?"

"No, no," he said. "I'm serious. Think about it. You know all those times that you've said, or at least thought, 'If I was rich, then I'd do so-and-so'?"

"Yeah?" I said cautiously.

"Well, consider. That's the first-level shit. The rich did that, whatever it is, years ago. They went wherever it is, they bought whatever it is, they joined whatever it is, they bedded whoever it is, they insulted whoever the hell they felt like insulting, and they've done it all as many times as they like, and they're bored with it. Now they have to go on to the second and third levels to find things and people that don't bore them."

"And what's on the second and third levels?" Agnes asked.

"How should I know?" Welsch replied. "I'm not rich."

"Of course not," Agnes told him. "You're a writer."

For the next few hours, after we were done examining the state of publishing and what bastards editors were, we wandered through politics (the Republicans were going to nominate Borah, Landon, or Childers, but it didn't matter; Roosevelt's reelection was as certain as a spring rain). We touched on sports (a Negro boxer named Joe Louis, Welsch reported, was creating respect for his people with his quiet dignity and with his sledgehammer fists—a good line; he'd probably use it in one of his stories); on music (the big swing bands maybe weren't as creative as the small jazz groups, but they gave work to a lot more people); and on the theater (musical comedy is an original American art form).

I was at home and in bed a little after two.

I gave myself an extra hour's sleep the next morning, since it was going to be a long day. We were collectively going out to Senator Childers's estate in New Jersey so that Brass could be a celebrity at his party, which started at about one in the afternoon and didn't end until after what the invitation described as a dress-optional dinner. It was about a three-hour drive, given the bad roads, and we were getting an early start. We could have gone by train; the president of the Delaware, Lackawanna & Western had arranged to put special cars on all the day trains just for the senator's guests, but being chauffeured by Garrett would give us an extra pair of eyes when we arrived. And nobody ever notices the servants; or so P.G. Wodehouse would have us believe.

It was eight-thirty in the morning when Brass's new black Packard sedan pulled up in front of the door. Garrett, in a dark blue suit and chauffeur's cap, was driving. I tossed my traveling bag in the trunk, climbed in front with Garrett, and swiveled around to say good morning to those in back. Brass was sitting between the two girls, who were dressed in the sort of skirt and jacket combination that is known, I believe, as "sport clothes." Exactly what sport a young lady is supposed to play in them, I don't know. I would like to watch. In keeping with the occasion, I was wearing gray slacks and a blue blazer with brass buttons that would have done an admiral proud. Brass wore his inevitable suit, but a red four-in-hand tie decorated his neck instead of the usual bow tie; his concession to country life.

We had no trouble finding the Childers's estate; large tin signs bearing the Childers family crest—a lion's head with a crown above but not quite touching it surrounded by thirteen stars—and an arrow pointing the way had been posted on all the roads starting about ten miles out. At about ten minutes to one a Negro lackey in what looked like court dress for the Emerald City of Oz checked our credentials and waved us through the pair of ornate wrought-iron gates. The family crest was centered on each gate and on the wrought-iron arch over them. The driveway was a lane of pale orange bricks majestically flanked by oak trees. After about half a mile we came to the house. I should say the main house, since there were a number of other hice scattered about the property.

A second fancy-dress lackey, also a gentleman of color, waved us away from the front door and around to the back, where a green and gold striped pavilion the size of the *Hindenburg* had been set up. Several costumed servitors stood about waiting for the chance to serve. We emerged from the car, all but Garrett, who was taken in hand by yet another minion of the senator's and guided off to wherever cars and chauffeurs were being kept for the duration of the party.

The senator was a broad-shouldered, ruggedly handsome man in his late fifties, whose plaid suit covered him with the inevitability of truly expensive tailoring. He stood inside the pavilion, flanked by men in blue suits with stern faces and precise haircuts, greeting the new arrivals. As I approached, I could see the amount of careful grooming that had gone into the ruggedly handsome exterior. "Alexander Brass," he boomed with the verbal excitement of a sideshow talker announcing a new act. "Welcome to my little place! Just great that you could get here—just great! Mighty glad to see you. Mighty glad! We must get together for a gab sometime before you leave. Off the record, of course, off the record. Just a friendly chat."

Brass smiled, muttered something noncommittal, and introduced his entourage. Childers barely nodded to me, but he enfolded Gloria in his arms and gave her a healthy peck on the cheek, and followed with the same exercise for Cathy. Impartial and fair in his treatment of women, was the senator, and who could blame him? Having bestowed his senatorial favors, he waved us on into the pavilion and turned to greet a carriage-load of guests that had come in behind us. The carriage was an open landau, pulled by a matched pair of chestnut horses, with a matched pair of dusky men in the senator's livery in the driving seat. One of several horse-drawn vehicles of different sorts that the senator kept around, it was being used to pick up guests who arrived at the train station.

On the drive down to Childers's kingdom we had discussed the possible ways to get the information we were after. The only problem was that we didn't know what information we might find, or whether we'd know it if we saw it. Brass had been pretty sure that he'd get a chance to have a talk with Childers; what politician could resist a tête-à-tête with an important columnist? But what should he ask and how should he phrase it? "Have you posed for any dirty pictures lately?" seemed a little crass. "Have you murdered or caused to have murdered any newsmen or photographers in the past week?" was a bit pushy. And what there might be to find was even more vague. It seemed unlikely that the room in which the pictures had been shot was on the Childers estate, and if it was, how could we recognize it? A naked couple cavorting on one side of the room, with a cameraman peering into his ground glass on the other, would be a definite sign. Mitchell had suggested that the room probably had a skylight. Perhaps we should ask Childers for a tour of his attic.

The pavilion covered a large serving area for the sort of snacks that one might desire before dinner: a roast beef, a ham, and a turkey, each with its own personal carver in chef's whites and toque; a crab steamer beside a mound of quiescent crabs; a wide variety of cold cuts, salads, mousses, gelatinous masses, pies, ices, and liquid refreshments. And by the tower of plates stood several servitors ready to help those who did not feel like helping themselves.

We paused at the pavilion flap to take in the view. The air was clear, the sky was blue, the smell of newly turned earth with just a touch of fertilizer perfumed the surroundings. Past the pavilion was a stretch of well-manicured lawn well furnished with lawn chairs and tables on which several groups of people were engaged in quiet social banter. A wide gravel walk semi-circled the lawn before continuing on its way. At about fifteen-foot intervals along the walk were marble statues of men in togas and women in very little.

Before we had a chance to go anywhere, a high-pitched drone surrounded us, seeming to come from all directions at once. After a second we could make out a lower, throbbing accompaniment. Imagine someone working the treadle on a sewing machine a little more rapidly than is actually possible, while at the same time rhythmically hitting a snare drum with a rolled-up newspaper. The noise was something like that. Half a minute later it got much louder and an odd-looking aircraft burst over the top of a nearby hill and headed straight toward us, at about two hundred feet off the ground. It was a single-engine monoplane fuselage with a tail but no wings, and what looked like a spinning parasol suspended over the pilot's seat.

The plane slowed as it reached the center of the field, and then dropped gently toward the ground with only the slightest forward motion. The various groups of people on the field were frozen in place, as though uncertain as to whether to approach this apparition or flee from it.

"What is it?" Gloria asked.

"It's an autogiro," I said, pleased that my monthly reading of *Popular Mechanics* was finally proving useful. "That thing that looks like a giant propeller above the cockpit is actually a rotating wing, which enables the plane to land and take off from very small fields."

"What makes it work?" Gloria asked.

I had no idea. "Gravity," I suggested.

The plane swung around and came to a stop.

"It's a Kellett," Cathy said. "I've never seen one up close!"

She started eagerly toward the craft and we followed. "It's a what?" I asked.

"A Kellett KD-1," Cathy said over her shoulder. "It's based on the Cierva design. I flew in a Cierva at Floyd Bennett Field a couple of years ago."

We stopped a few feet from the plane. There were two cockpits, one behind the other, and from each protruded a head encased in a leather helmet and goggles. "Let me get this straight," Gloria said to Cathy. "You flew an autogiro?"

"No, no," Cathy said. "Juan de la Cierva, the guy who invented it, flew it. I was his passenger. He's Spanish."

We looked at her. "I met him at a nightclub I was working at. I wasn't married then," she said defensively.

Senator Childers trotted up to join us. By now everyone on the field had come over, and a group of about fifty people surrounded the autogiro. The two leather-clad aviators pulled themselves out of the cockpits and lightly dropped to the ground. They raised their goggles.

Senator Childers stepped forward, right arm extended. "Chas!" he bellowed. "Good to see you. Nothing like making an entrance, eh?"

Charles Lindbergh pulled the leather helmet off, revealing his close-cropped sandy hair. "These things are truly exciting!" he said, patting the side of the plane. "They bounce into the air. Bounce. Never seen anything like it." He took the senator's hand. "Glad to be here, Senator. I've brought a guest. Well. Actually she brought me."

His flying partner removed her helmet and shook her head, cascading blond curls down to her shoulders. "Hi, there," she said. The surrounding crowd pulled in closer.

"Senator Bertram Childers," Lindbergh said, "let me introduce you to Amelia Earhart. She holds the altitude record in these things."

Earhart patted Lindberg fondly on the head. "Well, actually, it wasn't a Kellett. It was a Pitcairn PCA-2," she said. "I took it over eighteen thousand feet. Where's the food?"

Lindbergh and Earhart strode toward the pavilion, with Childers trotting alongside looking like the cat that had taught the canary to dance. The circle surrounding the plane slowly dissipated as the guests straggled back to the pavilion in the wake of Lindy and Amelia.

"We'll follow them inside," Brass said. He turned to me. "Morgan, let's keep you in reserve. Wander off on your own and don't join us unless I give you the office. See what you can see."

"Right," I said, and wandered. I could have made a pointed comment about the vagueness of his instruction, but as I had nothing better to offer, I kept my mouth shut. Past the pavilion were the sporting areas: three tennis courts, a swimming pool, a wading pool, a field on which indications showed that baseball might be played if one was so inclined, another field on which running, jumping, and general sportive behavior might not be discouraged, and a dirt track. There was a changing house by the pool, and several small shacks, probably for storage, scattered about the sportive grounds, all done in the style of European peasants' huts, complete to the thatched roofs. I would not have been surprised to see sturdy yeomen and yeowomen standing in the doors to the huts a-pulling of their forelocks.

Two of the tennis courts were in use, and an informal softball game was in progress on the informal baseball field. The joint was jumping with celebrities. Al Jolson and W.C. Fields, both immaculate in white shirts and trousers, were playing tennis in the near court, with Fanny Brice watching from a lawn chair by the side of the court, a large drink in her hand. I didn't recognize the people in the other court, who were younger and more enthusiastic but not noticeably better tennis players.

Among the guests who still dotted the landscape there were a number of attractive young ladies who did not seem to be escorted by young men, attractive or otherwise. After a little judicious questioning of passersby I determined that they were from the chorus line of *Girls! Girls! Girls!* an aptly named review that had just closed at the Eltinge Theatre after a run of 243 performances. They had been brought down in a railroad coach car provided for the occasion and were being chaperoned by several staunch matronly ladies from the Anna P. Waldo Club, which ran a boardinghouse for women in the theatrical professions on Forty-fourth Street.

I wandered down to the swimming pool, a monstrous rectangle of chlorinated water with three separate diving boards, the top one high enough to give nosebleeds to the sensitive, which was currently deserted. The air was cool, but the pool was heated. If anyone had felt like taking a dip, it would not have been an unpleasant experience.

I settled into a wood and canvas chaise by the pool and stared into the water, which was doing a poor job of reflecting the high-flying cirrus clouds stretched out overhead. I should have been peering into closets, stealthily opening hidden drawers in writing desks, and asking clever, pointed questions of the guests, but I had no idea of where to look or what to ask. I searched for inspiration in the steam rising off the water.

There was a noise behind me, and I turned as much of me as I could manage in the chaise without falling out of it. One of the girls had just come out of the pool house and was heading toward the tennis courts. She was wearing a short skirt and flimsy blouse that seemed a little skimpy for the weather, but I was not going to discourage her from dressing as she pleased. Personally I found the outfit, and the slender body under it, very pleasing indeed. My motion must have startled her; she jumped back a little with a sort of "oh!" sound coming from the back of her throat.

"Sorry," I said.

"I didn't see you," she said.

I sat up. Her hair was long and the color of a burnt-sienna crayon that I'd had as a child. It had been my favorite crayon. Her face was oval and her lips were wide and looked as if they might smile if provoked. She might have been twenty. "I saw you," I told her seriously, "and I'm willing to continue the experience indefinitely."

She smiled. "How nice." Her voice was deep and throaty, almost a purr.

"Thank you," I said. "It's always a risk."

"What?"

"Complimenting a girl's appearance. Some will smile and accept the compliment, and some will get all red and call you names and slap your face, if they can reach it. And you can never tell until you've made the experiment."

She perched on the chaise next to mine and stared down at me seriously. "So I was an experiment, was I?"

"You see?" I said. "I get in trouble whatever I say. If you were, you should be judged a success and used as a model for all women who come after you."

"I have been told that there are no others like me, that they broke the mold when I was cast," she said seriously. "And some of those who said so did not mean it as a compliment."

"Then they should be taken out and beheaded for spiritual blindness and general poor judgment," I told her.

She nodded solemnly. "I think I like you. Tell me, is there a real live person who I could get to know under the badinage?"

"Well," I said, "let's take the badinage off and see." I wiped my hand in front of my face without changing my expression, which I think was a sort of earnest smile. "There. Notice the difference?"

"Oh yes," she said. "Now I see the serious you, all ready to talk about world affairs and the situation in Ethiopia and the French governmental crisis and how it's all going to affect the stock market."

"My favorite topic of conversation," I said. "How did you know?"

She bent over and peered closely at my face. I peered up at hers. It was a face that stood up to close peering very well. "I think it's the amber specks in your otherwise light brown eyes," she said. "They speak of honesty and earnestness and strength and gentleness."

"All that in a few specks?" I asked.

"And the ability to play the cornet," she added, "and a tendency toward bilious attacks when you eat fish."

"I never eat fish," I said.

"And a good thing, too." She stood up. "My name is Elizabeth."

"Mine is Morgan."

"Like the pirate? What do you do, Morgan, sink ships, sack whole cities, and carry off the women and children?"

"It's not as easy as it sounds," I told her. "One must remember the proper order: first rape, then pillage, then burn. If you get it wrong, it could ruin your whole day."

"I can see where that would be important," she agreed.

There was a breathless quality to Elizabeth, as if she were always running even when she was standing still. There was something in her eyes—blue eyes, wide eyes, under long dark lashes—that dared you to see under the banter and take her seriously.

"I work for Alexander Brass," I told her.

"The columnist?"

"That's right. I am his amanuensis."

"Are you here amanuensing?"

"No. Off duty. We're just here as guests of Senator Childers. And you?"

She pouted. "And me what?"

"What do you do?"

"I look decorative. I smile at dull young men and tell them how clever they are. I smile at dull old men and tell them they shouldn't say such naughty things. I listen attentively while men explain to me things that I understand better than they do, and bite my tongue so as not to say anything when they get it wrong. And I smile. Most of all, I smile."

An insight into her character? Possibly a hint at her profession? I didn't know and I discovered that I didn't care. "I think I like you too," I said, "although you are a bit cynical and worldly-wise for one so young."

"I'm twenty-two," she said, "and I didn't ask to be born." She said it flatly and without affect, just stating a fact to her new friend. But I felt the chill of truth behind the words. I took her hand and tried to think of something to say that would wipe away the feeling without sounding banal to both of us. The silence stretched on.

"Damn!" she said. "I'm sorry, I didn't mean to—"

"Neither did I," I said. "Let's just—"

She stood up and pulled me to my feet. "Come with me," she said. She led the way back into the pool house and closed the door behind us. "This way," she said.

To the right were the showers and little cubicles for changing, but she took me to the left. We went through a door and were in a small suite of rooms: bedroom, sitting room, and bath. "What is this?" I asked.

"A little hidey-hole I found," she said, closing the door. She pulled me through into the bedroom, kicked that door closed with her foot. The bed was covered with a blue and white bedspread and had twelve pillows and a small teddy bear on it. The wallpaper was white with red flowers and the curtains on the one small window matched the wallpaper. Across from the bed was a bureau that looked too big for the room, and a small table was at the foot of the bed, leaving little floor space.

She sat on the bed and took both of my hands in hers.

"Yes?" I asked.

"Yes," she said. "Please!"

"I don't think—" I said.

"No need to," she told me. She pulled me with a gentle pull until she was lying on the bed and I was leaning on top of her, supported by my hands, which were still in hers. "Can you kiss?" she asked.

I showed her I could.

"That's nice," she said after a minute. "What else can you do?"

Ten minutes before I would have said, "Not much, really," but now, with the sound of her throaty voice in my ears, the fresh smell of her in my nostrils, the feel of her under my hands, I felt that I could do anything. I kissed her again, more thoroughly, and again. I moved beside her on the bed and fumbled at her blouse. She pulled my jacket off and her hands reached for my shirt and began unbuttoning it. My hands circled her and I found the hooks for her brassiere. I could feel my heart beating in my chest. I could feel her heart beating beside mine. My thoughts were befuddled and at the same time miraculously clear.

For a while neither of us said anything, but we conveyed a wealth of information with our hands, with our lips. And then, unexpectedly, Elizabeth sat up and pushed me away. I lay there for a second to catch my breath, and then rose to a more-or-less sitting position. She stared at me across the pile of pillows and discarded clothing.

I stared back at her, suddenly concerned that I was naked and visible in the light coming through the window. She was also both naked and visible, and a wonderful sight she was; but I've always thought that my best physical feature was the way my clothes hung on me when I was dressed.

"What?" I asked.

She leaned forward and cupped my face in her hands. She was crying.

"What is it?" I asked.

"I like you, I really like you," she said. "Please don't hurt me!"

That stopped me. For what seemed an eternity I could say nothing. Then I stammered, "Why on earth—? What makes you think—? How could you possibly believe—? You of all people? Now of all times?" I took her hands in mine and kissed each palm.

"I have been with many men," she said. "Since I was—much younger. It has nothing to do with love, or probably even sex, although it ends up as sex. I can't help it. I can't explain it. When the men I'm with find out what I am… this need I have… often they become cruel and hateful. I'm sorry."

I stared at her and thought over what she'd said. She sat,

her hands in mine, watching my face like a supplicant, or a dog waiting to be kicked.

"You like sex," I said cleverly.

"I *need* something," she said. "It isn't sex, but sex will have to do until I figure out what it is."

"You mean you really don't want to go to bed with me?"

"We are in bed," she pointed out. "I really do want to go to bed with you. Really."

"And you like me?"

"I really do like you," she said. "But if I hadn't met you I would have found somebody else. Not necessarily somebody I like."

I had pictured many scenarios in my head of what it would be like, the first time. This was not one of them. "I like you," I said. "Whatever happens, I like you. I would like to get to know you better. I would like to make love to you. I want more than anything else not to hurt you. I should warn you that I am amazingly inexperienced and I may not be very good at it."

She sighed. "You'll be wonderful," she said. She kissed me. "I promise."

18

I shall, as the Victorian novelists say, draw a curtain over this tender scene to save the delicate sensibilities of my readers.

Or maybe it's my delicate sensibilities I need to save. I will say that, as far as I could tell, each of us behaved in a manner befitting the occasion. I had never befat such an occasion before, but Elizabeth assured me that my befitting was as good as anyone else's and better than most.

An hour later and Elizabeth and I were lying under the covers talking about unimportant things like life and death and love and beauty and wars and breadlines. We touched lightly on our recent coupling and what seemed to both of us to be an important newfound relationship. I discovered that I honestly did not mind all the men she had had in the past, but I could not predict how I would feel about each and every man she would have in the future who was not me. She told me that she did not mind my being a journalist, that we all make mistakes in our youth.

"My mother, that sweet little old lady back in Ohio, does not know that I work for a New York newspaper," I told Elizabeth. "She thinks I play piano in a whorehouse."

Elizabeth considered this. "I didn't know you could play the piano," she said, rolling over on her side and staring at me. "There is much about you that I must learn."

"Like what?"

"Like who you are and where you came from and where you're

going and if you'll take me with you."

"I'll bet you say that to all the boys," I said. It was flippant and thoughtless and I could have bit my tongue. She looked as though I'd just slapped her in the face.

"Oh my God," she said. "If you think that—"

"No, no," I said, grabbing her and holding her in my arms. "I didn't mean it that way. I'm sorry!"

"You're different," she said. "It's true. I don't know why, or how. I want to be with you, stay with you. Most of the time, with most guys, I feel—dirty afterward. I want to go and take a real hot shower and scrub myself clean and hope the guy is gone when I get back. But you… I don't want to leave you. And I don't feel dirty. I feel happy."

She snuggled into my arms and I pulled the blanket back up over both of us. She didn't seem to expect me to say anything, which was a good thing as I had no idea of what I could say. I was happy and content and pleased and maybe a little smug. I felt warm and protective toward this strange little girl. Somehow, despite my lack of experience and her excess of it, she had made me feel like I knew what I was doing and was even good at it. And not just about making love, but about life itself. I seldom feel that I know much about life or how it should be lived. Perhaps that's why I want to be a novelist—an unconscious conviction that since I can't do it very well, I might, as well write about it.

I stared at the ceiling without seeing the ceiling and thought deep thoughts about nothing at all, or perhaps about too many things at once for any of them to make sense.

There were footsteps in the room outside and, as I pulled, the blanket up to my nose and tried to become invisible, the door opened and a large man in a plaid suit stood in the doorway. I had time to notice that it was Senator Childers, and that his hair was slightly messed, before I pulled the blanket over my head.

"Bitsy!" the senator said in a calm and reasonable voice. "There you are."

Elizabeth sat up, covering herself with the blanket, which pulled it away from me down to the knees. "Yes, Daddy," she said.

I scrunched deeper into the blanket, trying desperately to disappear. It didn't work. Large parts of me remained all too evident. I tried to think of something clever to say. Given the situation, "hello" seemed inept. Perhaps a literary allusion. Our revels now are over, I thought. Oh, that this too, too solid flesh could melt, I thought. Go not naked into the world, I thought. Everybody's got to be somewhere, I thought. I crammed a corner of the blanket into my mouth to keep from giggling.

"You must come out and entertain our other guests," the senator said. Except for his use of the word "other," he showed by neither word nor deed that he was aware that I was there.

"Yes, Daddy," Elizabeth said.

He turned and left the room, but a second later he reappeared in the doorway. "Don't marry this one," he said, and left again, slamming the door behind him with what I considered unnecessary violence.

Silence ensued.

I redistributed the blanket more equitably between us. "Senator Childers is your father," I said cleverly.

She nodded. "I know," she said.

"You didn't tell me," I said.

"Does it matter?" she asked.

I thought about it. "I guess not," I told her. "I just feel kind of silly, thinking you were one of those chorus girls."

She sat up and swung her legs over the side of the bed. "Unfortunately I'm not," she said. "And now you're going to be awed by Daddy or used by Daddy or want something from Daddy; and if we ever make love again you're going to be making love to Senator Childers's daughter, and not to me. Or he's going to want something from you, and then we'll never get it sorted out."

I didn't understand the last part of that sentence, but I decided that now was not the time to question her semantics. She reached for her stockings on the bureau and slid one over her right foot. I searched around for my socks on the floor. A silence stretched between us, and I figured it was my turn to break it. I took a deep breath. "Listen," I said. "This may blow our relationship to hell, which is a place I do not want it to go, but here it is. I am not a Republican. Usually I'm not even a Democrat. Perhaps I'm a Whig. I want nothing from your father. I don't support your father's policies. I don't even like your father; I think he's a stuffed shirt and a prig. And not only that, but every time I see him it reminds me of—ah—something I can't tell you about, and it makes me want to giggle. To me he's essentially a silly man."

"Really?" she asked.

"Really."

"Good," she said. "But he isn't silly. Trust me. Daddy is manipulative and narcissistic and self-important and wants to be president, and would happily walk right over you if you stood between him and the door. But he is not silly." She fastened on her garter belt. I watched. An endlessly fascinating contraption, the garter belt.

I gathered my own clothing from various places about the room and dressed. "When will I see you again?" I asked her.

She pulled her skirt up about her waist, and tucked the blouse in. "I'll call you," she said. "At the *World*. When I get to the city sometime next week. I'll ask for the piano player."

I bent over to tie my shoes. "I'll play an arpeggio just for you," I told her, "whatever that is." I stood up and wrapped my arms around her shoulders. "You will call?" I whispered. I hadn't meant to whisper, it just came out that way.

She kissed me. "I will," she said.

I left first, trotting toward the pavilion by instinct, my mind too busy to notice where my feet were taking me. My thoughts came fast, the new ones pushing out the ones that had arrived but a moment before. My emotions flipped from ecstasy to despair every few seconds. I was in love with Elizabeth the senator's daughter. The senator's beautiful, burnt sienna-haired daughter. The senator's neurotic, nymphomaniac daughter. I remembered some of the stories I had heard about "Bitsy," my Elizabeth. She went through men like a scythe through butter. She raised men up to the heights of passion, just to hear them bounce. She'd been married more times than the Isle de France.

My thoughts were not making sense, even to me. I stopped at the edge of the tennis courts and took several deep breaths. It didn't help. I sat down on the grass and took several more. You may think this confusion of thoughts and emotions I describe is literary license, I being a fledgling novelist and all. But it is as accurate as I can reconstruct my feelings.

A pair of legs encased in white flannels approached from the near court. "You look like you need a touch of liquid succor," a nasal voice drawled.

I looked up. W.C. Fields stood over me, white flannels, blue blazer, and a glass in each hand. "I happen to have acquired a spare glass of scotch whiskey," he said, extending one of the glasses to me. "They seem to have an endless supply of quite excellent booze here, a theory I intend to put to the experiment."

"Thank you," I said, taking the glass.

"Not at all," he said. "Always glad to do a service to my fellow man." He gave me a semiformal salute and wandered off toward the pavilion.

I took a gulp of scotch and realized that scotch was not what I wanted. What I wanted was to know for sure that Elizabeth Childers, Bitsy, the senator's daughter, was going to call me, was going to see me again. I put the glass down and stood up and brushed myself off. I was behaving, or at least thinking, like a lovesick adolescent, and for no good reason. She had said she would call, and why should I not believe her? We had been interrupted by her father, a not unheard of episode in the lives of young lovers. I would stop worrying. I would just go off somewhere and sit down and remember in detail the past two hours. There would be a silly smile on my face, and passersby would say…

My wallet was missing. I patted the pants pocket where it should have been, and reached in and felt nothing. I patted all my other pockets just in case. It wasn't there.

Had Bitsy stolen my wallet? While we were in bed, with my pants draped over the corner of the dresser, had her hand snuck away from its task of love to reach into my pants pocket? I felt guilty for thinking such a thing even as I reviewed our mutual activities in my mind. It seemed improbable. What must have happened was that the wallet had fallen from the pocket, and even now awaited me at the foot of the bed.

I turned around and started back toward the pool cottage. My mind circled about the prickly hedge of thoughts about Elizabeth and her father and her habits and her professed feelings for me and my evident feelings for her and refused to settle. But I'd have to settle my mind, and probably my stomach, later. For now I would just retrieve my wallet.

As I reached the cottage door, I could hear voices inside. It was Elizabeth and her father, but I couldn't make out what they were saying. The senator's voice sounded very positive and had the bark of command, as though he were planning to lead his daughter into battle. I paused. Entering at that moment did not seem like a good idea. I circled around to the side of the building to be out of sight when they left. Now I was beside the bedroom window and I could hear the voices more clearly.

"Daddy, just leave it be," she was saying. "We've had this talk so many times we both know it by heart."

"Talking doesn't help, that's for damn sure," Daddy said. "I don't know what to do. Sending you to alienists doesn't do a damn bit of good. Every time I send you to a new shrink, you end up in bed with him!"

"That's 'cause they're all father figures," she said.

There was the sound of a slap, and Elizabeth cried out.

"How dare you!" Daddy said, his voice vibrating with anger. "You're blaming me for this—this—insatiable craving of yours. When did you ever listen to me about men, or about anything else?"

I could hear Elizabeth sobbing softly. "You know when I stopped listening to you," she cried. "And you know why! I do what you ask. Why don't you just leave me alone!"

"You know who that was you were in bed with?" Daddy demanded.

"A very nice boy who works for the *New York World.* I'm sorry he wasn't a ward boss or a campaign contributor; I'll try to do better next time!"

He slapped her again. I almost jumped up and climbed through the window, but there was no way that my appearance could make anything any better for any of us, so I stayed where I was. "He works for that son of a bitch Alexander Brass," he said. "What did you tell him?"

"Tell him? Nothing. I didn't tell him anything."

"I hope that's true. If I read anything about me in Brass's column that he shouldn't know, I'll know where it came from."

Elizabeth blew her nose. "I didn't tell him anything, Daddy, honest."

"Are you going to see him again?"

There was a pause that seemed to stretch on forever before I heard her say, "Yes."

"Good!" the senator said. "Don't tell him anything, particularly about me. If he tells you anything about Brass's comings or goings, or any interest Brass has in me, let me know. You don't have to go out of your way to pump him; your standard acrobatics seem to inspire confidence in your men friends."

"Daddy!"

"Shocked, are you? Sure, you are. Now dry your face and go entertain my other guests!"

I heard footsteps and a door slam. After a minute I heard the door close again, and I peered around the corner and saw Elizabeth heading after her father. I waited until they were both far away, and then I went into the cottage and hunted for my wallet. It was under the bed.

19

I walked around for a time after that, I'm not sure how long. The size of the estate made it easy to keep away from other people, and so I did. I looked at new grass and old trees and small rocks and large clouds and thought a jumble of thoughts, one tumbling after the other unbidden into my brain and promptly out again. A heavy mist spread over the grounds, which suited my mood. I wandered, through the mist. When it turned into a steady rain I was in the ornamental garden in back of the main house. Damp is romantic; drenched is dumb. I headed for one of the row of French double doors leading into a ballroom larger than most train stations. Many of the other guests had managed to come in out of the rain before me, and groups of damp people were clumped loosely about the great room.

Scented candles were burning on sconces high on all four walls and the smell of oranges hung heavy in the room. A large bar occupied one corner of the ballroom, and its three bartenders were doing a steady business. A dozen musicians were clustered on a small platform in another corner, playing the sort of music that one could dance to, or sleep to, or talk over. Most of the guests were busily talking over the music. Some were in evening clothes, having already dressed for dinner, which was, according to my watch, about an hour away. The women's gowns were revealing without being daring, a good thing in most cases, and what was revealed was festooned with jewelry. I could not see Brass or

Gloria or Cathy in the room, nor was Elizabeth anywhere about.

A small door at the far end of the great room opened, and a conclave of men engaged in earnest conversation entered. The word spread in an echoing whisper from one group to the next: "It's Lindbergh!" "It's Lindy!" Within a few moments the scattered groups had all ceased talking and all heads had turned to face the royal presence. The musicians continued on for a moment but then, as though afraid to play into the silence, or perhaps they had just reached the end of their set, they stopped.

The conclave, made up of Senator Childers; John Pall, the governor of New Jersey; William David Sattler, who was a columnist for the *New York Graphic*, and whose politics were slightly to the right of Benito Mussolini's; and Colonel Charles Lindbergh, moved slowly through the room like a great ship coming into harbor. They were accompanied by two hard-faced, flinty-eyed young men in blue suits, who eyed the rest of us suspiciously and kept their hands near their sides. All lesser groups parted for them, and some of the men nodded slow nods as though they would have liked to bow but realized that it was somehow un-American.

Lindbergh was talking. His voice was not loud, but it was very positive, and in the expectant silence it filled the room. "Of course the Germans aren't even supposed to have an air force," he said. "But the Versailles treaty is pretty much a dead issue, with no Allied powers interested in enforcing it. And the planes that Herr Goering showed me—he's the minister of the air force they're not supposed to have—they call it the *Luftwaffe*—can fly higher, faster, and farther than anything we've got, and carry a heavier load."

"You believe that air power is going to be important in the next European war?" Senator Childers asked. He didn't seem to be in any doubt that there was going to be a next European war.

"Important? It's going to be decisive!" Lindbergh said firmly.

By now they had reached somewhere around the center of the room, and there they stopped. The people in the room gathered around them like iron filings to a magnet. Preferring not to be part of a group, and not to get into any sort of discussion with Senator Childers at the moment, I skirted the room, heading for a door that might lead to somewhere else inside the house.

"I don't think that Herr Hitler wants a war," Lindbergh said assuredly. "He told me that he doesn't, and I believe him. But he is determined that Germany regain her prestige, lost at the Treaty of Versailles. Germany is, and deserves to be, a great power, and her new chancellor is going to see that she is treated like one. Germany wants what's hers, what was taken away from her by the treaty, and England or France would be well advised not to fight over it."

"What about his treatment of the Jews?" Governor Pall asked. "I understand that German Jews are no longer allowed to practice law or medicine or hold government jobs."

"Well," Lindbergh said, "that may be so. But aren't there too many Jewish lawyers anyway?"

The crowd chuckled at the witty remark. The whole thing had the feeling of a set piece to me. Childers had maneuvered Lindbergh into the room and steered the conversation. Now everybody present would be able to say, "I was talking to Lindy the other day at Senator Childers's—yes, that's right, Colonel Lindbergh—his friends call him Lindy—and he told me..." I might even work it into a conversation myself. Perhaps Pinky would be impressed. I wondered if Lindbergh thought there were too many Jewish clowns.

When I reached the side door I had picked, I forewent the pleasure of listening to the rest of Herr Lindbergh's discourse and left the room. I found myself in one of those corridors that exist only in the very large houses of the very rich, a hallway placed for the passage of the servants so they can scuttle about out of sight of their betters. I followed the corridor until it terminated in a large kitchen, which I entered. A couple of dozen chefs, cooks, and assorted food choppers, slicers, and arrangers of both sexes and several different races were frenetically and loudly engaged in the process of food preparation and nobody paid the slightest attention to me.

I picked my way carefully through the kitchen, avoiding anyone who was yelling or handling a large knife. Past the stoves and the prep area a bank of ice boxes were set into the wall, and a couple of large electric refrigerators sat next to them in case the ice ran out. Past them a door led into a large pantry, in which a squad of workers, mostly young women, were giggling among themselves while carefully arranging endive salad on a collection of plates. When I entered the room all giggling stopped, and they stared covertly at me. Perhaps they thought I was a spy for management. I said, "As you were, ladies," and strolled through the room. But the giggling did not resume until I had passed through the far door.

I was now in what must have been the servants' dining area, a large room full of plain wooden tables and plain wooden chairs. A score of men in chauffeurs' uniforms were scattered randomly about the room reading newspapers, drinking coffee, smoking, and talking. Garrett was at a table by himself in the far corner, musing over a notebook. I went over.

"What's happening?" I asked.

Garrett looked up. "I have been contemplating the squid."

"The squid?"

"Yes. Or cuttlefish, if you like. I have constructed a poem."

I sat down. "About a squid?"

"Indeed." Garrett held up a hand to silence me, and then, with exquisite enunciation, read from his notebook:

> *"An unlikely fish is the cuttlefish,*
> *That sly, surreptitious and subtle fish.*
> *Quick as a wink*
> *He'll immerse you in ink,*
> *Thereby escaping the chafing dish."*

He looked at me expectantly. "I think you've captured it," I said.

"Notice the interior rhyme in the first two lines," he said. "I'm particularly pleased with it."

"And well you should be," I told him.

He eyed me suspiciously. "If you don't like it—"

"Oh, no!" I said. "I like it. Honest. It says something to the youth of America." I stood up. "How do I get out of here?"

"That depends on where you want to go," Garrett said reasonably. "There are changing rooms upstairs where gentlemen can change for dinner. In my capacity as chauffeur, I brought the bags up. You and Brass are in the same room. You might go up and try to convince them that you are a gentleman, as dinner rapidly approaches." Garrett put his cap on so he could touch the brim of it in mock salute. "Have a good time, sir. I'll stay here with the rest of the servants and eat my gruel." He grinned at me, took the cap off, and went back to his notebook.

Once again I realized that there was much more to Garrett than met the eye. And considering how much met the eye, the man was impressive indeed. If it wasn't for a supreme lack of interest in using his brain for anything beyond what caught his fancy from moment to moment, Theodore Garrett could have achieved greatness in any of several fields. I said something like that to him once, and he told me that in working for Brass he had achieved peace and security and a good supply of booze, and enough occasional excitement to keep his mind and body stimulated, and that was all he wanted.

Garrett pointed me toward a door which led to a hall, which opened onto the main hall, which terminated in a staircase that you could have rolled an elephant down, if you happened to be into that sort of sport. I went up the staircase, keeping a close watch for elephants, and found two neatly printed signs at the head of the stairs. One said MESDAMES and had an arrow pointing to the left, and the other said MESSIEURS with a right-pointing arrow. Next to the signs stood one of the liveried minions, presumably to make sure that my French was up to the task. I trotted down the hallway to the right. There were cards with names on them tacked to the doors, four names to a card.

After passing eight or nine doors I came to one with a card reading BRASS/DEWITT/CONVERS/PIGGORTY. I entered. The room had a brass bed and a bureau and makeup table of some well-aged dark wood, and a wash basin under the window. For some reason there was an old oaken rocking chair in the corner. Brass was standing in front of the makeup table and staring into the mirror, tying his formal black bow tie. Convers and Piggorty, whoever they were, were not in evidence. My suitcase was in the corner.

"Good evening, DeWitt," Brass said. "I trust you've had an interesting afternoon."

"You could say that," I told him. "Have you and the girls had any luck?"

He shrugged into the single-breasted dinner coat that he claimed was as close to informal as one could get at a Republican dinner, even one that claimed "dress optional," and stared critically at himself in the mirror. "I didn't really expect anything to come of this, but I was mistaken," he said. "We have learned many things, one of which is of particular interest, although I'm not sure just what to make of it yet."

I tossed my suitcase on the bed and undid the catches. "What's that?"

"Gloria pointed out—" Brass paused to consider. "No, wait until we go downstairs and I'll show you. Your independent confirmation, uncoached, would be valuable."

"Fair enough." I pulled my dinner clothes out of my suitcase and stared critically at them. "My dress trousers and my dinner jacket are both creased," I said in mock annoyance. "Where were the servants?"

Brass stared at me thoughtfully for a moment. "We are the proletariat," he said. "We are here for our entertainment value only. If we were one step lower on the ladder of social importance, we would have had to enter through the kitchen and dress in the butler's pantry."

"It's not that bad," I said. "I'm sure the senator wants to treat you right."

"I don't think Senator Childers would go out of his way to deliberately insult me," Brass said. "But I think that treating me, or any other columnist or reporter, right is pretty far down on his list of necessities. His interest is in influencing the owners of the newspapers, not the workers."

"Come to think of it, you're right," I said. "About an hour ago I overheard him refer to you as 'that son of a bitch Brass,' and yet here we are about to eat his food."

"Oh?" Brass said. "And under just what circumstances did you happen to overhear his remark?"

Good question. How much of my recent experience should I share with my boss? I'd have to think that one over. "It's a long story," I said. "I'll tell you about it later."

Brass checked his watch. "Meet me downstairs when you're ready," he said. "There's a half hour of cocktails before dinner. Don't drink; I need you alert."

"I am always alert," I told him, sitting on the edge of the bed and taking off my shirt.

"Nevertheless," he said, and exited the room.

20

Brass, in evening dress, looks like royalty; I look like an organizer for the Amalgamated Waiters' and Kitchen Workers' Union. I'm not sure what it is about formal attire that brings out the Bolshevik in me; perhaps it's the fear that any moment I'm going to be denounced as a fraud. Even though I now own my own tailor-made black single-breasted dinner coat with matching vest and trousers with a black silk stripe running down each leg, along with cummerbund, cravat, and patent leather oxfords, I am not comfortable wearing this rig. I play dress-up regularly as part of my job: at Broadway plays, nightclubs, the Metropolitan Opera. But evening dress still leaves me uncomfortable and unsure. I feel as though I'm in costume but whoever is in charge has forgotten to tell me what the play is or what part I'm supposed to be playing.

I stared at myself critically in the mirror as I tied my bow tie. I was not particularly handsome, nor was I particularly ugly. It would have been nice to be one or the other; being nondescript was to be unnoticeable, to fade into the background.

I pondered this as I made my way downstairs and followed the slow drift of humanity to the dining room. The room was not as large as the ballroom, and the ceiling was not as high, but if it were emptied of furniture it still would have made a useful roller skating rink.

Two large rooms flanked the dining room, each with its own bar; servitors weaved through the rooms with trays of hors d'oeuvres, and the dinner guests wandered about the three rooms with cocktail glasses in one hand, little plates of hors d'oeuvres in the other, and fixed smiles on their faces. The men were all in their penguin disguises, and the ladies were gowned and bejeweled in a dazzling display of Republican austerity. The waiters and bartenders were easy to differentiate because, not only were their faces varied shades of brown ranging to black, a feature not shared by any of the guests, but their dress suits were purple. Purple. Their bow ties were white and oversized, stretching across about eight or ten inches of shirt and jacket front.

I spotted Brass and Gloria from across the room at about the same time they spotted me, and we weaved our way toward one another. Gloria wore a red evening dress of some soft material that emphasized this and that, and suggested these and those. Cathy was not in sight. "There you are," Brass said. "I was beginning to wonder what happened to you."

"I've decided to organize the waiters," I told him. "We're going to strike for higher pay and the right to sing while we work."

Brass nodded. "Each of us must carry on the fight for truth and justice in his own way."

"Sing?" Gloria asked.

"That's right," I said. "If these gentlemen are required to look like a cross between a minstrel show and a chorus from a bad Sigmund Romberg operetta, they should be allowed to sing. Where's Cathy?"

"She has made a friend," Brass said. "She is cultivating that friendship." He glanced toward a corner of the room, and I followed his glance. Cathy was standing there in a white evening gown that flowed softly down her body and spoke of purity and vulnerability. She was in an animated conversation with a blond girl in a tight-fitting green-and-gold dress with a short, flared skirt. The blonde's dress, if I may be allowed to beat a metaphor to death, spoke of the secret desires of men when they look at beautiful women. The body encased by the dress aided in the discussion.

"Well!" I said. "And who is her new friend?"

"Her name is Heidi," Gloria said. "She is the niece of Dr. Erich von Mainard, a special guest of the senator's. That's him over there." She pointed to a thin man with a long face, close-set eyes, and a carefully manicured beard that came to a point several inches below where his chin would have been if he'd had a chin. I have no evidence that he didn't have a chin, but I'm training myself to be a careful observer and report only what I know.

"What sort of doctor is he?" I asked.

"He runs a clinic in New York City," Brass said. "The Mainard Clinic, as a matter of fact, specializing in diseases of the affluent."

"He could certainly build up a clientele around here," I said.

"Take a careful look at his niece," Brass said. "Look her over carefully, take your time, and see if anything occurs to you."

"Yes, sir," I said. "But if I'd known I was going to be forced to stare at beautiful women, I never would have taken this job." I crossed the room to the bar in the next room and got myself a scotch and soda and then headed back. I stared at Heidi as I passed. I didn't have to be too subtle; she must have been used to men staring at her. Her complexion was a pale white with a hint of red at the cheeks, her chin was noble, her nose was straight with an aristocratic flare at the end, her shoulder-length blond hair softly framed her perfect oval of a face. Her dress was artfully designed to emphasize what it was concealing, but her body needed little emphasis. I could go on like this, but you get the idea.

Dr. von Mainard, he of the pointed beard, had stalked over to Brass while I was contemplating his niece, and was giving him the lowdown on the Mainard Clinic. I think he expected Brass to whip out a pad and pen and take notes for his next column. "It is our psyche that responds to and directs our physical body," he was saying with a controlled intensity, his eyes bright with the fervor of a true believer. He spoke with the overly precise pronunciation of the well-educated European. "It is the repression of physical emotion, Mr. Brass, that curls up inside the stomach of our psyche and sours the spiritual food with which we nourish ourselves. Modern society forces us to accept too many of these repressions, which do us great harm and prevent us from achieving our potential."

"Indeed," Brass said, taking a step backward as von Mainard continued to advance as he spoke.

"At my clinic we remove these repressions and allow the psyche, and thus the persona, to become whole."

"Fascinating," Brass said.

"You must come and visit us. I, myself, would be delighted to give you a tour and—why not?—a session so that you can see of yourself how powerful this can be. I insist."

"I'll call you," Brass said.

Dr. von Mainard, his missionary work done, brought his heels together, bowed, and stalked off to convert someone else.

Brass took a deep breath. "My psyche needs refreshment," he said, artfully removing a glass of wine from a passing tray.

Brass and Gloria turned to me and waited patiently while I took a thoughtful sip of my drink.

"She's a lot prettier than he is," I said.

"Nothing else?" Brass asked.

"Nope," I said. "Except for the fact that she sure as hell doesn't look anything like her uncle, I don't see whatever you see."

"I didn't see it either," Brass said. "There is some advantage to having a woman around to appraise other women."

I looked expectantly at Gloria.

"Picture," Gloria said, "that paragon of department store magnates, Mr. Ephraim L. Wackersan."

"Junior," I said. "I'd rather not," I said.

"Picture him naked, lying on his back, his eyes crossed in concentration, with a young woman, also naked, straddling him somewhere around the midsection."

"You mean..." I said. "Heidi—"

"I mean Heidi," Gloria said.

I slowly turned for another look. A minute or so later I turned back. "It could be," I said. "It could very well be."

"It is!" Gloria said.

I thought it over for five or six seconds, but nothing clever occurred to me. "Well, what are we going to do about it?" I asked Brass.

"Cathy is doing what has to be done," Brass said. "She seems to have a talent for making friends. Man, woman, or small animal, they all love her."

"What is she telling Heidi?"

"Whatever is appropriate. She is, of course, omitting the fact that she came here with us. Cathy is very bright and highly motivated. She'll manage."

"And then what?"

"That depends on what Cathy discovers," Brass said.

A few minutes later Senator Childers and his wife entered the room têtes-à-têtes with Charles Lindbergh and Amelia Earhart. A thin-faced man with dark, deep-set eyes and a Leica camera with a flash gun came in with them and, as Lindbergh and Earhart circulated through the rooms, he scrambled about, taking pictures of either or both of them standing with some eager patron of the senator's.

We stayed where we were, unobtrusively eyeing Cathy and Heidi. It would have been wiser to ignore them on the slight chance that Heidi would notice us watching, and we couldn't see anything anyway, but there you have it. After a while Lindbergh's circuit brought him to where we were standing, and someone introduced him to Brass. He stuck out his hand. "You're the chap who writes the column about nightclubs and showgirls," he said.

Brass shook his hand. "I have occasionally touched on other subjects," he said.

"Yes, I remember," Lindbergh said. "Politics and foreign affairs."

"Occasionally," Brass admitted.

Lindbergh shook his head. "You should stick to nightclubs and showgirls," he said, and moved on.

Several flashes had gone off while the two great men had met, and the thin-faced photographer came over as Lindbergh pulled away and handed Brass his card. "If you want some prints, suitable for framing..." he said, and then continued in Lindbergh's wake.

Brass stared after Lindbergh, the card in his hand and a tight smile on his lips. "Framing," he said as though it were a dirty word. Then he glanced down at the card. He looked at it intently for a long moment and passed it to Gloria. "Curiouser and curiouser," he said.

Gloria stared at the card. "Well, well," she said. "The long arm of coincidence is certainly beating us about the head and shoulders today."

I took the card and looked at it.

DIETER VOGEL
PHOTOGRAPHER

229 East 77th St.
New York City • Atwater 9-1537

"So he's a German, and a photographer, and he lives in Yorkville, close to the scene of the action," I said. "You're going to be seeing coincidences under every rosebush if you're not careful. Sometimes a cigar is just a cigar."

"How's your German?" Brass asked.

"Heil, Hitler and *gesundheit,* and that's about it," I told him.

Gloria leaned close and smiled up at me. *"Vogel,"* she murmured, "is German for *bird."*

"So?" I said.

She continued smiling.

"Oh!" I said. I handed the card back to Brass. "Bird. As in the name on the Dworkyn folder. I see what you mean."

"Good," Brass said.

"We seem to be making progress," I said. "What do we do now?"

A waiter came to the doorway of the dining room and artfully stroked a dinner gong. "We eat dinner," Brass said. "Then go home. Tomorrow we'll consider the possibilities."

21

Sunday I slept late. While I was asleep a ten-year-old Jersey City boy named Kappy Osterman and two of his friends rowed out into the Hudson River to fish. They pushed off at 6 A.M., having absorbed from their elders the ancient wisdom that it is necessary to sneak up on fish in the dark. At six-forty, as the sun was rising somewhere behind the Manhattan skyline, Kappy hooked onto something that would provide him with after-dinner conversation for many decades to come. "It was awful," he told his mother a couple of hours later, after the police sent him and his friends home. "Fish-belly white, but it wasn't no fish. It was a arm. A human person's arm."

By quarter past seven the Jersey City police had fished the arm, and the body attached to it, out of the Hudson. At ten o'clock they called the New York City police. At quarter to eleven Brass called me.

It was shortly after noon when the unmarked New York City police car pulled up in front of the vaguely Gothic, redbrick building that housed the Jersey City morgue. Inspector Raab got out of the front seat and Brass and I emerged from the back. Captain Niall McVinnie of the Jersey City Police Department, a squat, powerful-looking man in an immaculate blue uniform plastered with gold braid, was waiting for us at the curb. He shook hands with Inspector Raab. "Glad you could come, it being a Sunday and all."

Raab introduced Brass and me, and a mighty frown crossed the captain's brow as he shook our hands. "Newspapers," he said, turning to Raab. "Did you have to bring the newspapers?" He turned back to Brass. "Not that it isn't much of an honor to meet yourself, Mr. Brass, but we could do without the newspapers at the moment."

"I am not a newspaper," Brass told the captain. "Not even a newspaper reporter. I am under no obligation to write about whatever I see here."

"Calm yourself, McVinnie," Raab said, slapping the captain on the shoulder in a gesture of solidarity. "I asked Brass and DeWitt to come along because I thought they might be able to help. You want us to take jurisdiction, don't you?"

"I want you to take this goddamn body out of here. Just because it was a Jersey City lad that hooked onto it in the river doesn't make it a Jersey City killing. We're having enough troubles with the citizens' groups right now, and with the local papers having a sporting day over the department's troubles. I could sure do without adding a mutilated body to their list of incidents."

"I assure you I will not write anything detrimental to Jersey City or its police force," Brass joined in. "I don't want to do anything to add to your troubles."

Brass was being less than ingenuous. He wouldn't write anything at all about Jersey City because, even though it was just across the Hudson, Jersey City could be Mars as far as readers of the *New York World* were concerned. But the mention of his troubles took the captain's thoughts away from the implausibility of the head of New York City's Homicide North and a major newspaper columnist crossing the river on a Sunday to view an unidentified floater. He shook his head sadly as he led the way up the front steps. "Four of me own lads," he said. "Who would of thought it?"

"I've heard the story. Did they do it?" Brass asked.

"There don't seem to be much doubt," McVinnie said. "They were caught leaving the loft building at four in the morning with their arms full of fur coats; the tools used to go through the floor into the fur vault were right where they'd dropped them and had their fingerprints all over—and the mothers' sons were wearing nothing but their long johns at the time."

I tried unsuccessfully to suppress a grin. "They robbed a fur vault in their underwear?"

McVinnie nodded, his face a cloud of indignation. "Burglarized," he corrected me. "It's not funny. They thought that if they were spotted it would be harder to identify them. Whatever is the world coming to?" He held the door open for us and we went past him into a cold, dark corridor. What little light there was came through a frosted-glass panel in a door at the end of the corridor. We headed toward the light.

The sign painted below the frosted glass read: OFFICE OF THE CORONER—HUDSON COUNTY, NEW JERSEY. From inside came the murmur of subdued voices. We went in.

There was a desk facing the door, and a couch to the right of the door. Five chairs were pulled up to the desk, and six men were playing stud poker on the desktop.

The dealer looked up as we entered. "McVinnie," he said.

"Charlie," the captain acknowledged. "This is Inspector Raab, NYPD; and these are a couple of New York newspaper fellows come to help."

Charlie nodded. "Charles Drier, Drier's Full Service Funeral Home. I'm also the coroner. Let me finish this hand and then I'll take you all inside for a viewing."

There was a minute of intense concentration before one of the policemen took a pot of something over two hundred dollars with a pair of tens up and one in the hole. Then the coroner gathered the cards, dropped the deck in the middle of the table, took his money off the table, and stretched. "I'll be back shortly," he told the other players. "If you're going to mark the cards while I'm gone, don't use mustard; it makes them sticky and hard to deal."

"As if we didn't know who's been sticking his little finger in the mustard," one of the cops said, reaching for the deck.

Drier led us into an inner room, and through that to a metal staircase which let out a thunderous ringing as we tramped down one flight to the basement. He pushed through two more doors and turned the lights on in a large, white room with metal tables and oversized file drawers set into the far wall. "Refrigeration's been acting up," he said, "but it seems to be all right now." He crossed the room and pulled open one of the drawers. "Haven't autopsied her yet. Doc won't be here until Tuesday." He pulled the white sheet down, revealing the object under it that had recently been a woman.

Brass and Raab moved forward to stare down at the body. I stayed a little back, but I looked. What had caused us to give up our Sunday and cross the river was Captain McVinnie telling Raab that the corpse had been "mutilated." His description of the hacking done to the body reminded Raab of the corpse of a certain defunct photographer, and so he had called Brass, and Brass me. And so we were staring with interest at the body of a young girl, and McVinnie was wondering why we cared, and nobody would tell him.

The girl was blond, in her early twenties or even younger, and had been very good looking. This was no longer so. Her body was pale white, blotched with brown and crisscrossed with welts. My impression was that she had been thoroughly beaten, as well as slashed at with a whip or belt. It didn't appear to be nearly as severe as the torture poor Hermann Dworkyn had suffered, but she couldn't have enjoyed it. For a couple of minutes nobody said anything, and then Raab turned to the coroner. "Do you mind if we turn the body over?" he asked.

"I don't mind if she don't mind," Drier said.

Between them Raab and Brass flipped the body over. The back showed a regular pattern of parallel stripes as though the girl had been whipped by someone who was practiced and precise at his job. I stepped closer to get a better look, recognizing in myself a growing callousness toward dead bodies. I suppose this was good if I was going to keep running into them.

After a minute they returned the body to its supine position. Brass took the bag I was carrying, opened it, and pulled from its depths a roll film camera with a bellows lens and a flash gun. He turned the dead girl's face sideways, stepped back, and took four flash pictures from varying distances.

"Say," McVinnie said, "what'd you do that for? You're not going to use them pictures—"

"You know I couldn't do that if I wanted to," Brass reassured him, tossing the camera, the flash, and the spent bulbs back in the bag. "The public isn't ready for photographs of corpses in their morning papers. This just might help identify her, that's all."

"Yeah," McVinnie said. "I guess that's right."

"I would say we've seen enough," Brass said, drawing back from the table.

"Yes," Raab agreed. "I think we can take this problem off your hands, Captain. If you'll bring the remains over to our side of the river, I'll tell the ME to expect it."

"I'll get the complete paperwork to you tomorrow," Captain McVinnie said. "But I'll sign 'one unidentified white female, deceased' over to you right now. Charlie, if you'll take one of them fine hearses of yours and deliver the body to the morgue at Bellevue Hospital sometime in the next couple of hours, I'd appreciate it."

"Fine," Drier said. "Who do I bill?"

We stared at him. He looked back unabashed. McVinnie sighed. "Bill the department, Charlie."

We returned to Manhattan through the Holland Tunnel and headed uptown to the *World* building. Raab dismissed his driver and came upstairs with us. Brass tossed me the roll of film and I took it downstairs to the photo-processing department and gave it to the on-duty man, who promised to call as soon as he had prints. I went out to pick up some sandwiches since we hadn't eaten lunch. I had to go about six blocks to find a joint that was open on Sunday, but that's the great thing about New York. At any time of the day or night there's always someplace. I got meatball sandwiches on kaiser rolls from a little luncheonette on Tenth and Sixty-fifth that catered to cabbies.

When I returned to the office, Raab was lying on the couch and Brass was in his desk chair, his back to the room, staring out at the river. I put a sandwich on Brass's desk and on Raab's chest and flopped into an armchair next to the couch. Neither of them moved. I stared from one to the other. "Well," I said, "what do we know?"

Raab raised his head from the couch cushion to look at me. "Too damn much," he said. He let his head drop back down.

"I've called Gloria," Brass said without turning. "She was home. She is coming up. We are going to share information with Inspector Raab. He is not happy about this, as there is nothing he can do with the information at the moment."

"What information?" I asked.

Brass swiveled in his chair and picked up a handful of eight-by-ten photographs from his desk blotter. "Here," he said, tossing them in the general direction of my chair. "These were on the desk when I got here." There were twenty of them and they scattered to twenty separate destinations around the room.

I retrieved them. "Good toss," I said, pulling one from under the couch, but I was speaking to Brass's back; he had already returned to analyzing the traffic patterns on the Hudson River. I dropped back down in my chair and examined the pictures.

They were photographs of naked women. No; they were all photographs of the same naked woman in a variety of poses. Unlike our previous collection, there was nobody else evident in any of the pictures, and the poses didn't seem particularly erotic. The pictures were fairly grainy and seemed to have scratches or lines running through them. Then I realized what I was seeing: the lines weren't on the photograph; they were on the girl. "She's been cut!" I said.

"Whipped," Brass said. "Whipped and beaten. Use the glass." He pushed a large magnifying glass across the desk and I got up and retrieved it.

"Where did these come from?" I asked.

"They're blowups of the contact sheet Bobbi Dworkyn found in her brother's files," Brass explained. He unwrapped his sandwich and turned back to contemplate the passing garbage scows.

I studied the photographs through Brass's magnifying glass and reached two conclusions: that it was the same girl we had recently viewed on a slab in Jersey City, and that she was alive when these pictures were taken. She didn't even seem particularly unhappy, morose, or angry. She was just standing passively with her arms raised or leaning forward or with her leg up on a chair displaying the inner thigh, the clear intent being to document her cuts, slashes, and bruises.

"Somebody was beating up on this girl," I said. Brass turned to stare at me without saying anything.

"And now she's dead," Inspector Raab said without bothering to look up. "Can we assume there's a connection? Don't all speak at once." He had covered his shirt and tie with the butcher paper his sandwich had been wrapped in, and was eating the sandwich without raising his head. I decided not to mention the strong possibility that he would choke on a meatball if he didn't sit up.

Gloria came in about ten minutes later. Brass had the original batch of pictures on the desk and was slowly going through them and comparing them with the new group. Gloria smoothed her skirt and sat in the chair next to the desk. "It's just started to rain," she said. "I understand you've had a hell of a morning."

"We've been to New Jersey," Brass told her. "This seems to be our month for going to New Jersey. We went to Jersey City and examined the body of what had been an attractive young girl."

"So you said over the phone," Gloria said. "What killed her?"

Raab sat up and crumpled the butcher paper in a ball and threw it at the wastebasket. He missed. "She was fished out of the Hudson," he said. "Couldn't have been there long, not as long as a day. But she's been dead two or three days, which means…"

"Which means what?" Gloria asked.

"I'm not sure, but it's strange. Somebody's been warehousing a corpse, which is a dangerous and unlikely thing to do. She was beaten and whipped, but that was at least a week before she died. The pictures we have here, pictures taken while she was still alive, were taken shortly after the beating. The bruises hadn't had time to develop yet. And the other mutilations to the body, they were done after she was dead. Which is even odder. As far as what actually caused her death, there were no obvious fatal wounds, so we'll have to wait for the postmortem."

"You have pictures of the same girl when she was alive?" Gloria asked.

"They're from the Dworkyn collection," Brass said. "Which is why we're assuming that this is all related."

"Some kind of strange sexual deviate?" Gloria suggested.

"I don't think so," Raab said. "Too many different things happened to this poor girl. It would take a clan of deviates, each with his own particular deviation. Although that, itself, is not outside the bounds of human possibility."

Brass leaned forward and laid out six photographs across the front of his desk, *slap, slap, slap,* one at a time, like a gin rummy player laying out his hand. "One more piece of the puzzle," he said.

Inspector Raab and I came up next to Gloria and stared down at the exhibits. Two pictures from the original collection, given to us by Dworkyn, and four of the new ones. Just then a copy boy came in with an envelope holding the newly printed photographs of our Jersey City expedition. Brass went through them and picked out two, which he added to the six.

Raab straightened up. "Son of a—" he said. "It's the senator!"

Brass looked from one to the other of us. "Are we agreed?" he asked. "The girl whose corpse showed up in the Hudson River this morning is the girl who is sharing an intimate moment with Senator Childers in these two photographs?"

Inspector Raab put a finger on one picture contemplatively, and then shifted it to another. "Romans, six, twenty-three," he murmured.

"What's that?" I asked.

"'For the wages of sin is death,'" Raab said.

"Don't get mystical," Brass said. "The wages of everything is death. Some of us just have to wait longer to get paid off."

22

Inspector Raab stared glumly at the litter of photographs in front of him and then raised his eyes to gaze out the window behind Brass. He pushed his chair away from the desk. "Well," he said, "only one thing for me to do now."

We looked at him. Brass made a grunting sound that could have been a question.

"Retire," Raab said firmly. "If I put the paperwork in today it'll go through in a week or two, maybe—I can stretch the investigation for a couple of weeks; slow, methodical work is good police work—and then Johnson or O'Farrell will have the pleasure of arresting a United States senator."

"You think Childers killed that girl?" Brass asked. "That's kind of a leap."

"We don't have enough to hold him now, although if he were a regular citizen we'd certainly bring him in for questioning. I'm not even sure that you can arrest a United States senator. I think they have immunity."

"That's only on the floor of the Senate," Brass told him.

"Yeah, well, I'd have to go into New Jersey and get some local police chief to agree to help me. And Childers owns most of New Jersey and rents the rest. But it for sure looks like somebody's going to have to ask him something. First he's photographed with the girl, then pictures are taken showing that she has been truly and thoroughly beaten, and then she turns up dead. During this time a photographer who is somehow involved with the first set of photographs and a reporter who was following that photographer for reasons of his own are both killed. There are men who like to beat women, some for sexual satisfaction, and others just to show what big men they are. Is Childers one of them? If he has a record of it, it's certainly been suppressed. Money and power buy a lot of suppression. But I can ask a few questions of the New Jersey State Police. Their chief, Colonel Schwarzkopf, is a good guy. They might know something. I'll do that. They may tell me off the record; they may not. I wouldn't want to bet my house that Childers killed the girl, but neither would I want to bet my front porch that he didn't. As for Fox and Dworkyn, perhaps he was eliminating witnesses. I don't say he killed them himself, but he could have had it done. There's no question about that. You have a better suggestion?"

"Who took the photographs?" Brass asked.

Raab slumped in his chair and stared at the ceiling, silently thinking that one over. We silently watched him. After a minute he sat up. "Those middle photographs—the ones that show her alive but whipped and contused—where'd you get those?"

A smile crossed Brass's face. "*Contused,*" he said. "Right off a police report. I like it." He fished in his pocket and pulled out a business card. "We have no proof yet, but this gentleman may have had something to do with it." He flipped the card across the desk.

Raab picked up the card and examined it while Brass explained where it came from and why the name "Vogel" was of interest.

"I knew we should have spent more time questioning that stripper," Raab said. "Bird, eh?" He tapped the card. "Vogel. Also a photographer. Also lives in Yorkville. And you saw him at a party at Senator Childers's estate. The connections are getting inescapable. It would be pushing the bounds of coincidence if Herr Dieter Vogel were not the bird in question. And yet another reason to wonder about the senior senator from New Jersey."

Raab stood up. He had come to a decision. "I'll take those pictures," he said. "Not the first set; the ones from the Bird folder. We will ignore the fact that you've been withholding evidence—"

"Come on, Inspector," Brass said. "We didn't know they were evidence of anything until we had them blown up, and then you saw them at the same time I did."

Gloria smiled sweetly. "Is this the thanks he gets for letting you sleep on his couch?" she asked.

"Yeah, I read the column," Raab said. "We'll discuss that some other time." He gathered the photographs and stuffed them into his pocket. "I'll pull this Vogel bird in and see what he has to say about taking pictures of the dead girl." He reached for the telephone, but then pulled his hand back. "I guess I'd better set this up in person," he said. "Then if anything goes wrong, I know who to blame." He grabbed his hat and headed for the door.

"Well," I asked Brass after Raab had cleared out, "what's your vote? Did Childers do it?"

"There seems to be a confluence of events around Senator Childers," Brass said. "But when a cyclone hits a barn in Kansas, you don't blame the barn."

I paused for a moment to admire the rustic metaphor. "Then you think he didn't do it?"

Brass drummed his fingers on the edge of the desk. "It remains to be seen whether Senator Childers is the barn or the cyclone," he said.

"Do you think Vogel is our missing pornographer?" Gloria asked.

"He probably took the pictures of the girl after she had been damaged," Brass said. "Dworkyn filed them under his name. But how did he get them? We don't know. And even if Vogel brought Dworkyn the first batch of pictures, we don't know whether he took them or not, and if so, what the circumstances were." He raised an arm and pointed it in the general direction of the wall safe. "You think he did that?" he asked me. The door was still hanging at a strange angle from the body of the safe, and the wall around it showed minor battle scars. Brass had ordered a sturdier replacement from the Ouiga Safe Company, but it would be another week before they could install it.

"Not himself," I said. "He wasn't one of those three men. But maybe he sent them."

"Why?" Brass asked.

I stated the obvious. "To recover the pictures."

Brass shook his head. "It won't do," he said. "If he took the pictures, he had the negatives. If they were being used for blackmail, the threat is in no way diminished if I have copies. He must have known I wouldn't use them."

"Not everyone is as aware of your honesty and rectitude and high moral principles as we are," I said. "But I see what you mean. The people most likely to have wanted the pictures badly enough to send a trio of thugs to retrieve them are the subjects."

Gloria stretched and turned around in her chair. "But they would have to have known that we had the pictures," she said. "How would they have found out?"

"Whoever killed Dworkyn tortured him first," I said. "Probably to discover what he did with the pictures."

"And on that happy note," Brass said, "I have a column to write. And I have nothing in mind. Nothing. Considerations of murder and mayhem, when you have a reason to take them personally, can drive all lesser thoughts from your mind."

"Tell the world about Senator Childers's idea of what the ideal dinner party should be," Gloria suggested. "The bourgeoisie always like hearing about how their betters live and frolic."

"That's what caused the French Revolution," Brass said. "That reminds me," he turned to me. "Just when did Childers call me a son of a bitch, and how did you happen to overhear it?"

"I met his daughter, Elizabeth, and we got friendly," I began.

"So that's what they're calling it now," Gloria said. I glared at her, and I think my ears turned red. She said, "Oops, sorry," and shut up.

Brass stared at me patiently. "Your relations with Bitsy Childers are your business," he said, "but anything you know about her father should be shared."

He was right. I paused for a few seconds to think of a way to say it, and then decided, what the hell, tell it like it was. I took a deep breath and plunged in. "Senator Childers caught us being friendly in the pool house," I told Brass. "And he was very mild about it. I sort of expected an explosion, but it didn't happen. He is not a normal father. A while later I was standing behind the pool house, and he and Bitsy were inside and I heard him yelling at her. But it wasn't what he caught her doing with me that he was angry about; it was that she might be telling me things about him, which I would pass on to 'that son of a bitch' you. She said she wasn't. He just about told her that, in that case, she should see me again and get me to talk about what you know about him and what you're doing."

"Well," Gloria said. "I wonder what secrets little Bitsy knows that her dad is worried about her telling to random partners—sorry, I didn't mean that the way it came out."

"I like the girl," I said. "I don't care what her reputation is, or how much of it is true, and I imagine a lot of it is."

"Are you going to see her again?" Brass asked.

"I hope so," I said. "She's supposed to call."

"Well, don't pump her about her father; he might hear about it. Whatever she might know, we can get at some other way."

"Let me make something clear," I said, perhaps less mildly than I intended. "I have no intention of interrogating Elizabeth about anything, unless and until I get a compelling reason to do so. I'm sure she knows many interesting things about her father, but I doubt if any of them have anything to do with our concerns."

"Don't get upset," Brass said. "I was just telling you not to do what you're insisting you won't do. Just be careful not to tell her anything about what we're doing, or what we suspect."

I got up and glowered across the desk. "If you don't trust me—"

"And for God's sake don't take offense," Brass said. "We haven't got time for that now. Men have been known to tell their inamorata secrets that were better untold. That's how Mata Hari had a career."

"She got shot," I said.

"Right," Brass said. "Now get out of here and let me attempt to work." I went home.

Pinky came back from his gig at the children's hospital around eight o'clock, and I talked to him. My subject was women; specifically senators' daughters. A very polite clown, Pinky pretended to be interested for over an hour before announcing that he had to go to his room.

When I returned to the office around ten-thirty Monday morning, Gloria and Cathy were there, but Brass was not. Cathy was looking pleased with herself.

"Morning," I said. "What's up?"

"I," Cathy announced, "just got offered a job."

"You have a job," I said.

Gloria was sitting behind her desk. She smiled up at me. "That was her job," she said, "getting this job."

I propped myself up on the edge of the desk, leaned forward, and smiled back. "You lost me," I said.

"My new friend Heidi suggested I might like to work at the Mainard Clinic, where she works," Cathy explained. "I led into it very gradually so she has no idea that it wasn't her own idea. I told her I was a nightclub singer, but I wasn't doing very well. She was very sympathetic. According to Heidi, I can make a lot of money at the clinic. The tips are very good."

"I'll bet," Gloria said.

"I never realized I could be sneaky like that; it felt funny. And then I realized it's what girls do with men all the time; I just never did it to another girl before."

Gloria nodded. "The ancient art of letting men think they're making the decisions," she said.

"Isn't Dr. von Mainard her uncle?" I asked.

"In name only," Cathy said. "When an old man goes out with a pretty young girl, he's either her uncle or he's a dirty old man. We called them 'sugar daddies' at the Hotsy Totsy Club."

"I thought Wackersan the department store prince was her sugar daddy," I said. "Isn't Heidi the girl in the photograph with Wackersan?"

"She didn't say, and I didn't ask. If she isn't, I've taken the wrong job."

"You've taken the job?"

"I had an interview with Dr. von Mainard yesterday at his office."

"Sunday?"

"One has to work Saturday and Sunday in the clinic, as a lot of their patients are important men who can only come in on the weekend."

"Just what is your job?" I asked.

"I'm to be the receptionist," she said.

"I'll bet that's not where the good tips are," Gloria said.

Brass came in, nodded hello to all of us, and went through to his office. We followed in a couple of minutes, giving him enough time to sit down, twirl around in his chair a couple of times, and check the traffic on the river.

"Cathy has got herself a job," Gloria told him. "At the Mainard Clinic."

"Very good," Brass said. "So your new friend Heidi works for her uncle?"

Cathy explained about uncles and sugar daddies.

"Wonderful," Brass said. "So she's an employee as well as a niece. I wonder if Mr. Wackersan ever visits the clinic."

"I wonder if it has a room with a skylight," I added.

"Be cautious," Brass told Cathy. "If there's anything to discover about the clinic or the doctor, let it come to you. Don't take chances. If these people are involved, they're very dangerous."

Cathy nodded. "Believe me," she said, "I'm too scared to do anything silly."

The phone dinged, and Gloria reached around Brass's desk to pick it up. "It's the lobby," she told Brass. "A group of Germans wants to come up to see you." Since our incident with the three thugs, lobby security had instructions to check with us before letting people on the elevator. It was either that or hire two large bodyguards to stand at the door.

"What group?" Brass asked.

Gloria relayed the question. "It's the Verein for Whosis and Whatsis," she told him.

"Send them up," he said.

There were five of them this time: the four originals and their leader, who had obviously been released from jail. They paused to bow politely to the ladies as they came in the room, and then turned to face Brass, a clump of five middle-aged European intellectuals standing at attention, hats clutched in front of them. "We have come to give you thanks," Grosfeder, the stout journalist, announced.

Max von Pilath took one step forward. "I am owing you much thanks," he said. "I am not ungr-gr-grateful." With that the entire group marched forward to crowd around Brass's desk, right hands extended. Brass stood up and gravely shook hands with each of them, and they each took a step back at the completion of the ritual.

Brass looked them over. “Obviously Mr. von Pilath has been released from jail,” he said, “and obviously you think I had something to do with it. Much as I would like to take credit, I think you should save your thanks for Inspector Raab of the New York City Police Department.”

“But this inspector,” von Pilath said, “you t-told him of my innocence, yes? And he listened to you, yes?”

“I told him I thought you were innocent, yes, but he made up his own mind.”

They all chuckled, possibly at the idea of police inspectors having minds of their own.

“It is as I said,” Grosfeder said. “In this country journalists are of some account. They are not locked up when they disagree with the authorities. It is the freedom of the press.” They bowed to the room at large and turned to leave. Before they had taken a step Schulman turned back and thrust his chin forward, pointing his beard at Brass. “You should use your admittedly great skills to write columns about the travail of the workers, Mr. Brass,” he said, nodding his head for emphasis. “You must grant that the capitalist system has been shown to—*ergh*—”

Grosfeder’s large hand came up and grabbed Schulman by the collar and pulled him out of the room, his hands waving in the air.

23

The bird had flown. Inspector Raab went to call on Vogel late that Monday afternoon, and his studio was empty, deserted, cleaned out. A lady in the office across the hall told Raab that movers had come early that morning to take everything away and that Vogel, "such a nice man, always so polite," had told her he was going away for a while. He didn't say where.

"And I don't even know what he looks like," Raab said. It was a little after five Tuesday afternoon, and he was in his usual corner of the couch in Brass's office, a cup of coffee in his hand and annoyance in his voice. "You saw him, Brass; describe him to me."

"Gloria's better at describing than I am," Brass told him. "But it isn't necessary. I can do better than that." He fished in his drawer and came up with a manila envelope, which he skimmed across the room to Raab. "Can't you trace him through the moving company?"

"I've got two men on that right now," Raab said, opening the envelope and shaking the contents onto the couch cushion. "What are these?"

"The negatives of those photographs were in the Bird folder. The *World* photo lab just printed them up for me."

"More information you've been withholding?"

"I didn't mention them before because they weren't relevant."

Raab scowled. "Someday, just once, I wish you'd let me decide that. Just once."

He switched on the table lamp by his side to better stare at the photographs. I peeked over his shoulder. There were eight pictures, all taken on a New York City street, judging by the background: a couple of Vogel in a suit, three of a plump but attractive girl in the sort of skirt and blouse that makes you think of European peasants, and three of both of them standing together.

"That's Vogel?" Raab asked. "Who's the girl?"

"That's Vogel," Brass affirmed. "I don't know the girl. She's not one of the young ladies in our exotic picture collection."

"I'll take these two," Raab said, stuffing the one of Vogel alone and the one of the girl alone in his pocket. He tossed the other two back on the desk. "You want a receipt?"

Brass shook his head. "My gift to the NYPD."

Raab pushed himself to his feet and jammed his hat on his head. "I'm meeting Colonel Schwarzkopf at Luchow's in an hour," he said. "I was kind of vague about what I wanted to talk to him about over the phone, but I think he got my drift. And I think he has something to tell me if I ply him with roast beef and dark beer."

The phone rang in the outer office as Inspector Raab left, and a few seconds later Gloria stuck her head through the office door and pointed to me. I returned to the little cubicle I call an office and picked up the phone. Gloria had already patched the call through to me.

"Hello?"

"Morgan the Pirate?"

For a second I didn't know who it was. I think I didn't really believe she'd call. "Elizabeth?"

"I'm so pleased," she said. "You can recognize my voice from all the other girls that pester you with phone calls."

"They all call me Mr. DeWitt and try to sell me subscriptions to *The Saturday Evening Post.*"

"How's your sales resistance?"

"Wonderful. I now have twelve subscriptions."

"Good. Can I interest you in *A Girl's Life*?"

"Is that a magazine?"

"It's an autobiography, and I want to add another chapter. Have dinner with me tonight and help me decide what the subject should be."

"I think I can work you in," I said.

"Eight o'clock at Pietro's?"

I paused for a quarter of a second before I said yes to show her I wasn't easy. We chatted about this and that for another minute, and hung up.

Pietro's is a small steak and spaghetti house in the West Forties. Dark wood walls, subdued lighting, quiet, friendly service, good food. It's the perfect place to meet a lover for a romantic dinner. It would also be the perfect place to meet a city commissioner for a bribe payoff, or a professional killer to arrange the elimination of your spouse. It's all in how you look at it.

Elizabeth, my beautiful Elizabeth, was waiting for me at the bar when I arrived ten minutes early. My heart beat faster when I saw her and I stammered when I spoke. She broke into a wide smile when I came in and hugged me. She was wearing a black pleated skirt and sweater with a sort of tan (café au lait, she told me) jacket with large black buttons and an oversized black beret. "Simple yet elegant," I told her.

"Expensive yet costly," she said. "It's Balenciaga."

"Is that good?"

"It's what every shop girl will wear," she said, "if she marries rich. And buys her clothes in Paris."

We sat at a table in a corner in the back and Elizabeth ordered dinner, since she knew more about it than I did and spoke Italian: *fichi con prosciutto* (a plate of figs with thin slices of Italian ham over them, another reason for leaving Ohio) to start; house salad and *spaghetti alia bucanier* for her, in honor of my being a buccaneer, she said; a spinach salad, a rare T-bone, and *spaghetti con aglio e olio* for me, in honor of my being hungry. We talked about many things during the meal. We held hands.

"I can't get over it," she said, staring into my eyes over dessert—a piece of cheesecake for me and a warm zabaglione for her. "I never tire of looking at you."

"I like looking at you," I told her, "among other things."

She smiled. "It's funny, I've known you for all of two hours spread over two days, and I feel like we already share all the secrets in the universe. I care about you so much, sex isn't important. We could just wander through Central Park holding hands and I'd be wonderfully happy."

For a minute I enjoyed the image, and then a random thought hit me and I suppressed a sudden impulse to laugh, but not quite well enough.

She frowned. "Are you laughing at me?"

I shook my head.

"What, then?"

"A stray thought; it's unimportant."

"Tell me!"

I told her: "I have resolved to be honest with you, whatever the cost. It just occurred to me: in you I have every man's dream—a beautiful nymphomaniac. And now you tell me you love me so much you don't want to sleep with me. Just my luck!"

Elizabeth stared at me for a moment, then broke out into quiet giggles. Thank God! It could have gone either way. "Am I beautiful?" she asked.

"Helen of Troy had nothing on you, babe," I told her. "'Were you not the face that launch'd a thousand ships and burnt the topless towers of Ilium?'"

"They can't blame that one on me," she said, hiding her face behind the napkin. "I was elsewhere at the time."

She lowered the napkin and smiled at me. "Can we go up to your place?"

"What?"

"After dinner, can we go up to your place? So we can be alone and I can show you that sex isn't totally unimportant."

"I live in a rooming house," I told her. "I'd have to sneak you in. We're supposed to keep the door open if members of the opposite sex are in our rooms. The landlady has been known to patrol the corridors, protecting the chastity of her female residents. It wouldn't be practical. I'll move tomorrow."

"What a nice offer," she said. "But you won't have to. Usually we can go up to my place. Park Avenue and Seventy-third. But for some reason Daddy's in town. It's the family place, a great big duplex penthouse apartment, but nobody ever uses it but me and sometimes my brother. Except now, of course, when the fates are conspiring against us."

"Doesn't your father know that Congress is in session?" I asked. "Why isn't he in Washington doing his little bit to soak the poor?"

"I don't know," she said seriously. "He's been acting strangely the past few weeks. Worried. He thinks your boss is plotting against him."

"Really?" I asked. Was she being Mata Hari or was I? What was the masculine form of Mata Hari—Mato Haru? Was this turn of conversation just a coincidence? I tried looking nonchalant and not feeling guilty.

"Really," she said. "But that's not it. Daddy always thinks that anyone who isn't for him is plotting against him. And some of those who claim to be for him, too."

"Ah!" I said.

"And sometimes he's right," she added.

"It's the constitutional duty of every American citizen to plot against their elected representatives," I told her. "It's a sacred trust. But the usual target is the president, not a senator. Ask Father Coughlin."

We fought over who should pay the check. She insisted that, after all, she had invited me, and I cited the commandment handed down by Moses that a man should pay when he takes out his date. We compromised: she paid for me and I paid for her. Since mine was more expensive, I put down the tip.

"Perhaps we should go to my room and chance the landlady," I said.

"Perhaps we should," she agreed.

Perhaps we did.

It was almost eleven when I arrived at the office the next morning, after stopping at Danny's for a cup of coffee and a couple of doughnuts to go. Brass had not yet arrived. Gloria was at her desk, and Inspector Raab and one of his minions were sitting in a pair of the pseudo-Louis chairs across from her. Raab looked relaxed the way a fighter looks relaxed in his corner between the rounds. His minion, the well-dressed young detective first grade I had seen at Dworkyn's studio, was in an attitude of frozen attention, like a praying mantis. "Well," I said, taking off my topcoat and hat and hanging them in the closet. "Good morning, Inspector. What gives?"

"You're doing me a favor," Raab said.

"I am?"

"Actually, Miss Adams is, in Brass's name."

I looked quizzically at her, and she smiled at me. "We are sending a radiogram facsimile to London even as I speak," she said. "At Inspector Raab's suggestion."

"Why are we doing this?" I asked.

Raab shifted in his seat and the chair creaked alarmingly. "We traced Dieter Vogel this morning," he said. "His furniture and equipment were brought by the moving company to the secondhand store which had purchased them. Herr Vogel himself boarded the *Europa* shortly before she sailed yesterday, bound for Bremen."

"A wise man who manages to flee before he's being pursued," I said.

"Perhaps he's just visiting the old folks at home," Gloria suggested.

"I've suggested to the British police that he be held for questioning," Raab told me. "He'll be taken off the ship when she docks at Southampton." Raab fished in his pocket for a box of cough drops and popped one in his mouth. "I'm having the *World* send a radio facsimile of that photograph of Vogel to New Scotland Yard. The New York City Police Department doesn't have the equipment."

I nodded wisely and went to my cubicle to begin sorting the morning's mail. A few minutes later Brass came in and heard about the absconding Vogel. "Interesting," he said. "If he didn't know you were after him—and how could he have?—then why did he run?"

"If you get any ideas," Raab said, getting up and reaching for his hat, "pass them on. I got to get back to catching the bad guys."

About an hour later I went in and stood in front of Brass's desk. Brass was staring out the window and fingering an ivory letter opener supposedly carved from the tusk of a narwhal and given to him by the Grand Duke Fyodor Androvitch, whom Tsar Nicholas called cousin and who now ran Balalaika, a small bistro on the East Side that had great borscht and pretty good blinis. "Is there anything I can do more useful than answering letters?" I asked.

He swiveled in his chair and looked up at me. "I think not," he said. "We await events."

"What events?"

"I don't know. I know what I want, but I'm not sure how to best make it happen."

"What do you want?" I asked.

He opened his desk drawer and pulled out one of the pictures of Vogel and his, I suppose, girlfriend posing in a doorway. "Cathy came by last evening," he said. "She has to be careful coming to the office because she's now staying with Heidi. She wanted to look over our dirty picture collection to be sure she was right. She recognized three of the girls from the pictures and the boy who was with Suzie Frienard; they all work at the clinic. She also saw this picture." He tapped it with his finger. "The building that Vogel and his chubby inamorata are standing in front of—that's the Mainard Clinic."

"I see," I said.

"Do you?"

"I see that all the pieces are interconnected, but I'm not sure how."

"The missing piece of the puzzle is somewhere inside the Mainard Clinic," Brass said.

"So Cathy is looking for it? Just what is she looking for?"

"Possibly a room, possibly a photograph collection, possibly clinical records; I don't know. But Cathy is under strict instructions not to actively look for anything. I don't want her body to be fished out of the Hudson."

"So how are we to find it, whatever it is, without looking?"

"That's what I've been considering," Brass told me.

"It would seem that von Mainard himself is a piece of the puzzle," I said. "Do you want me to see what I can find out about him?"

"Ah!" Brass said. "A sensible question." He pulled a scrap of paper from his pocket and smoothed it out on the desk. "Herr Doctor Erich von Mainard is an Austrian national. He received his medical degree from the University of Munich in 1911 and served as a medical officer with the Austrian Army during the World War. After the war he published a paper on the use of certain drugs to alleviate the symptoms of shell-shock. He went into private practice as a psychoanalyst in Vienna until 1926, when he had a feud with Dr. Sigmund Freud over the use of drugs, specifically an alkaloid derived from the *Rauwolfia serpentina* plant, in his practice—von Mainard's, not Freud's. Freud said that the unconscious should be neither examined nor controlled by psychopharmacology until much more was known about the working of the brain. He felt that perhaps someday severe psychoses would be treated by psychoactive drugs, but that neuroses were best handled by analytic psychotherapy. Von Mainard called Freud a "busybody know-it-all who practices Jew medicine," and moved to Berlin. He set up a successful clinic for alleviating the stress of the wealthy. He came to New York about a year ago and opened his clinic here. I'm not sure whether the one in Berlin is still operating."

"Yes," I said, "but what does he have for breakfast?"

"I think we're going to have to go find out," Brass said.

24

It was two o'clock Friday morning, and Brass and I were standing in front of the Mainard Clinic on Seventy-ninth Street between Park and Madison, planning a felonious entry. The Packard sedan was parked just in from the corner of Madison Avenue, with Garrett in his chauffeur's disguise feigning sleep in the front seat. To make our felonious plans feasible, since neither of us had the requisite skill, Brass had brought along a felon: a thin, short man in his forties with bunchy muscles, a bony face, and almost no hair named Alphonse "Shoes" Mallery, who shyly admitted to being something of an expert in these matters.

I had been with Brass earlier that day when we went looking for Shoes. He was at the third place we peered into, a piano lounge called the Abigail Room in the Hotel Quincy, drinking club soda and playing chess with the hostess, a blonde named Vicky, who wasn't busy hostessing yet, it being only three in the afternoon.

"I'm in," Shoes said when Brass explained our needs. "It would be something, having you owe me one for a change."

"I dislike asking you to commit a crime," Brass said, at which Shoes almost spilled his drink.

So here we were contemplating the front door of the clinic, a wide wooden door with an iron gate up five steps from the street; the window to the left of the front door, which was crisscrossed with iron bars; and the side door of the clinic, which was down a short alley and looked to be solid iron with a window barely big enough to peer through. There were no windows facing the alley. Cathy, who had drawn us a plan of the interior, as much as she knew it, that morning before she went to work, had volunteered to try to leave the front door unlocked for us when she left, but Brass had nixed the idea as too dangerous for her.

Making his decision, Shoes went up to the front door and rang the bell. "Much better to find out if there's anyone inside while we're still outside," he explained.

"At two in the morning?" I whispered.

"Especially at two in the morning. And don't whisper. Don't yell, but don't whisper. Whispers carry."

"I knew that," I said in a weak approximation of my normal voice.

After a minute of ringing, there was still no sound from inside. Shoes, working with several small devices that looked to my untrained eye like dental implements, had the gate opened in under a minute. The front door took a bit longer. He stepped inside and shone a small flashlight around the edge of the door. "No alarm," he said. "Put your gloves on and come on in."

We pulled on our black cotton gloves, Woolworth specials at ten cents the pair, and sidled past Shoes into the hall. Shoes closed the door behind us, leaving it subtly ajar in case we had to make a hasty retreat, and we shone our flashlights around the hall, carefully keeping the beams away from the window. To our right was a large waiting room fixed up with carpeting, comfortable couches, and high-backed easy chairs to look like a living room. Past it was the reception room, where Cathy spent her day greeting Dr. von Mainard's wealthy patients. There was a staircase ahead of us to the left, and a hallway straight ahead, going to the back of the building, with rooms off to each side.

"The office first, I think," Brass said softly, heading down the hall.

"What the hell are we looking for?" Shoes asked. "They don't keep money in cribs like this."

"Dirty pictures," I told him.

Shoes shone his flashlight in my face for a second. "You ain't smiling," he said.

"It ain't funny," I told him.

Brass paused at the office door and turned to Shoes. "Ignore him," he said, sounding annoyed. "We don't know what we'll find."

Shoes shrugged. "Most guys have some idea what's in a crib before they b-and-e. But it ain't any of my concern. Mine is not to reason why," he said. "Mine is but to pick locks and stand back."

"See what you can do with this office door," Brass said. Shoes went over and opened it—*click, click*—like it wasn't locked, and the three of us went in. The office had two desks, one to the left and one to the right, and a row of file cabinets against the back wall. Brass started in on the file cabinets and I pulled out a couple of the desk drawers. Shoes contented himself with shining his flashlight on the pictures on the wall and making little appreciative clucking noises.

Earlier I had asked Brass to give me a better idea of what we were looking for besides photographs resembling the ones we already had, and he had told me, "Just ask yourself these questions: Does this tell us anything we didn't know before? And, if so, is it worth knowing?" I went through the desk drawers methodically, asking the questions of everything I saw. I learned that the secretary used a shade of nail enamel called Rose Empassionata, and that she—I assume it was a girl—kept several pair of sheer black silk stockings in an envelope in the bottom drawer. I wouldn't know whether it was worth knowing until I got a look at the secretary.

The desk yielded nothing else of even passing interest, so I crossed to the other one and pulled open the top drawer.

I found a rectangular case of stiff brown leather, about six by eight by two. I unsnapped it and pulled it open. It was lined with red fabric and was designed to hold snugly in place two hypodermic syringes, one medium sized and one large, and a row of needles, each with its own little glass needle-holder. The syringes were glass tubes inserted into silver frames with silver plungers. Just the sort of gift a doting mother might have given her son in medical school twenty or thirty years ago. Nowadays doctors preferred all-glass syringes, which had less places for germs to hide while they were auto-claved.

There was a clicking noise, and then another, and Shoes, with something approaching awe in his voice, said, "Well, I was wrong!" Brass and I turned. Shoes had swung aside an oil painting of a sailboat, revealing the wall safe behind it. He had also opened the wall safe, revealing the stacks of money within, all neatly wrapped and banded. "My fedora is off to you, Mr. B.," Shoes said in an admiring undertone. "You did know what you were doing after all." Shoes pulled out the stacks of bills and piled them up on the desk, counting under his breath. "We got maybe sixty grand here, give or take a dollar," he announced. "Mostly twenties and fifties. All used bills." He pulled a bill loose from its stack, rubbed it between his fingers, and then stared at it with the flashlight held behind it. "And not the queer," he added.

"I'll be damned," Brass said. "There's more money in psychiatry than I imagined."

"Blackmail?" I suggested.

"The doc in question is, maybe, putting the black on a bunch of Germans," Shoes suggested, affectionately riffling one of the stacks.

"Germans?" Brass asked.

"Take a look," Shoes said. He shined the flashlight on the paper band wrapped around one of the stacks. It was stamped with a stylized eagle perched on a swastika, with the words *Reichsbank Berlin* below.

"That is worth thinking about," Brass said. "Put the money back now."

Shoes stared at him. "What?"

"Put the money back, please. We're not thieves."

"Speak for yourself," Shoes said.

"It's important that they don't know we were here," Brass told him. "More important than the money."

"To you."

"That's right," Brass agreed. "To me."

Shoes stared at Brass. "The way you've been moving things around, they're going to sure as hell know somebody was here."

"An inquisitive cleaning lady," Brass said.

There was a long moment of silence, and then Shoes shrugged. "It's your show." He retrieved the stacks of money and jammed them back into the safe, at first grudgingly, but he grew increasingly cheerful as he completed the job and slammed the safe door closed.

We finished our investigation of the office in another few minutes, having found nothing further of interest, and retreated to the hallway. Shoes locked the door behind us. None of the other doors along the hall were locked, and none looked as though they were worth searching. "Upstairs," Brass said.

The second floor contained the therapy rooms, each furnished to create a different illusion, foster a different aspect of the psyche, encourage the release of a different repression. There was the nursery, with an oversized blue crib; the schoolroom; the jail cell; the gym locker room with a row of wooden benches and steel lockers; and a room with a thickly carpeted floor and no furniture but an oversized bathtub in the middle of the room. "Does this stuff work?" I asked, staring at the bathtub.

"Do you mean is the tub functional?" Brass asked. "Probably. Do you mean is this therapy useful? If you believe it will help you, then it probably will. The mind can find all sorts of excuses for getting well, or for assuming rightly or wrongly that it now is well."

"This is not the time for chatting," Shoes interrupted. "Time is passing, and we got to get out of here before daylight."

"You're right," Brass said. "Onward and upward!"

We proceeded up the stairs to the third floor and discovered a closed door at the head of the stairs. It was metal, it was locked, and it had a small peephole with a sliding panel that worked from the other side of the door. I had a hunch things were going to get interesting.

Things got interesting. Shoes had just started to work on the door when it was abruptly pulled open from the inside and three men stood facing us from the other side. Two of them were large, stocky, square-headed muscle men holding oversized automatic pistols, which they were pointing at us; the third was a smiling Dr. von Mainard.

We froze. It seemed the sensible thing to do.

For at least two complete eternities, from the creation of the universe to the heat death of our sun, nobody moved. Then one of the weight lifters gestured with his automatic, and we three filed past him into the hallway.

Von Mainard broke the silence. "Alexander Brass, I presume?" He gave a little rasping chuckle, as though he'd just said something clever.

"Dr. von Mainard," Brass said, his voice more unconcerned than mine would have been. "An unexpected pleasure."

"I could just shoot you, you know," von Mainard said, his head nodding rapidly up and down in agreement with his thoughts. "Your American law allows me to do that to protect my home. *Bang, bang*. But first there are some things that I must know."

The two goons prodded us down the hall and into a large white room decorated with five or six white metal chairs and a white metal table. There was a door in the far wall and two in each of the side walls. Against the wall to our right was a white metal cabinet with glass doors, which held several rows of stoppered bottles and various bits of medical apparatus. Cathy sat motionless in one of the chairs. Her eyes turned to watch us as we entered, but she gave no other sign of recognizing us or even being aware that we had come into the room. I must have shown that I was startled to see her, because von Mainard swung around and thrust his face a few inches from mine. "Yes?" he demanded.

His breath stank of tobacco and halitosis. I took a step backward. Now was not the time to discuss his dental hygiene. "Who's the girl?" I asked.

He chuckled again. "Very good, Mr.—DeWitt, is it? As fine a bunch of burglars as I've ever seen. And just what did you expect to find in my little clinic?"

Shoes shook his head in disgust. "We rang," he said, sounding aggrieved.

Von Mainard examined him with the interested air of an entomologist who has collected a hitherto unknown specimen. "I don't believe I know you," he said. "But I shall—I shall." He rubbed his hands together. "We never answer the bell after midnight unless it is rung in a special manner." He tapped on the table to illustrate the manner. "All others we ignore."

The two bodybuilders searched us roughly and thoroughly, relieving Shoes of a small revolver and a sand-filled sock, and sat us down on the metal chairs. While one of them stood in front of us looking menacing with his automatic, the other came behind us, one at a time, and attached our arms firmly to the backs of the chairs with shiny silver handcuffs.

Von Mainard stood in front of Brass and peered down at

him. "It is fortunate that we were here to receive you. I spent the evening at the penthouse of Senator Childers. A delightful man, the senator. Curiously, I returned here to question the young lady, who was detained after Hans recognized her from his little expedition to your office. But, as we have you now, I will go straight to the horse's mouth, as you say." He raised a hand to hush Brass, who had given no sign of being about to speak. "Do not attempt to say anything now. Whatever you say could not be trusted. I have more reliable methods." He turned to the cabinet behind him and took a hypodermic syringe from its case. It was one of the newer sorts, without the silver chasing. "You should feel honored, you three," he said, meticulously fitting a needle on the end and filling it from a glass vial. "You are being given the opportunity to test one of the latest advancements in interrogation procedures."

The doctor approached me. I contemplated kicking him in the balls, kicking the syringe out of his hand, suddenly springing up, chair and all, and somehow overpowering von Mainard and his two henchmen. Heroes in the pulps did it at least once an episode. The Shadow and Doc Savage made it look easy.

One of the muscle men impassively came behind me and held his large gun to my temple as von Mainard pushed up my sleeve and thrust the needle into my arm and pressed the plunger. "This will not hurt you," von Mainard said in a mild voice, the doctor reassuring his patient. "It will merely rob you of your volition, an appendage you have small use for at the moment, anyway. Later, and in another place, we will kill you."

He moved away from me and wiped the needle down with alcohol, and then repeated the procedure with Alphonse. Sterility must be maintained, even unto the death. I tried to shift my head around to better follow the action, and discovered that I couldn't. I was still completely awake and alert, but I couldn't move anything but my eyes. It was as though my body had forgotten how to follow the instructions my brain was sending it. I was suddenly overwhelmed by the horrible conviction that I was going to forget how to breathe. I screamed—but no sound came out.

Von Mainard refilled his syringe from another bottle and again carefully wiped down the needle. "And now, Mr. Brass, a slightly different preparation for you. It will take longer to work, but it is more sure." He pushed Brass's sleeve up and aimed the syringe.

There was a sudden commotion from downstairs: the sound of running feet and raised voices.

With a gesture of annoyance von Mainard turned toward the door, listening, the hand holding the hypodermic now poised above his head. The sounds got louder. "Kurt," von Mainard said, "go see what is happening!"

One of the muscle men stalked out the door. About ten seconds later he came running back in. *"Der verdammt Polizei!"* he yelled.

"So you did bring the police!" Von Mainard glared at Brass. "Well, I am prepared." He thrust the hypodermic at Brass's arm, but Brass twisted in his chair and kicked von Mainard's hand. The hypodermic flew into the air.

Von Mainard cursed and slapped Brass across the face. "If I had time—no matter, there will be another time."

"All right, men, upstairs—quickly!" came a barked command from below, followed by the thunderous footsteps of a horde of men racing up the stairs.

The two goons slammed and bolted the door, while von Mainard disappeared into one of the side rooms. In a few seconds he was out again carrying a stuffed briefcase. By this time men were up the stairs, pounding at the closed and bolted door. "Bring that ax over here, O'Malley," cried the voice of authority from behind the door, a voice that I recognized.

Von Mainard and his cohorts ran to the door at the other end of the room and pulled it open. In a trice, or maybe a trice and a half, they were all through it and had slammed it shut behind them. There was the sound of hammering at the other door and then, after a few seconds, a methodical thunking sound as of an ax against metal.

I was content to sit and wait to be rescued; I had little choice. But then, after perhaps thirty seconds, I smelled smoke. By peering to the left as far as I was able, I could make out a thin haze of black smoke coming from the room von Mainard had been in. The haze thickened as I watched, and puffs of deep black smoke billowed into the room.

The chopping continued at the door, with nothing visible from this side to show progress. "Brass, DeWitt, are you in there?" the familiar voice called. It was Garrett. So near and yet so far. Would he get to us before the fire did? There were other questions, like what was he doing out there, and how had he roused the police, and I hoped to be able to ask him really soon.

"We're here, Mr. Garrett," Brass called. "Hold on a minute and I'll get the bolts." He tried to get up, and fell back into his seat. "Damn!" he called. "I'm handcuffed to a chair, and it's bolted to the floor!"

Someone was moving. I turned my eyes and was able to make out Cathy lying on the floor, dragging herself toward the door. Her legs were not working, and her arms were not doing much; most of her painfully slow progress was by rolling herself from side to side and inching forward. It was the silliest-looking, most beautiful form of locomotion I had ever seen.

She reached the door. She sat up against it. With a tremendous effort of will she reached up and slid one of the bolts over. She couldn't reach the other one. She rolled over onto her stomach on the floor. A layer of black smoke now filled the room. I could hear the crackle of flames.

Slowly she pulled her legs under her as if practicing some obscure yoga exercise. She raised her body. She fell forward onto her face. It was painful to watch. In a minute she raised up again; this time she made it to an approximation of a kneeling position by leaning against the door. It was wonderful to watch. She raised her hand and reached the other bolt. She pushed it and it moved, but not enough. She pushed it again, and it slid free. She collapsed.

The door was pushed open and Garrett, ax in hand, came bounding in. Behind him came two or three drunken citizens, who were definitely not policemen. One of them stumbled over to me and peered at my face. "Where's the booze?" he demanded.

25

It was two hours before the effects of Dr. von Mainard's concoction began to wear off. Garrett and his soused platoon did a splendid imitation of the Keystone Fire Department, but they did manage to extinguish the blaze. Garrett searched von Mainard's inner sanctum until he found a key of a strange pattern that worked on our handcuffs. Shoes and I were still unable to walk, so a pair of drunks carried us downstairs to the bathtub room to get us away from the smoke. Being helplessly carried down a flight of stairs by two men who can't walk a straight line is better than any roller coaster for causing absolute panic. But we got down safely, and were gently laid on the carpet next to a recovering Cathy, who had wisely staggered down on her own. Brass and Garrett went off to explore the house.

In the meantime, although the fire had been put out, one of the drunks, or possibly someone on the street, called the fire department, which brought several fire trucks and the police. The firemen ran around chopping holes in the wall to make sure the fire was truly out, and the police asked many questions and stared curiously at me and Shoes. Brass mollified the police, who went away shortly after the firemen departed, leaving two men at the door and promising to send Inspector Raab along as soon as they could locate him.

Garrett came in and sat with Shoes and me until we regained the use of our bodies. He sang to us and recited poetry, mostly

Kipling, Service, and Levy, as well as some of his own, to keep our spirits up. He did explain his timely arrival: He had become concerned and, as he put it, "tippy-toed up the stairs" just in time to hear us being captured. Upon which he trotted over to Lexington Avenue and rounded up the customers at a bar called The Shamrock, jumping up on a bar stool and, with spellbinding oratory, promising them free booze and maybe a good fight if they came with him. A dozen men had followed him from the bar and joined him in his assault on the clinic. Most of them were eight or nine sheets to the wind, and they had stumbled around enough to sound like a whole platoon of gendarmerie.

By six in the morning the rank and file of Garrett's drunken army had gone home, except for two who had been laid out in the waiting room, having been rendered hors de booze after finding a cache of schnapps in von Mainard's office. Cathy had recovered completely except for a headache and an abiding anger at von Mainard and all his works, and Shoes and I were more or less able to stagger about on our own. Garrett went forth into the world and returned with paper cups of coffee and an assortment of doughnuts, and we ate and drank of them and were glad.

At seven-thirty Inspector Raab showed up with a quartet of plainclothesmen, who began a systematic search of the building from the ground floor up.

"I won't ask you how you got in here," Raab said, after hearing an abbreviated version of our adventures. "We'll assume that you were rudely snatched from in front of the building, and my old friend Shoes is with you to discuss the Giants outfield. That is your team, isn't it, Shoes, the Giants?"

Shoes nodded without rancor. "Opposites attract, Inspector."

"Quite right," Brass agreed. "That's just how it was."

"Just what has been going on here?" Raab asked. "I mean, before you arrived?"

"I think I can tell you a little bit about that. Follow me," Brass said. He led the way upstairs to the scene of our rerent excitement. "Through that door did the doctor and his cohorts escape." He pulled at the door. "It is barred from the inside, but judging by its position, it can't be more than three or four feet wide. From which I infer that it contains a ladder leading to the roof. Such forethought shows that they had an escape route planned, and are probably well on their way out of your jurisdiction by now. It also shows some sense of guilt, since you don't plot your escape unless you have reason to think someone might be chasing you."

"And just what is it I'd be chasing them for, aside from all the things we suspect but cannot yet prove?"

"We could begin with the kidnaping of Miss Fox. That should do to hold them for a while. And there is more. I've found several things that plant the finger of suspicion firmly on von Mainard's nose."

"Photographs?" Raab asked.

"No. I fancy von Mainard took those with him. But this," Brass pushed open the door to the left, behind the row of metal chairs, "this would seem to be the location at which they were taken."

The room was about twelve by twelve, with no furniture but a light-colored carpet. Rolled up in one corner was a large, white, fluffy throw-rug, with several oversized pillows perched atop. A large mirror was centered on the wall to the left, and the ceiling was mostly filled with a multipaned skylight of frosted glass, to discourage the prurient interest of anyone who happened to be restating the roof.

"The camera is mounted on a brace on the other side of the mirror, which is one-way glass," Brass said. "The wonders of modern science once more serving to improve the condition of mankind."

"So the Mainard Clinic was just a front for a whorehouse for the affluent," Raab said, looking into the empty room with disapproval.

"No, no, much more than that," Brass said. "Do you know the story of Hasan ibn al-Sabbah, the 'Old Man of the Mountain'?"

"*The Arabian Nights*?" Raab suggested. "Isn't that one of the tales?"

Brass decided that he wanted more relaxed surroundings for his storytelling, so we followed him back downstairs and settled in the overstuffed furniture in the waiting room. "It is not a tale at all in the sense that you mean," he told Raab. "Hasan ibn al-Sabbah was the leader of a secret sect known as the Hashshashin in eleventh-century Persia. From a fortress called Alamut—'the Eagle's Nest'—high on a mountain in central Persia, he terrorized the Muslim, and much of the Christian, world. His followers were few but much feared and completely dedicated to his will. That their name is the root of our word *assassin* should give you some idea."

"Charming," Raab said, "but I don't see the relevance."

"Patience," Brass said. "Hasan got this complete obedience from his disciples by telling them that, if they died bravely in his service, they would go to Paradise, where they would feast on rich foods and be serviced nightly by beautiful houri. And they believed him because he had taken them there once to give them a foretaste of what was to come."

I had been staring at the ceiling, but now I looked over to Brass. "He what?" I asked.

"The word *hashshashin* means 'hashish eater,'" Brass said. "Hasan would drug his faithful followers with wine doped with hashish and take them into a secret garden hidden in his palace. There they would taste of all the delights that he had promised them. The next morning they would wake up in bed, and Hasan would tell them they had been to Paradise."

Raab was skeptical. "And they believed him?" he asked.

"They did," Brass assured him. "Why not? Would their leader lie to them? And they would gladly die for him—because they knew where they were going."

"I can believe it," I said. "Look at some of the people who are being blindly followed today, without even drugged wine as an excuse."

Alphonse "Shoes" Mallery appeared in the doorway with his overcoat bundled under his arm. "I'll be going now, if there's no objection," he said. "It's been a fascinating night."

Brass waved at him. "I thought you might," he said. "Go in peace." Shoes waved back and headed out the door.

Raab had been thinking over Brass's narrative. "Are you saying that's what was happening here?"

"Sort of," Brass said.

"Von Mainard was turning a group of middle-aged politicians and executives into an assassination squad?"

Brass grinned. "A wonderful image," he said, "but no. The not-so-good doctor has apparently developed a drug, or combination of drugs, that will release inhibitions in the user and induce a quasi-dream state. It's what he was going to give me. With my inhibitions removed, I would have told him anything he asked. But what he was using it for with the senator and the judge and the lawyer, all of whom shall henceforth remain nameless, was to induce pleasure. They would all remember in a sort of foggy way that they were alone in a room with a lovely girl, or in one case, boy, who made love to them. Non-judgmental, nonthreatening, with no responsibilities; just pleasure."

Raab thought it over. "Well, drugs or no drugs, any court in the state would see it as prostitution and pandering, which is good for a few years in the joint. I guess he took those photos without his, ah, patients' knowledge, but if he hasn't actually tried to use them yet, we can't get him for blackmail."

"I think his goals were more ambitious than that," Brass said. "His drugs cause a state of extreme suggestibility. My guess is that he was going to suggest things to them while they were under the influence."

"What sort of things?"

"That is the question. Judges, attorneys, senators—what sort of things indeed. And the secretly taken photographs were for extra persuasion, should such prove necessary." Raab sat up. "Speaking of senators... I had lunch with Colonel Schwarzkopf yesterday. We discussed Senator Childers."

"And?"

"Schwarzkopf was very circumspect. He didn't actually *say* anything. But the impression he managed to leave me with was that the senator does not have a record of sadistic treatment of women."

"Does not?"

"Does not have a record," Raab reiterated. "But off the record, there is the suggestion that he has paid large sums of money to several women to keep charges from being filed. Apparently the senator loses control occasionally in what would otherwise be just a little playful spanking. I believe in the trade it's called 'the English vice,' but Childers occasionally takes it to an un-English extreme."

Brass nodded. "One man's foreplay is another man's five years in the penal institution of the state's choice," he commented. "Just one more thing that money can buy."

Three shots, one after the other, sounded dull and distant from somewhere outside. Raab jumped up and ran for the door, Brass and I right behind him. We paused in a clump at the front door at the thought that the shots might be aimed in our direction.

The two uniformed officers who had been at the door were standing in the street with their guns drawn, staring up at something over our heads. Inspector Raab drew his revolver. "You two stay here until I find out what's happening," he whispered, and cautiously made his way toward the curb, looking up at the building.

More shots from overhead, louder now that we were outside. And then a continuous firing, every few seconds for what seemed like ten minutes but was probably less than one. I could make out two distinct weapons being used; one had a higher-pitched *crack* than the other, but what they were I couldn't have said.

After a pause of another minute, a head appeared on the rooftop, looking down. For a moment it surveyed the street. And then a voice called, "Inspector Raab?"

"Yes?" Raab called back.

"It's Framingham. You'd better get up here."

We were two steps behind Raab as he ran upstairs. One of the detectives was on the phone to Bellevue when we entered the third-floor room, and he gestured toward the far door and continued telling the other end of the phone where to send the ambulances.

The door that von Mainard had escaped through had been battered open, revealing a closet-sized room with a wooden ladder fastened to the far wall. Brass was right again. Raab went up the ladder and Brass and I followed. The roof of the building was the usual flat, tarred surface with various pipes and oddments sticking up randomly and a knee-high wall around the edge. A plainclothesman was sitting on the tar a short distance from the ladder, clutching his right leg with both hands, a look of fierce concentration on his face. Blood was slowly oozing out from under his hands.

Framingham was standing by the side wall, his hands on his hips, staring across at the next building. We joined him. "What the hell was all that?" Raab asked.

Framingham pointed. There was a three-foot gap between the clinic roof and the next rooftop, an easy jump. Three men were lying in various positions at the far corner of the next roof, blood pooling under them. "They started shooting at us as soon as we came up the ladder," he said. "So we started shooting back. They lost. I don't even know who the hell they are."

"It's Dr. von Mainard and his two associates," Brass said.

"So. What the hell are they still doing up here?" Raab turned to Framingham. "Cover me!" He jumped the gap and cautiously approached the bodies. They remained dormant as he squatted by each one, holding the back of his hand in front of each nose. "This one's alive," he said, indicating one of the thugs. "I think the other two are dead, but we'd better get them downstairs just in case."

Brass jumped across with studied nonchalance. I followed, trying not to let the fear show on my face. A three-foot jump is a snap, but when the gap is a three-story drop to the street, it becomes more imposing. I went over to look at von Mainard. He looked dead to me, a wide stain of blood across his chest, which had already stopped flowing, and an angry, puzzled look in his eyes, sightlessly staring into eternity or possibly at the water tower on the roof across the street.

"Here's the answer," Brass said, peering over the far edge of the building. I went to look. There was about three feet of iron ladder leading down from the roof, and then nothing but blank wall.

"A ladder to nowhere," I said.

"There was a fire escape here until recently," Brass pointed out, indicating some rusty iron bolts still protruding from the wall of the building below the ladder. "My guess is that it rusted out and either fell down of its own accord or was taken down because it was too dangerous to use."

"And von Mainard didn't know it was gone," I said.

"That's my guess. And once they were up on the roof, they were trapped. There's no entrance from inside this building, and they couldn't go back into the clinic with all the police and firemen there."

"They didn't have to shoot it out," Inspector Raab said. "We didn't have that much on von Mainard. I don't even know if we could have gotten a conviction."

Brass went over to von Mainard. "He died an aphorism," he said. "'The wicked flee when no man pursueth.'"

"So that's an aphorism," Raab said. "I thought it was a proverb. Well, we would have been pursuing soon enough."

"That's so," Brass agreed, staring down at the defunct doctor.

"I think, as you go through the building, you'll find more than enough to convict him for a variety of crimes. He certainly had Fox and Dworkyn killed, but I don't know whether we'll be able to prove it. If his henchman lives, perhaps we can establish it. But I guess that doesn't matter now. Which reminds me—" He picked up von Mainard's overstuffed briefcase and hefted it. "Perhaps it might be wise if I keep this for you and, ah, do a little editing before you have to turn it in as evidence."

"That would be irregular," Raab said. He paused, and added, "I'll get it from you this evening."

A stream of people emerged from the ladder to the other rooftop, carrying stretchers and medical bags and other paraphernalia, which made it a good time for us to leave. Downstairs we ran into a passel of policemen with thick layers of gold braid on their uniforms and hats. Two of them cornered Raab and insisted on a complete report then and there. We elbowed by and onto the sidewalk.

A short, bald, bemused-looking elderly man carrying an oversized doctor's bag was being escorted up the steps by two detectives. "The safe's in a downstairs office," one of them was telling him. "How long do you think it will take you to get it open?"

Brass chuckled silently to himself as we headed down the street.

"What's so funny?" I demanded.

"They won't find anything in the safe," he told me.

"Why not?"

"Shoes left carrying an overcoat, but he didn't have one when we came in," he said.

"Oh," I said.

Garrett was waiting in the car, peacefully sleeping behind the wheel. Cathy was curled up in the backseat, covered by a red and white blanket, but she was awake. "What's been happening?" she asked.

"You may tell William," Brass said gently, "that those who sent him to heaven are now on their way to hell."

26

Brass spent the weekend pondering and considering and playing with his toys. He took the Lagonda out for a long solo drive to somewhere in Connecticut and back. I contented myself with deep breathing and lighting joss sticks. On Monday morning Inspector Raab called. Herr Vogel had fled the *Europa* when it docked at Southampton and asked for asylum in England even before Scotland Yard had gone after him. A steward on the ship, who also sought asylum, had warned Vogel that a Gestapo welcoming party awaited him at Bremen.

According to Vogel, he had taken the picture collection to his pal Herm as insurance, because he was beginning to suspect that Dr. von Mainard's motives were not pure. You can believe as much of that as you like.

Dworkyn made the mistake of going to Dr. von Mainard, thinking that Vogel had snapped the pictures without von Mainard's knowledge. Apparently Dworkyn had shown the same sort of reticence at explaining himself that he had demonstrated in Brass's office, and von Mainard thought that Dworkyn was trying to blackmail him. The good doctor had tortured Dworkyn and gotten Vogel's name as the picture supplier and Brass's name as the person holding the other set. Vogel thought he had convinced Dr. von Mainard that Herman had stolen the pictures, but the steward's story had shown him the error of his beliefs.

"Very efficient, the doctor," Brass commented. "Sending Vogel home to be killed eliminates the problem of disposing of the body."

Brass sent me to Senator Childers's apartment with a photograph and a note commanding the senator's presence in his office. The senator did not want to come to Brass's office. People came to the senator, he did not go to them. But the photograph was a powerful incentive. Childers didn't ask me any questions, he just put his jacket on and stomped to the elevator. He stormed out of his building and jumped into a cab, and if I hadn't been quick it would have left without me. He did not speak to me or even look at me during the brief ride. But he hadn't become a member of the country's most exclusive men's club without learning how to fight in the trenches.

"Just what does this mean?" Childers demanded, stomping to Brass's desk and slamming his hand down on the polished walnut. With the other hand he waved the photograph at Brass. "What do you and your pinko newspaper think you're going to do with this?"

Brass, who had been staring out at the Hudson when Childers came in, slowly swiveled his chair around to face the senator. "Sit down," he said sharply.

Childers gave the desk a series of sharp slaps with his hand. "If you think this phony—this obvious composite is going to frighten me—"

"Sit down, Senator," Brass repeated. "I have brought you here to ease your mind, not to add to your burden."

Childers dropped into the chair. "What?"

"Although I don't know why I should. I find your politics abhorrent, your ethics Byzantine, and your sexual practices repulsive. You almost deserve to continue thinking that you killed that girl."

Childers jumped to his feet. "Excuse me, sir! What girl? Of just what is it you're accusing me?" He leaned forward until his pugnacious nose was scant inches from Brass's. "If you print one word of that libel, I'll sue you for everything you're worth! Bigger men than you have tried to harass me, accuse me of things, horrible things, but they all went away. I saw to it—and I can see to you!"

"Sit down, sir!" Brass bellowed, with a voice louder and deeper than I had ever heard come from his throat before. Childers slowly lowered himself back into the chair. "Among your other qualities, you don't listen," Brass said. He reached into his desk drawer and took out a stack of photos. Leaning forward, he lined them up on the desk in front of Childers, one by one, as though he were laying out a hand of bridge for his partner. "You have seen these before?"

"Clever forgeries," Childers said, leaning back in his chair and staring at Brass.

"These show you making love to a woman," Brass said, pointing to the first photos in the row. "These show you beating the same woman with a belt and—is that a squash racket? These show the woman dead from her beating. The photos are all genuine. I have had them looked at by an expert. I have seen the girl." He added two photos to the line. "Her body is in the morgue at Bellevue."

Childers started to say something, but the words didn't come out. He slumped in his chair. "She was found then," he said. "They assured me... no matter." He gestured toward me. "Send him out of here. I want to talk to you."

"Mr. DeWitt stays," Brass said. "If you like, I'll do all the talking. There is nothing you can tell me that I do not already know, except possibly some corroborating details."

Childers stared at something on the desk for a while, and then he straightened up and stared out the window behind Brass. He wasn't seeing anything. "I can tell you," he said finally, "because you already know. But even so, it isn't easy. God, how I've wanted to tell someone, but who?"

"I don't need details," Brass said hurriedly. "Please, spare me the details. In broad outline, you occasionally like to beat women as part of what, I suppose, we must consider sexual foreplay."

"It's not that I like to," Childers said. He looked down at the floor and crossed his arms in front of him and hugged himself as though to equalize a great pressure from within his chest. "It comes over me sometimes, an irresistible impulse. But I've never actually hurt anyone before."

"You mean you haven't damaged them beyond the ability of your money to repair," Brass said harshly.

Childers looked up at Brass, and then looked away. "Yes, I suppose..."

"But you were in a room with this girl in Dr. von Mainard's clinic, and you lost control," Brass said.

"Yes."

"He gave you an injection first?"

Childers thought for a second. "Yes. He always did. Vitamins."

"Vitamins. And during this—session—you beat her."

"Yes. I remember hitting her, but not that badly. I must have gone into a rage. I blacked out."

"And Dr. von Mainard had pictures."

"Yes. Of me hitting her, and of her lying dead. I didn't mean to kill her."

"And Dr. von Mainard wanted something in return for his silence?"

"Yes. Sort of. He said he would occasionally come to me with a request. Nothing onerous."

Brass shook his head. "You are a fool," he said. "Von Mainard was a Nazi, working for the German government. We found documentation; the Germans, apparently, keep records of everything. God knows what he would have asked—demanded—of you. First, you were given a powerful drug that released your inhibitions. And we already know where that would take you, don't we? But, second, you didn't kill the girl."

"But I… the body."

Brass passed Childers two more pictures. "This is the damage you did. It's not pleasant, but notice that when these photographs were taken the girl was very much alive. Dr. von Mainard decided that a very badly beaten corpse would be a much stronger hold over you."

"So he—"

"That's right. And then he realized that a photographer he used was stealing negatives. And so several more people died. But you didn't kill the girl."

Childers was silent for a long time, his gaze shifting about the room. And then he said to Brass, "What do you want?"

"I'd like you to leave the senate, but I suppose that's too much to ask," Brass told him. "I'm not going to blackmail you. But I am going to hang on to a selected few of these pictures. If I hear of you assaulting another woman, I will consider using them. You can't buy me off, and you can't buy this girl off; she's dead."

Childers stood up. "I won't offer to shake your hand," he said.

"But you have relieved me of a terrible burden, and I thank you." He went to the door, and then paused and turned back to Brass. "I am thinking of remaining faithful to my wife henceforth," he said. "She is an Epping and, like all of her clan, has a will of iron. I wouldn't dare touch her. I am afraid of her." And so he left.

"How on earth," I said to Brass, "did you figure all that out?"

Brass shrugged. "There were two or three other possibilities," he said, "but that was the most probable." He stared out the window for a minute and then said over his shoulder, "Go open the mail and let me think. I have a column to get out, and I have no idea what to write about."

A few last notes: Brass made a date with Bobbi Dworkyn to fill her in about her brother. He may have had more than talk in mind, since he didn't have to take her to the Sky Room for conversation, but Brass keeps his personal life very personal and I want to keep my job. Cathy is singing at the Opal Room, backed by a quartet called the Spirit of Swing, and is packing them in. Glen Miller has made her an offer to front his band, but he's on the road all year and she's not sure she'd like that. She's still thinking it over. I'm up to page forty-three of the novel. I'm still seeing Elizabeth, but—well, that's my business. Garrett is writing an opera for dogs called *The Barker of Seville.* Gloria is—Gloria. Inscrutable as always. And a good thing, too.

ACKNOWLEDGEMENTS

I would like to acknowledge the material assistance of Sharon Jarvis at a time when I truly needed assistance. And I thank Keith Kahla for intelligent editing that improved the book.

ABOUT THE AUTHOR

Michael Kurland is the author of more than thirty books, but is perhaps best known for his series of novels starring Professor Moriarty. The first volume, *The Infernal Device*, was nominated for an Edgar Award and the American Book Award, and received stellar reviews, including this from Isaac Asimov: "Michael Kurland has made Moriarty more interesting than Doyle ever made Holmes." It was followed by *Death By Gaslight*, *The Great Game*, *The Empress of India* and *Who Thinks Evil*, published over a period of more than thirty years.

Kurland is also well known as a science fiction writer, and is the author of *The Unicorn Girl*, as well as the bestselling T*en Little Wizards* and *A Study in Sorcery*, fair-play detective stories set in a world where magic works. He has edited several Sherlock Holmes anthologies and written non-fiction titles such as *How to Solve a Murder: The Forensic Handbook*. He lives in California.